MW01171755

NIGHT'S DECENT

JESSIE NIGHT THRILLER BOOK TWO

JESSIE NIGHT THRILLER

EMBER SCOTT

1

Bird's Eye Horror

The drone hummed as it lifted off and quickly ascended to a bird's eye view of Pine Haven. The town was the hidden gem in the heart of the North Carolina mountains, and this late in the summer, the golden light of the sun softened the rugged edges of the mountain peaks.

Beneath the electronic eye, the emerald-green of the forests began to dull, preparing for cooler days and nights of fall to reshape mother nature's color palette. From this vantage, the lake shimmered like a mirror, reflecting crystal blue, almost cloudless skies; the surface a still haven only occasionally broken by the ripples of a fish hunting insects or turtle poking its head up for air.

Mountains flanked the town on all sides, like ancient guardians standing watch, mineral veins of quartz and granite striating their faces. White ribbons in the form of waterfalls flowed down their sides, feeding streams that eventually led to Pine Haven Lake.

Kevin Hicks watched his control screen as the images of the town itself, dotted buildings and farmscapes, disappeared, giving way to the vast swathes of open, untouched land that made up the Blue Ridge mountains. Peppered with verdant meadows filled with wildflowers, to sunlight dappled groves, and outlined by scenic trails carved from centuries of foot traffic, the sights opening before him made Kevin's artistic mind swell with possibilities.

He flew the drone high and fast, letting the scenery blur before him, trusting his mind's eye to tell him when he had found the right backdrop for his next project. He reached into his pocket and withdrew a microfiber cloth to rub a tiny smudge from the screen. The DJI Mavic 3 Pro drone had cost him his entire summer's pay at various odd jobs around town, as well as birthday and Christmas money from the past two years. It was easily his most prized possession, even more than the Yamaha TW200 bike he and his dad had put together years ago.

Thinking about the bike brought the start of painful memories to mind that he quickly vanquished. He refused to think about a drunk who had run out on him and his mom when things got tough. If he hadn't needed the bike to get from job to job, he would have taken a sledgehammer to it by now.

He had taken any and all work he could get over the past couple years. Not just to buy the drone, but to live. He hated the way he felt trapped in Pine Haven. It was the only place he'd lived in his scant twenty years, and it felt like it would be the only home he'd ever know. He took whatever work he could land, not really saying no to anything. Shoveling snow in the winter, yard work of all kinds in the summer, handyman when it was something he knew how to do, cleaning pools for the rich lakesides who never noticed him beyond a puzzled nod every now and then. Still, it was barely enough to feed himself with a paltry bit leftover for bike parts and art supplies.

He wanted to go to college. Every year he collected the brochures for art school down in Queen City, but the tuition was way more than food, utilities and bike parts. He couldn't go without making more money first, and he couldn't make more money because he didn't have a degree. Not that it would have mattered if he had. Pine Haven was a town of those who have and those who need.

And he definitely didn't have anything.

All he had was his art. Black and white still life was his specialty, and he was forever on the lookout for new places or faces to make the target of his camera. While he had only taken rudimentary aerial shots with his drone, people seemed to respond positively to them. But he needed more, and they needed to be better.

Better shots, better money. The tourists that flooded the town each year loved to think they were lifting the local arts community out of impoverishment, and he was more than happy to play along with that if it meant paydays that could one day get him into an actual arts college.

He had an idea for his next photo series, but he needed shale rock for the basis and that meant exploring the mountain passes. As the drone sped along, he would occasionally pause, hover and click a few random shots, just to get used to the angles and shadows created by the sun from an angle he couldn't appreciate with a hand-held camera.

He passed over black tarmac that led to a gravel path cutting through a winding pass over mountainous terrain he didn't recognize. There was a car sitting on the side of the road he mindlessly captured before buzzing across the treetops to the interior of the pass.

And that was when he saw her.

A woman, standing on a dirt path, arms raised as she slowly walked backwards. She was naked, which, in and of itself, was not that shocking to Kevin. In the short time he had been flying over these ranges, he had seen a few couples who were hiking their way up the mountain and decided to stop and take advantage of the desolation. When that happened, he would immediately angle away, leaving them to their intimacy, and he was about to do the same here when something caught his eye.

Movement from in front of the woman as a man stepped out of the brush. No, two men. Both were fully dressed, and what bothered Kevin was the fact that they weren't dressed season appropriately. They didn't seem to be dressed for hiking or exploring the North Carolina mountains in late summer. They were wearing black jackets and dark trousers. There was also something distressing about the way they moved.

They were shifty, like they were used to being watched all the time, even when they did things no one else should see.

He slid a button on his controller, shifting the camera from static bursts to video record. He shifted the camera back to the woman, trying to capture more of her face. It was hidden by the wildness of her dark, unkempt hair. She was shaking her head violently, pleading silently on his screen with the men standing before her.

More movement and Kevin drew back enough to get both men and the clearly frightened woman in view. She had ceased backing up and had clasped both hands in front of her, her pleading now begging. She dropped to her knees, her head shaking violently back and forth.

Kevin watched as the smaller of the two men reached into his jacket and removed a pack of cigarettes, tapping it against the palm of one hand before removing one and lighting up. The second reached into his jacket, but instead of cigarettes, pulled out a small, dark gun.

Without hesitation, he pointed it at the woman. His hand jumped with the recoil and the woman's head snapped back as she slumped to the ground. The smoking man had his back turned as he took a long drag.

Kevin instinctively recoiled from what he saw, causing the drone to roll to one side. The sudden change in motion, or the sound of the rotors and stabilizers engaging, attracted the smoker's attention. He looked up, his mouth hanging open, the cigarette falling as he saw the drone. Grabbing at his friend's jacket, he pointed at the drone.

The second man aimed his gun squarely at Kevin and squeezed off a shot. Then another.

Kevin zigged the drone through the air, heading for a group of trees on the far side of the opening. Whether they were still shooting at him he didn't know. He criss-crossed his way through the woods before shooting straight up through the canopy and high into the sky. Swinging the drone around, he risked a quick look to see if there was any sign of the two men.

Nothing.

Still, he wouldn't take any chances, deciding to fly the drone as far away from him as the range would allow, before circling around, dropping beneath the canopy, and returning.

Once the drone was in his hands, he stood there, staring in shock.

That couldn't have been real. Could it?

He stared at the drone before packing it up, then looked at the controller's screen. His hands shook as he hit the playback button.

Christ. That really had just happened.

The cracking of a tree branch to his left caused him to nearly jump out of his skin. He froze, staring at the undergrowth, ready for the two men in dark jackets to come blazing forth, riddling his body with bullets.

Instead, it was a doe and her fawn that stepped forward, ears twitching as they took notice of him. The deer stared, assessed that he wasn't a threat, and casually moved on, nibbling at the dark shoots of grass surrounding them.

Kevin let out a breath, the sudden surge of adrenaline leaving a dank, metallic taste in the back of his throat. His mind raced.

He should destroy this footage and never think about what he just saw.

No. He needed to turn this over to the police. Or the FBI.

He needed to run. To hide.

And then, something began to play at the back of his mind. Something he knew he shouldn't even entertain. But there it was. The beginnings of an idea.

A very bad idea.

2

Old School Record Keeping

"Okay, you've had more than enough."

Jessie Night looked down at Blizzard, the white shepherd she had adopted, as she took another batch of extra crispy bacon from the pan and placed it on paper towels to drain. "And don't give me that me-so-pitiful look either. You've had your breakfast and plenty of bacon. Go lay down."

The shepherd turned and headed for the fireplace, curling up with his giant Kong bone and tossing a few grumbles Jessie's way.

"And no backtalk. I don't know who you think you're talking to like that..."

She looked at the wall peninsula that shot off from the counter. It was covered in pancakes, fresh fruit, bacon, sausage, scrambled eggs and a pitcher of freshly squeezed orange juice. "I might have overdone it just a bit."

The buzzing of the doorbell told her it was too late to rethink things as she turned off the stove, wiped her hands and headed for the door. She opened it to Alex's smiling face.

He stepped inside. "I don't know what is going on in here, but it smells amazing."

She laughed and headed back through the front room into the open kitchen. "Well, I have been promising you food. I feel bad that every time you've been here, my shelves were bare."

He looked at the mound of deliciousness on the peninsula and stopped short, eyes widening. "I thought the Taste of The Pines festival wasn't until next week. Looks like you've got a jump on things."

She pursed her lips. "I might have gotten carried away. Hope you brought your appetite."

He smiled, licking his lips. "Always."

Considering he was at death's door only a few months ago, Jessie had to admit she was happy to see him getting back to normal. "How's the stomach?"

He patted his midsection. "Really good. Doc says I've healed up nicely. Now this area" —he held up his arm and swung it about like he was serving a tennis ball— "That's still a bit stiff. Doc says I might develop some early arthritis in it. Hey, maybe I'll be one of those people who can predict the weather from their aches one of these days."

Jessie shook her head playfully. The man was shot twice and still had jokes about it. She went to the cabinet and brought down two plates, some glasses and then two mugs. "Well, dig in. The coffee's fresh as well if you don't want orange juice."

They heaped their plates and made their way to the small dining table where Blizzard had already camped out.

"Ignore him," Jessie said, pulling up her chair. "He's had enough already."

As they settled in, Alex chomped on bacon and chased it with a bite of pancakes, a wolfish grin spreading over his face. "This is really good, Jessie. Where did you learn to cook like this?"

"Military brat, remember? I was making breakfast for my dad and Bro—" She stopped and looked down at the forkful of eggs she had stabbed. "Brody, since I was six."

Alex let it rest, chewing in silence, before clearing his throat. "How are you doing? You can see that I'm healing, but what about you?"

She purposefully stuffed her mouth, knowing it would only delay his questions for so long. She felt ashamed for what she thought, but part of her would have given anything to trade places with Alex. She was so thankful that he had survived, but deep down she felt that recovering from gunshot wounds was infinitely easier than healing from what she had done.

She swallowed, looking up to see Alex patiently watching her. "I'm...getting there. I'm not going to lie and say I'm fine because obviously I'm not. But I'm coping as best I can."

He nodded. "And that's really all any of us can do. Have you had any more attacks?"

She took a deep breath, reaching for a knife to cut her

pancakes. "Thankfully, no. Catatonia isn't a train; it doesn't run on a schedule." When Alex winced, she immediately regretted her words. "Sorry. I didn't mean to come across so...assholery...if that's even a word."

He laughed lightly. "Well, it is now. And you're forgiven. I tend not to know my boundaries. Always been a problem with me."

She put her cutlery down and looked at the police officer sitting across from her. "It's alright. You didn't do anything wrong. If it weren't for you, I probably wouldn't be here right now. It's just hard for me to acknowledge my weaknesses. And that condition, is the biggest of all of them."

Alex didn't respond as he absentmindedly handed a piece of bacon to Blizzard, choosing to ignore the look Jessie gave him. "What about the manifest we got from John? Anything jump out at you from it?"

She shook her head, grateful he had changed the subject. "Jordan wasn't stupid. It's written in code of some kind. Or shorthand."

"Are we even sure it's a cargo manifest?"

Jessie pushed her chair back and went over to the coffee table in the living room. It was strewn with folders and papers of various colors. She rifled through them, found what she needed, and returned to the dining table. "This is definitely a manifest. It's some kind of mashup between commercial shipping companies and military cargo lists. The layout is the same. Headers, footers, even destinations. But all the entries...I have no idea what this is. It's all dots and dashes in weird combinations." She pointed to multiple columns on the list. "At first, I thought maybe it was braille. But that's not it." She sighed in frustration. "Jordan didn't create this. She stole it from whoever did."

Alex was staring at the paper. "Yeah, and it got her killed. If something is this important, why isn't it digital? An encrypted hard drive or something?"

"Old school physical record keeping is starting to make a comeback. I saw more and more of it in the military. Believe it or not, there are a lot of criminal organizations that are realizing the benefits of physical media like this. Reduced risk of accidental leaks. No chance of it accidentally being emailed to the wrong person. And it's easy to destroy. Fire can reduce this to nothing. In this age of forensic analysis, it's pretty much impossible to destroy a digital copy of something. And most importantly, with something like this, there is no electronic footprint. No IP addresses, no login times, no accidental metadata that can reveal dates, times, or even the type of device used to create the document."

Alex smiled appreciatively. "But when we use pen and paper at the department, you nearly have a stroke."

"Ugh. Don't even get me started on that mess of a police station. Speaking of, how are things with the chief?"

He lifts both shoulders, dropping them with a sigh. "He's been very quiet lately. Not as in he's checked out, but he's definitely not as engaged as he used to be. He's been focusing on recruitment. Bringing in the right people for the force. Ones that are heavily recommended and vetted. Even though no one is talking about it, it's going to be a while before the stench of corruption Todd left is washed away."

Jessie shook her head in disbelief. "Wow. I still can't believe that whole department hasn't been razed and rebuilt. No offense, of course."

He held up both hands. "None taken. But this is a small, locked community. The people of Pine Haven just wouldn't feel safe under the eye of a department they don't know."

Jessie frowned. "Does the community know just how close they came to being fodder for a drug cartel? Or whatever these people are trading in? No. Don't answer that."

"Everyone trusts you now. Word spread pretty quick how you saved the mayor."

She didn't reply, her eyes playing over the manifest one last time. The series of dots and dashes playing through her consciousness as she looked for any identifiable repeating patterns. "You know, this might be easier if we sent this to the FBI and see what they can make of it."

Alex shook his head. "You know how the mayor feels about outsiders. Besides, without anything concrete to connect this to, there's nothing the FBI can do."

He was right of course. They needed to get a better grasp on what was going on before they could even hope to bring in the big guns.

"And what about you? Given any more consideration to taking the detective's test? You could be the first on the force here."

He twisted his mouth to one side as he chewed on

another bite of pancakes. "I've thought about it, but then I think what would really change? Someone still has to pound the pavement day to day here in town. I think I can do a lot more good being out and seen on a daily basis rather than waiting to solve a specific crime once it happens."

She could understand and appreciate that. Still, Alex had shown a real aptitude for detective work in solving the Jordan Myer case. It was a shame to let such innate abilities go to waste. Still, in the end it was his decision and she had to respect that.

"And you?" he said. "Have you thought any more about getting that private investigator license? You could be a huge asset to the community."

She gave a half laugh. "Honestly, how many people in Pine haven would have need of a private investigator?"

"You might be surprised. Plus, you'd be able to continue working with the police department in a capacity other than consultant."

Jessie was about to answer when Alex's phone buzzed.

"Hold that thought," he said, lifting it to his ear. "Eric? What's going on? Okay. Sure, I can be there in about twenty." He hung up and glanced over at Jessie. "Want to take a ride?"

She gave him a puzzled look. "What's going on?"

"That was Eric Jensen. He and Mark are out at the bed and breakfast and said they found something that I probably need to see."

Jessie looked down at her watch. "Well, I have some time to kill. My friend from back home is coming for a visit, but they're notdue to arrive until closer to the evening."

He snapped his finger. "That's your, uh, therapist, right? What's her name again?"

"Doctor Corinthia Jasmin Anderson. Cora for short. She was my psychiatrist, and she also happens to be my friend. Weird, I know. She's going to be at a convention down in Queen City, and I offered her a place to stay. It will be good to catch up."

He smiled. "And show her just how normal your life now is."

Jessie laughed as they began clearing away the dishes. Her life in Pine Haven might have calmed down a bit, but it was anything but normal. Once the table was cleared and the dishwasher running, she grabbed Blizzard's leash and they piled into Alex's department-issued Ford Bronco.

"Wonder what those two have found," Alex said, pulling out.

Jessie didn't answer. The more time she spent in Pine Haven, the more she was realizing that this sleepy little town could hide some big secrets.

She gritted her teeth. Who knew what the owners of a one-hundred-and-twenty-year-old Victorian might have unearthed.

3

Welcome to the Cage

The smell inside the cage was both clean and nauseating at the same time. The antiseptic used to wipe down the cell floor and launder the bedding was overpowering in its effectiveness. But underneath, the scent of stress-induced sweat, the coppery tint of blood that sometimes permeated the air, and the ever-present smell of fear still hung in the air.

The women watched as the two men in the black jackets walked back into the room. Not that it would have protected them, but they instinctively drew closer together, away from the sides of the cage. Their heads were down, eyes cast to the floor.

Only one of them risked looking at the men. It was a quick glance, her dark, almost jet-black eyes sweeping across them before returning to the polished concrete.

The shorter of the two, who was also the meaner of them, slammed the heel of his hand against the bars.

"She's dead." His voice was little more than a bark. "Let that be a lesson. You get sent back one too many times and there's no place left for you to go." Bright blue eyes squinted heavily as he fixated on the women. "So, make damn well sure that when you go out you make yourself as useful as possible. Remember, three strikes and you're out." He slammed his palm against the cage bars once again for emphasis.

The room was lit by massive, overhead fluorescent lighting that illuminated every inch of the cell and the women. Blemishes and imperfections in the skin needed to be monitored and reported, so the lighting was important for daily inspections.

Walking past the cell, the two men keyed into an electronic lock on a large wooden door and entered a new space. It was surprisingly well-appointed and comfortable. Despite the inherent darkness of a space with no windows and natural light, the abundance of desk and accent lighting surrounding leather couches and chairs added a certain ambience to the space. There was a central seating area comprised of a large sofa, two love seats and two wing backed chairs arranged on a large, red and gray printed area rug.

To one side of that was a massive desk with a large filing cabinet behind it, and beyond that was a fully stocked bar filled with bottles of amber liquids that reflected the light in mirrored shelves behind them.

The larger man walked straight to the bar and grabbed one of the bottles, pouring two generous shots into gold-rimmed glasses. "Christ. They're going to kill us, you know that, right?"

The smaller of the two calmly took one of the glasses and downed the liquor. "Don't be ridiculous. No one's going to kill us." As much as he tried to control it, his voice quivered.

"Someone fucking saw us!"

"We don't know what they saw. Chances are it was some kid flying his new toy and has no clue what was going on. And if they did, who are they going to tell? We'll know if they march into the cops."

The taller one poured more drinks. "Maybe at one time, but Todd and Wesley are dead. We don't know who we can trust in the department anymore. Christ. We're both dead when the boss finds out."

The smaller man's mind raced as he considered his friend's words. He was probably right. "We will fix this. We were doing just fine before we took on investors and we'll be just fine after we buy them out. You'll see. When is the next exchange due?"

The tall one walked over to the desk and flipped open a large, well-worn receipt book. "Three days. The buyer for number A-714 is arriving."

"Good. She's trouble, that one. Always giving us the side eye when she thinks we aren't watching. I'll be glad to get rid of her. She's someone else's problem now. Let's get her updated, and then we can worry about our other problem."

They finished off their drinks, then the smaller man went to the filing cabinet, opened the top drawer, and withdrew a second, smaller ledger, along with a metallic box. Together, they went back to the room with the caged women.

Upon seeing the small metal box, the women gasped, covering their mouths to stifle their cries as they moved away from the cage door.

The tiny, cruel man smiled. "You." He pointed to the dark-eyed woman. "You're in luck. We got a buyer for you. Here's hoping you do a little better than your friend did."

He reached into his jacket and pulled out a black taser, firing it up enough that the woman standing next to the dark-eyed one yelped and fled from her side.

He opened the cage door and moved toward the one with dark eyes. She didn't flinch, didn't try to fight. In her experience, that only got you hit or put into one of the tiny, individual cages meant for punishment. This would be her third update, and as painful as it was, resisting would do her no good. She gave in, letting him drag her out of the cell and to the chair that was outfitted with wrist and ankle restraints. She was actually grateful they were going to put her out for transportation. If she was lucky, she wouldn't wake up while she was being worked on.

He strapped her in, leaning in close as he tightened the ankle restraints.

She gritted her teeth as he opened the metal box and took out a syringe. She bit down on her lip. No matter what, she wasn't going to scream.

4

___

A Dark Find

The majestic Victorian commanded an envious cove on Pine Lake. With a couple hundred feet of beach frontage, it was the crown jewel of the impressive homes dotting the waterfront. The majority of the rooms were along the back and far side. Their water views were unmatched, and that, coupled with the privacy, ensured they stayed in demand for seasons at a time.

Even now, with the season winding down, the no-vacancy sign swung on the wooden crest hanging above the double-door opening on the sweeping front porch. As they walked up, the doors swung open to reveal Mark and Eric standing just inside.

"Well, it took you long enough," said Mark.

Alex frowned. "I'm sorry. We literally rushed right over."

Mark's eyes swept them up and down. "Uh-huh. Sure you did. Together I see."

Jessie stepped forward. "We were having a perfectly good breakfast that we would be more than happy to get back to." She gestured over her shoulder and made to turn back towards the cars.

Eric, the taller, more powerfully built of the couple, reached out quickly. "No, please. Forgive Mark. He's feeling a bit stressed over...things."

Mark slapped playfully at his husband's arm. "Don't you *mansplain* how I feel." He gave Alex a look. "I'm sorry. Whatever is or is not going on between you two is not my business. But what we just found is my business and you better make it yours too."

"Follow us," Eric said.

Together, Jessie and Alex filed in behind the couple and made their way past the little greeting office and welcoming living room, past the double-sided staircase that led to the guest rooms and into a small anti-chamber at the back of the house. It led to a small pantry and butler's station and then out a screened back door to a concrete pad where a gleaming new generator, along with the air conditioning units and water heater stood.

Behind them, almost invisible against the siding of the house, was a narrow door.

"When we first purchased the house, we didn't even realize this was here," said Eric, indicating the door. "Then, once we started upgrading the HVAC system, the installers discovered it. It was locked and we could never find the key."

"Until," chimed in Mark, "we redid the butler's pantry, adding a coffee bar, and we found this. He was wearing an apron over his jeans and tee shirt and reached into the front pocket, drawing out a metal ring with various keys attached to it. They were iron and obviously very old, original to the house no doubt. "We started fiddling around with them and, wouldn't you know, one of them opened this door."

He fished through the mass of keys until he found the one needed and slid it into the lock. He struggled for a bit, trying to engage the corroded locking system, but was finally rewarded with a series of clicks that allowed him to push down on the handle that served as a doorknob.

He pushed at the door, moving it only a few inches, and stepped back. "The hinges are pretty rusted. Eric, would you?"

The larger man stepped forward, putting his weight and muscle into the door. While it looked like wood, it sounded like metal as it groaned and creaked its way open.

"Watch your step," Eric said, taking out a small flashlight from his pocket.

He pushed his way in, followed by Mark, Jessie and Alex. They stood still, letting their eyes adjust to the darkness, slowly making out the space around them illuminated by Eric's light. Mark took out his own flashlight and added it to Eric's beam.

Jessie blinked, taking in the dank space. "So, you called us here to see your secret wine cellar?"

Mark rolled his eyes, placing a hand on his hip. "Yes. We placed an urgent call to a police officer and his... friend, just to show them where we can keep wine." He stopped and looked around. "Although, this *would* make an amazing wine and cheese bar—"

Eric cleared his throat. "Mark. Not the time." He turned to face Jessie. "How many wine cellars come with their own dungeon?"

Jessie and Alex exchanged looks in the dim light and followed them through the space. The dim glow of the flashlights revealed a vast, oppressive chamber, its heavy air tainted with the tang of damp and ancient decay. The floor beneath them was uneven, compacted dirt. Every step they took kicked up a light mist of dust that tickled and scratched at the backs of their throats.

Bare, rough-hewn stone walls enclosed the space, their cool surfaces marred by rusted chains and tarnished shackles that dangled like grotesque ornaments. Eric played his light across them as they continued walking forward, before settling it in the corner of the room. There, corroded iron cages, their doors hanging ajar, squatted. They were of varying sizes, some no bigger than a medium-sized dog kennel, while others were large enough for a full-grown man to stand up in. They looked hauntingly out of place, grim sentinels that harkened back to a time of pain and bondage.

Jessie felt the chill of sweat clinging to her back as she stared at the horrors before her. She had seen things like this before while in the military. Testaments to inhumanity and cruelness. There were ghosts that still lingered here, and she could almost hear them rattling the cages.

"What in the world?" said Alex, his tone hushed.

"That's what we were wondering," said Eric. "Do you think this was some kind of torture site, or jail in the past?"

"Something like that," said Jessie. She took the light from him and stepped closer to the cages, sweeping the light across them to get a closer look. "My guess is these were slave pens."

Mark gasped. "Are you serious? Are you telling me that we own an old...slave plantation?"

Alex was shaking his head. "This isn't a plantation home. Almost all of those that are still standing are on the historic registry of homes listed as plantations. This Victorian is old, but it isn't listed as a plantation. And there is no farmland associated with it. The locale is all wrong."

"Maybe it was just owned by some old-timey freaks," Mark said, hopefully. "You know. Some *Eyes Wide Open* kind of people."

"Shut," said Jesse. "Their eyes were shut. And I don't think that's what was happening here. But Alex is right. The climate and topography here is very distinct. It has a different agricultural profile than the coastal and Piedmont regions. Still, there are a multitude of things slaves could have been utilized for."

Mark was shaking his head. "This is too awful. I wish we had never found this."

"There's something else," said Eric. "Follow me. I hope you're not claustrophobic."

The narrow entrance to the tunnel was hardly visible, hidden behind a jumble of old crates and dust-laden cobwebs. As Jessie and Alex bent to enter, the air immediately grew cooler, the musty scent of earth and time greeted them. The walls were rough, unworked stone that felt clammy to the touch, occasionally dripping with the condensation of subterranean moisture. Stooping down, they followed Eric into the cramped space, each step setting off puffs of aged dust, making the already limited air feel thick and hard to breathe.

The further they moved, the denser the darkness became, swallowing more of the weak light being cast before them. The ceiling was so low that they had to hunch over, their backs protesting the unnatural posture. Jessie looked at Eric's silhouette and wondered how the big man was even able to move.

After what felt like hours to Jessie, the tunnel began to incline upwards. The air grew slightly fresher, tinged with the scent of moss and lake water. As they climbed, a faint light started to become visible, a mere pinprick at first but grew steadily brighter. The diffused, silvery light of the outside world filtered through the dense overgrowth that concealed the tunnel's exit.

In moments, they were standing on the wet, muddy shores of Pine Lake. They exited the tunnel through a canopy of overhanging vegetation, root systems from trees growing along the embankment, and entanglements of vines that kept the exit all but hidden from view. Looking back at it, the opening was all but invisible, looking like just another play of shadows among the muddy banks of the lake.

Jessie breathed deeply, taking in a lungful of air that tasted sweet after the dank confines of the tunnel. "Well, I wasn't expecting that."

She and Alex turned, surveying where they had come out. The roof of the Victorian was barely visible in the distance and the area of the lake they had found themselves was a quiet, inlet away from the bustle of the main lake traffic. Jessie stepped through the mud and walked the few feet to the water's edge.

"Rocky, murky water makes it difficult for boaters to see the bottom here so most wouldn't risk their boats coming to this little shore. Also, with the dense, overhanging vegetation from the bank, there isn't really any beach access visible. That means that only someone who knows about this little tunnel would be using it," she said.

Mark was shaking his head. "Well, that's good, because obviously, no one has been in there in many, many years. Do you see anything wrong with sealing it up?"

Alex had been studying the ground and looked up at Jessie. "Eric, how many times have you been out here?"

Eric looked at him and frowned. "Only once, when I first discovered the tunnel earlier this morning. Why?"

"I don't know about sealing it up, but I do know that it hasn't been years since someone has been here." He pointed at the muddy earth. "There were tracks here when we came out. Someone has been inside this tunnel. And recently."

5

Bad Decisions

The inside of the trailer was dim, the single overhead bulb barely emitting enough light to reveal the frayed edges of the used-to-be-white sofa, the threadbare rug, and the bare, faux wood paneled walls of the tiny living room. The drone, an out-of-place piece of modern tech in this setting, sat on the worn-out coffee table, its blinking light reflecting in Kevin's anxious eyes.

He replayed the footage one more time, the quiet hum of the drone's playback overshadowing the distant sounds of laughter and arguments filtering in from other trailers nearby. The chilling scene unfolded on the screen; and each time he looked away at the apex of the violence. He didn't have the stomach to watch that again.

He sighed, cast the drone remote aside, and leaned back into the worn couch, closing his eyes. Somewhere, a kid started crying. Again. He hated this place, but also knew that for better or worse, it was home. He wasn't going anywhere, at least not anytime soon.

Unless of course the two men in the video found him. Then he knew he'd be headed six feet under. And if that happened, would anyone even miss him? Who would mourn him? He had no idea if his father was dead or alive and couldn't bring himself to care. He had no siblings; at least none that he knew about. It's possible his father had started over. Maybe he had a new family somewhere.

For some reason, that thought was more unsettling than if two men in dark jackets showed up on his doorstep.

He had a decision to make. One that really wasn't a decision. He looked at the drone again. He should march down to police headquarters and turn this footage over. But the thought of that was just as scary as all the other scenarios that had run through his mind over the last few hours. Everyone had heard the rumors about how corrupt the Pine Haven police could be. Well, everyone on his side of the tracks at least. If you had enough money to live on the right side of town, then you didn't have to worry about shake downs and planted evidence.

Or worse, if some of the rumors that floated around were true.

He froze for a moment, deep in thought. There was someone new working with the police he had heard about. A woman who was working with Officer Thomas. Everyone in town was whispering about her, said she was someone that could be trusted. They said she had done the unimaginable to protect the town back when everyone was scared of a potential serial killer running around. Plus, he had always liked Officer Thomas. He was one of the few policemen who didn't snicker when Kevin walked by wearing shoes with soles that had been superglued on one time too many.

But still. What could one officer do? And what if one of the officers that wasn't on the up and up were to learn what Kevin knew? Maybe some of them were on the payroll of whoever had killed that woman. If that was the case, he wouldn't last long in town.

Fear gnawed at his insides as he imagined the killers discovering his footage, tracking him down. The drone was his only protection, his bargaining chip.

What if he offered it up to the two men? Promised them there were no backups, and that in exchange for letting him live, they could have the only copy. But why stop at that? Men like this would probably do anything to get what Kevin had.

Maybe even pay anything.

He didn't need much. Just enough to get out of town and pay for a semester of college. Then he could get a job doing something—anything—to pay for the rest of college. He just needed a jumpstart.

He looked at the drone again, shaking his head. What he was thinking was wrong. He thought of his mother and how disappointed she would be if he went through with it.

"It won't always be easy, Kev, but just remember; do the right thing." It was something she always used to tell him. Right up until her last days spent coughing up blood on the same couch he was sitting on.

He looked around, his meager belongings suddenly making him feel smothered. All he needed was enough to get out of this town. Enough to start over. Anywhere. He stared at the drone.

He had what he needed to make it happen. But now, the question became, how?

6

Saying It Out Loud

"What did you think about that?" Alex asked. They had just pulled back into Jessie's driveway and stood on her porch, watching Blizzard run around in the yard.

"I think that Eric and Mark were just happy we didn't shut them down in order to investigate that tunnel."

Alex nodded. "There wasn't really anything criminal about it. I mean, it was obviously used for criminal activity at some point, but right now, it's just a creepy dungeon with a tunnel leading to the lake."

Jessie wasn't so sure as she watched Blizzard amuse himself with a large turtle that was trying to make its way unharnessed across the yard. "I'm not so sure. I didn't want to say it in front of them, but remember how the Chief said whoever has been buying up property really wanted the bed and breakfast? What if this is why?"

Alex turned to face her. "I didn't make that connection. I know Brody said they weren't involved in drugs, but it just seems like the most likely thing going on. That tunnel emptied out to an area of the lake that is isolated. It would make for a perfect spot to load and unload something illegal."

Jessie nodded in agreement, but she still had her doubts. Despite the horrific incident with her brother, she was pretty convinced that he hadn't lied to her about anything. He wasn't forthcoming with all aspects of the truth, but what he did say seemed to be factual. "The dungeon aspect bothers me. That, and the fact there were fresh footprints outside the tunnel, needs to be looked into further."

"I can check around. See if there are any experts around that might specialize in knowledge about the history of Pine Haven around the time of the slave trades. Maybe someone can give us some clues as to what we may be dealing with."

Jessie's eyes lit up. "You know, I may know just the person, and as luck would have it, she's actually on her way for a visit."

Alex arched an eyebrow. "Your friend is an expert at this?"

"Well, not officially, but it was part of her undergraduate coursework, I believe. I'll let you know more after she arrives."

"What do you have on tap for the rest of the day?"

"Cleaning the house and running some errands. Cora and I haven't seen one another since I left Colorado, so I have a feeling we are going to go through a couple bottles of wine as we catch up. Time to stock the bar. And you?"

"I have a couple of reports to type up at the office, and then I'm going to go do a bit of furniture shopping. I still need to replace that glass coffee table."

The mention of the table made Jessie wince. In her mind's eye, she could still see the look of shock on her brother's face when she drove that piece of glass into his neck.

Alex noticed her change in mood and immediately regretted his words. "Hey, I'm sorry to bring that up. I really do have a taste for my own foot."

Jessie laughed. "It's okay. It's something I've accepted. I'm just not ready to talk about it just yet."

Alex pursed his lips and gave a single nod. "Okay, well, I need to head out. But I'll check in later." He moved over to Blizzard and ruffled the dog's head before climbing into his vehicle.

Jessie watched as he pulled out and drove away before turning her attention to the shepherd. "Alright, big boy, it's time to clean the house and then run some errands."

She spent the next hour sweeping up enough excess dog hair to build another shepherd and then vacuuming and dusting the hard surfaces. After cleaning the kitchen and bathrooms, she looked around, pleased with the progress she had made. She made one last check of the spare bedroom where Cora would be staying, and then headed out of the house with Blizzard.

The first stop she made was at Angel's bakery. She left Blizzard in the Jeep and made her way inside. There were a couple of women standing at the counter speaking in animated, yet hushed tones with Angela. One of the women turned and saw Jessie and her mouth dropped open. The fact that they were obviously talking about her was comical, and the two women all but blushed as she approached the glass counter to inspect the array of pastries on display.

Angela smiled upon seeing her, said something to the two women, and then made her way over to Jessie. "Hi, Jess. Good to see you."

Jessie watched the two women give her a discreet glance as they walked to the door. "Maybe for you. What was that about?" She thumbed in the direction of the two ladies who had just exited the bakery.

Angela smiled. "Haven't you noticed that you're the talk of the town. Well, at least among the locals. Those two were actually in the process of asking me just what I knew about you. Martha, the one with the short bob, was telling me about how her son is thinking of moving back home and what a catch he would be—if you're single that is."

The last part was more question than statement, and Jessie ignored the pointed, yet playful, tone. "If that topic comes up again, feel free to tell them I am not interested. But thank you." She deliberately sidestepped the question and was grateful that Angela didn't push it.

"So, what brings you in today? Looking for something in particular?" Angela asked.

"Actually, yes. I have a friend visiting from out of town and I'd like to have something special for her to snack on. She loves fruit but *really* loves chocolate. Anything that you can suggest would be greatly appreciated."

Angela looked down, lost in thought as she considered the request. When she looked up, her eyes gleamed and she had a wide smile on her face. "I might just have the perfect desserts. A fresh apple tartine with a cheesecake filling that I have been experimenting with. As for the chocolate, might I suggest these chocolate cream truffles, dusted with gold powder? They are exquisite, if I must say so myself."

Jessie smiled broadly at the woman. "Sold. Load me up." As she waited for the order to be filled, she let her eyes wander around the bakery and cafe. It was definitely one of her favorite places in town. Angela was a master at her craft, and she also happened to brew some of the best coffee Jessie had ever tasted. She didn't go for flavors and whipped additives; it was coffee. Pure and simple and strong and magnificent.

There were a few small tables and chairs in the space as well as a couple of larger leather chairs meant for relaxing and reading. Jessie felt eyes on her and casually turned to see a young man sitting alone in the corner, a coffee mug sitting on the table before him. As soon as she looked his way, he quickly cut his eyes away, turning his attention to the window where he sat.

A rustling behind her caught Jessie's attention, and she turned to see Angela boxing up her order and placing it in a large paper bag with rope carrying handles.

"Thank you, Angela," Jessie said as they made their way to the cash register.

"You are more than welcome."

Jessie rummaged in her jacket, taking out her wallet as Angela rang everything up. "Hey, Angela, who's the kid sitting back there?" She indicated to the corner where the young man had taken up residence.

Angela looked over and frowned. "Who?"

Jessie looked over her shoulder, only to see the coffee mug sitting on the table, but the boy wasn't there. She glanced at the front door, trying to remember if she had seen him leave. "Oh, never mind. Thank you again for these. I'm sure they'll be delicious."

She left the bakery and jumped in her Jeep. "One last stop, boy." Blizzard barked in response, and they made their way down Main Street to the grocery store where she loaded up on cheese, snacks and wine.

With the passenger seat stocked with bags, she headed home. She smiled as she checked her watch. "Just enough time to unpack and feed you." The shepherd's ears perked up at the mention of food.

An hour later, with Blizzard taken care of and the house given one last going-over, Jessie was satisfied and ready for visitors. Glancing at her watch, she heard tires crunching on the gravel outside.

"Good old Cora. Right on time."

She stepped out onto the front porch as the blue Prius came to a stop, the driver's side door opened and one of her closest friends in the world stepped out. She rushed down the steps to greet her, throwing her arms around Cora.

"It is so good to see you," she said, her face all but buried in the soft cloud of natural hair that framed her friend's face.

"And you, Jessie. Look at you. You look amazing." She held Jessie by the shoulders at arm's length and took her in. "This mountain air definitely agrees with you."

Reaching into the back seat, Cora took out an

overnight bag and turned to take in the house. Her eyes were immediately drawn to the large, white shepherd sitting at attention on the front porch, his amber eyes trained on her.

"And who is this?" she asked, the faintest hint of weariness in her voice.

"Cora, meet Blizzard," Jessie said, motioning for the dog to join them.

Cora held perfectly still as Blizzard sniffed around her, then tentatively held out her hand for him to sniff. His rapidly wagging tail let them both know he approved of the new human and had adopted her as part of his pack.

"That is a seriously big animal," said Cora.

"I told you I adopted a dog."

"You said a dog. That's a small pony."

She followed Jessie inside and looked around admiringly at the home she had created. "Jessie, I love it. This feels like you."

Jessie smiled. She had to admit that once she made the decision to remain in Pine Haven, she had enjoyed turning her aunt's house into her home. Putting her own little stamp on things had helped her to feel settled.

And distracted her from everything that had happened with Brody.

Jessie showed her to her room where she could drop her bag and then led her back down the stairs and over to the small peninsula where the prepared charcuterie was on full display before them.

Jessie picked up the board and headed for the couch. "Grab the wine."

Placing the wine on the coffee table, Cora plopped down with a sigh.

"You know, I would have driven down and picked you up," Jessie said. "Or, you could have flown into the regional airport that's only a half-hour away."

Cora shrugged. "I know. But with the conference being down in Queen City, I wanted to take the opportunity to drive up to the mountains. See what makes this place so special that you're willing to settle down here." She playfully kicked a foot in Jessie's direction.

"Settle for now. And yes, there is definitely something to Pine Haven that I feel an attachment to. I can't explain it."

Cora relaxed back into the couch, a glass of red wine in her hand. "So. How have you been after everything that happened?"

Jessie blew out a lungful of air in a deep sigh. "I don't know if we have enough wine for that conversation." Her eyes focused on something in the distance, and she bit lightly on her lower lip. "I killed my brother, Cora." It was the first time she had said it like that. It sounded so final.

And then the dam burst.

Tears, raw and scalding and angry flowed. All Cora could do was gather her friend in her arms and let her cry.

When there were no more tears left in her, Jessie sat up, rubbing at her face with both hands. "I am so sorry. I don't know what just happened."

"Grief," Cora said. "You're finally allowing yourself to experience what you lost. And no matter how you or anyone else spins it, you lost something that was special to you."

Jessie sighed. "You should have seen him—heard the things he was saying. At the end, that man wasn't my brother anymore. I don't know what he was."

"And again, that's something else you're grieving. The loss of Brody as your brother, and the man you remember him as. It's going to take some time for you to heal. And you've got to be honest with yourself about a lot of things that maybe you don't want to acknowledge."

Jessie smiled at her friend. "Is that coming from the official Dr. Anderson?"

"That's coming from your official friend."

Jessie reached out and squeezed her hand. "There is so much we need to talk about. I hadn't realized how much I needed to talk to someone."

Cora cleared her throat. "Indeed. Well, if I remember correctly, I'm pretty sure I sent you the name of a therapist nearby who is more than willing to work you into her schedule."

Jessie felt her cheeks color. "You're right. You did, and I...didn't. But I will. I promise." She looked down at her hands, noting the tremble that had set in.

"Any new episodes since the last one?" Cora said.

Jessie shook her head. "No, thankfully. Hey, before I forget, didn't you minor in African American history in the south, or something like that?"

"I did. African American Studies." Cora frowned. "Is there something I can help you with along those lines?"

"I hope so. Or at least give a couple of friends of mine some peace of mind about something." She started to say more but was interrupted by the buzzing of her phone. She looked at the screen and then picked it up. "Hey, Alex, what's going on?" She listened intently for a few moments, a frown settling over her face. "Text me the address. I'll meet you there."

Cora looked concerned when she hung up. "What's going on, Jess?"

"Two hikers found a body. Alex wants me with him to look at the scene." She looked around, shaking her head. "I'm sorry. I'll be back as soon—" She stopped speaking as Cora stood, moving to retrieve her jacket from the coat rack standing just inside the door. "Um, what are you doing?"

Cora gave her a confused look. "What does it look like? You're in no condition to be driving yourself to look at a dead body. Honestly, you probably shouldn't even go. So, the least I can do is drive you there." She held up a hand as Jessie started to protest. "Besides. You know how anxious I am to check out this police officer of yours."

Jessie blushed for the second time. "He's not *my* police officer."

"Uh huh. Whatever you need to tell yourself, girl. Now get in the car."

7

A Brutal Discovery

The drive up the mountain was filled with twists and blind curves where one lapse in attention or judgement could result in a one-hundred-foot plunge off a cliff. Cora had a white-knuckled grip on the steering wheel of the Prius while Jessie tried not to snicker at her friend. Halfway up the mountain, Jessie had started to feel better and she realized that Cora was right; she was not in the right headspace to have attempted the drive.

She kept checking her phone for more messages from Alex, thinking he might send her information about the body that was found for her to digest prior to arriving. But the cell remained silent as they made their way to the site. "Looks like this is where we park." She pointed to a spot behind Alex's SUV. There were other police officers there as well as the sedan marked as belonging to the Medical Examiner.

Cora pulled onto the narrow shoulder ahead of Alex's car, and Jessie hopped out.

"Aren't you coming?" she asked Cora.

"Nope. Not the least bit interested in seeing any of what's going on over there. I'll hang here and enjoy nature. You do...whatever it is you do in these situations, and I'll be here when you get back."

Jessie patted the car door as she pushed it closed. "This won't take too long."

At least that was what she was hoping. She made her way off the road and down a dusty trail, following the sound of voices that grew louder with each step.

As she walked down a small hill, she rounded a bend in the path and was greeted by a couple of officers Jessie recognized. They were standing next to a young man and woman sitting on a fallen tree. The couple was visibly upset, and the man had a protective arm around the woman's shoulder. The two officers saw Jessie and nodded.

Out of the corner of her eye, she noticed the intense flash of a camera going off and walked over to find Alex and Dr. Lindquist standing together, speaking in hushed tones. Alex had his notebook out and was scribbling furiously.

He looked up and smiled at Jessie. "Hi. Sorry to pull you away from your friend. But when the call came in about this, the mayor was in a meeting with the chief, and she insisted you be contacted."

Jessie looked around. She could make out a couple of bare legs visible behind some brush. "No problem at all. What have we got?"

Dr. Lindquist cleared his throat. "It appears we have a young lady, in her early twenties at most I would say, of Asian descent, with two bullet wounds to the head. The stippling from the first indicates it was delivered at extremely close range. From what I can see about the angle of entry from the second shot, the killer stood over her body and fired down."

Jessie took a deep breath. "Execution style."

"So it would seem," added Alex. "Doc, what about a time of death?"

He shook his head. "I'll need to get her back to the lab to be certain, but judging from the rigor that has set in, I would say sometime in the last twelve to eighteen hours."

"No clothing or identification found in the immediate vicinity," said Alex. "We've already started searching the missing person's database for anyone fitting her description. Maybe we'll get a match."

"And of course, I will start looking at dental records as soon as I get her back to the office," said Dr. Lindquist.

Jessie held up a hand. "Doctor, can you also make sure to do a full drug panel as well?"

He gave her a curt nod. "Always do." He returned to examining the body. "I'm going to go over her one more time. Make sure I collect any possible trace evidence before she is moved."

Alex and Jessie left him to his work, stepping away from the body. Jessie thrust her chin in the direction of the two kids sitting on the fallen tree. "What about them? What's their story?"

Alex flipped a few pages in his notebook. "Matt Elder and Lana Devins. They said they were here hiking over to Devil's Peak when they stumbled across the body."

Something in his tone gave Jessie pause. "You sound like you don't believe them."

He shrugged. "Considering their car is parked not far from here, and they really don't have any hiking gear other than" —he pointed to the girl— "the blanket she has wrapped around her shoulders..."

Jessie gave him a slight smile. "So, they were up here to make out. Does that happen a lot?"

"More than you might think. Young people looking for some privacy that they can't get at their respective homes. So, they venture out to the far trails for some alone time."

"Did those officers take their statement?"

Alex nodded. "They did. I told them we have a consultant who would probably want to ask them a few questions as well. That's what they're waiting on."

Jessie walked over to the couple, making note of their body language as they leaned into one another. The young woman had her head on the man's shoulder as he protectively held her shoulder, pulling her closer.

Jessie nodded to the two officers, letting them know they could step away while she and Alex spoke with the couple. "Hello, I'm Jessie Night. I'm a consultant with the Pine Haven Police Department. Would it be okay if I asked you a few questions?"

The man dropped his head, removing his arm from around the woman. "Look, we've answered everything they already asked. Can't you get it from the other officers? We're tired and cold and want to go home."

The woman, Lana, smacked at his arm. "Matt, stop. A woman is dead." She looked up at Jessie, her eyes bloodshot. "Whatever you need to ask. We want to help in any way we can."

Jessie nodded. Despite Matt's demeanor, she knew what they must be feeling. That was why it was important to speak with them right away; the shock and mental trauma that accompanied stumbling across a dead body would set in soon. And with it, their memories of the event may change.

She kept her tone warm, reassuring and patient, so they didn't feel pushed or pressured. The popping in one of her knees made her wince as she squatted down to their level. Years of infiltrating military personnel had taught her that if you stand over someone when questioning them, it automatically puts them on the defensive.

"Matt. Lana," she began. "I know this is incredibly difficult for you and I'm sorry you're having to go through this. We're going to make it fast so we can get you out of here. Some of the questions I'm going to ask will be the same as the other officers, but it's important I hear it for myself. Is that alright?"

Despite her earlier words, Lana still looked to Matt to take the lead. Slowly, the man nodded. "Yeah. That would be fine."

"Good," Jessie replied. She looked up at Alex, who took out his notebook, pencil poised above an empty page. "Why don't we start with you telling me why you were up here. The real reason." While she doubted the answer would have any real bearing on the case, she wanted to establish a baseline of truth with them. It would make the next questions much easier to answer if they felt like she could be trusted. "It's okay. It stays between us."

Matt hesitated and then let out a small sigh. "We just wanted to be alone. Our families hate each other, and I'm not supposed to even be seeing her. So, we sometimes come up here just to be together; away from our parents."

Lana leaned forward. "My family thinks Matt isn't good enough because he's in training to be a mechanic and doesn't have a house on the lake like we do." She rolled her eyes, crossing her arms over her chest.

Alex gave Jessie a quick told-you-so glance before returning to scribbling in his notebook.

Jessie returned her attention to the couple. "How did you stumble across the body? And did you touch it at all?"

Lana wrinkled her nose at the thought. "We parked down the mountain at the overlook, then hiked up the creek to the access road. There's a spot not far from here that is secluded and beautiful. It's a field filled with daisies that we've been to a couple of times. Matt stepped away from the trail because he had to...relieve himself."

"And that's when I saw the body," Matt finished.

Alex cleared his throat. "Matt. When you were answering the call, did you...?"

The young man's eyes shot up. "Oh, no way. The minute I saw that I didn't need to go anymore."

"He screamed," said Lana.

Matt blushed. "I didn't scream. I just yelled out loud. We called 911 and...well, here you are."

"You called the police right away? No time lapse there?" Jessie asked.

Lana nodded. "Immediately."

"Good. Now for this one I need you to think hard. Did you see or hear anything prior to arriving on the scene? A gunshot, car pulling away; anything at all?"

Matt furrowed his brow for a moment. "No. It was so quiet. We figured there was no one around, like usual."

"Did you take anything from the area?" Jessie asked.

"No, nothing," Matt replied, glancing over at Lana. The girl agreed but shifted her eyes away.

Jessie zeroed in on her. "Lana, did you take anything?"

"No. I didn't...remove anything."

Jessie paused. "Did you take any pictures or videos of the area?"

This time Lana's body grew stiff. She began to wring her hands. Matt gave her a curious look.

"Fine," she said. "I might have snapped a pic or two. Maybe a video. But it's not like I was planning to post them online or anything."

Matt gave her a genuine look of horror. "Why in the hell would you do that?"

She raised her shoulders, dropping her hands onto her thighs. "I don't know. It's not like I've seen a dead body before. And I wanted to share it with my mom."

Matt drew in a deep breath, but before he could say more, Jessie held out her hand.

"You'll need to turn the phone over, as well as your password. Our forensics team will get it back to you once they've removed the photos."

Lana opened her mouth to protest but then thought

better of it as she reluctantly took her phone out of her pocket and handed it over. "The password is 2-2-2-2." She answered Jessie's stern look with a sheepish one of her own. "What? No one steals phones anymore."

Jessie just gave a small shake of her head as she stood and handed the phone over to Alex. "Thank you both. I know what you've been through can't have been easy for you. But thank you for all the help you've given." She handed each of them her card. "If you think of anything else you think we should know, feel free to call that number. Do you need an officer to take you home?"

"No, I can manage," said Matt. He placed his arm around Lana and led her away from the police, Jessie, and death.

Once they disappeared from view, Jessie turned to Alex. "They definitely didn't have anything to do with this."

Alex frowned. "You thought maybe they did?"

"In my book, when it comes to murder, everyone is a suspect until they aren't."

A female officer, one of the ones originally questioning the young couple, came rushing up, nearly out of breath.

"Alex, you need to come over here. I think we found the crime scene."

8

Casings and Cracked Branches

"Officer Nevins, is it?" Alex asked as they trudged through an area off the trails.

"Yes. But just Lyla, please," she replied, breathing hard.

The officers had been making sweeps outward in a spiral formation from where the body was found. The area that had attracted the attention of the officers was only a little over a half-mile from the body, but the terrain leading to it was almost impassable.

Jessie was thankful she had worn hiking boots instead of her sneakers. They made their way through what looked like a dried creek bed, through another patch of thick undergrowth and forested area to another trail.

"Is this part of the same trail system where the body was found?" Jessie asked, looking around.

"No," said Officer Nevins. "This one is not even

marked. It's part of an old farming and livestock footpath that farmers used to use to drive livestock down the mountainside to the more accessible main roads for the truckers to haul to the meat markets."

"So, unless you know it's here, there's not much chance of just stumbling upon it," said Jessie.

"That's correct," she said.

"How do you know so much about it?" Alex inquired.

"I grew up in this area. My father didn't raise livestock, but he did farm hemp. It grows well in the high altitudes," she replied.

Clear of the tree line, they made their way around a bend to where another officer was standing.

"What did you find?" Jessie asked.

The officer pointed to a dark red stain on the ground that bloomed outward, and a second stain pooled in one place. They had dropped yellow evidence markers in various places around the site.

"Casings?" Alex asked.

Officer Nevins nodded. "Two of them found. We've already bagged them and will be sending them off to match against the wounds on the victim."

"Great work," said Jessie. "Mind if I look around the scene?" She really didn't have to ask, but with the department now being made up of so many new officers, she wanted them to know how much she respected what they did.

A look of surprise crossed the woman's face. "Of course. Do your thing, Jessie."

With a nod to Alex, they walked slowly away from the scene.

"What are you looking for over here?" Alex asked.

She stopped and turned to face him. "All things indicate this is where that woman was killed. But why? Why kill her here, on an unmarked trail, isolated from foot traffic, and then move her to a trail where she had every possibility of being found?"

Alex lifted the cap he had been wearing and scratched at his head. "Well, in all honesty, both trails are pretty isolated. If those kids hadn't come up here, it might be days before anyone else came through here. These aren't hiking trails that tourists know about. Like Nevins was saying, you either know they are here, or you don't."

Jessie was nodding in agreement. "This trail must feed to a main road somewhere. How else would the killer have gotten her up here? Doubtful he would have made her walk the whole way through the terrain we just crossed. Too many chances for her to run. Have someone check the feed points to the trail for tire marks or any other sign of a car or truck." She turned, continuing her observation of the ground around her as Alex spoke quickly into the radio transmitter attached to his uniform's shoulder.

Something to the side of the trail caught her eye and Jessie stooped to investigate.

Alex followed her. "What did you find?"

She pointed to the ground in front of her. "It looks like the growth here has been trampled down. Broken twigs, cracked branches, smashed vegetation. Looks like someone ran through here in a hurry."

Alex's brows furrowed. "Witness maybe?"

She stood, looking around. "Could be. Only one way

to find out." She took a step into the grassy area and began to follow the broken reeds.

Alex spoke into his transmitter as he walked behind her. "I'm having some of the crime scene guys come photograph the area. See if they can get any shoe impressions."

"Good idea. Of course, that means we now have to give them ours. To rule us out from the scene."

She stopped suddenly, pointing downward. "Bullet casing."

Alex took a few steps to her side. "More here. A lot more." They looked around, seeing roughly six casings spread about the immediate vicinity.

Jessie stared into the distance in all directions. "What the hell were they shooting at?"

"Had to be a witness. Someone saw them."

Jessie eyed the closest tree line and then the array of bullets. She stiffened her arm, thumb up, forefinger pointing straight out in front of her as if she were holding a gun. Looking down at the casings, she then pretended to fire the 'gun'. "I could be wrong about this, but it really looks like whoever did this shooting was turning in circles...or something like that."

"Well, this will be a good test for the crime scene guys we hired."

Jessie nodded. After her near-death experience the mayor had been very forthcoming with the release of emergency funds to upgrade the police department. The money had gone toward a much-needed IT improvement, as well as new equipment and personnel for a small crime scene investigation team.

There still wasn't a detective on the force, but Jessie was more than thankful to see Alex and the team get the tools they needed to make their jobs a lot easier. A detective would come in time.

Alex's radio crackled and he leaned his head to the side listening. "The team will be out here as soon as they are finished with the other scene. Shouldn't be long. In the meantime, I'll walk you back to your car. I know you had plans for today. Sorry about ruining them."

Jessie was still vaguely distracted as she looked around at a crime scene that made no sense. "Um, yeah, not a problem. You know, if there was a witness they were shooting at, the bullets would have struck somewhere in the tree line in front of us." She started in the direction of the trees, only to be stopped by Alex.

"The team can handle it from here. You've pointed them in the direction, let's let them do what they're getting paid for. Don't you have a houseguest you're supposed to be hosting?"

Her eyes widened as she looked at her watch. "Cora. How long have I been out here? She's waiting on me in the car."

Alex just gave her a bemused look as they turned and headed back towards the trails. On the walk, Jessie's mind was turning over everything she had taken in regarding the two crime scenes.

"As soon as Dr. Lindquist is finished with the autopsy, will you let me know? Also, someone needs to canvas any homes in the area. I know with the layout here it's unlikely, but maybe someone heard something. With as many shots as were fired off, it might have attracted attention. Oh, and be sure and send me everything the CSI team digs up."

Alex chuckled. "Don't worry. As soon as I know it, you'll know it."

Thirty minutes later, they arrived back at their respective cars. Cora was standing outside her rented Prius, leaning against it, casually thumbing through her phone.

Jessie rushed up to her. "Cora, I am so sorry. Time completely got away from me."

Cora looked up and smiled at her friend. "Don't even worry about it. I knew we might be out here all night. I just got to level twenty-four on Candy Smash so I'm all good." She gave Alex a very obvious up and down. "And who do we have here?"

Jessie cleared her throat and waved a hand in Alex's direction. "Dr. Cora Anderson, may I introduce you to Officer Alex Thomas of the Pine Haven Police Department."

Cora smiled appreciatively and extended her hand. "So, you're the famous Alex I've heard so much about."

Alex shook her hand, his brows dipping slightly. "Well, I don't know about famous. But I am the only Alex in Pine Haven."

"You saved Jessie's life a couple of months ago. Thank you for that." The sincerity in Cora's voice made the man blush.

"Well, I'm really not sure who saved who. But thank you," he said.

Jessie turned to Cora. "Well, I'm sure Alex has a lot to do still, and you and I need to get back to the house. I'm sure Blizzard is starving by now. And I bet you are as well."

"Oh, I'm fine," she said, giving Alex another quick glance and a smile. "Very fine."

"Okay, it's definitely time to go," Jessie said, giving her friend a playful push towards the driver's door.

After Cora closed her door, Jessie made her way to the passenger's side and climbed in. Alex stopped her before she could close the door.

"Um, aren't you forgetting something?" he said. She looked at him quizzically and he smiled, looking down at her feet. "I need your shoes for the forensics guys."

Jessie looked at him confused for a moment before it hit her what he was saying. "Oh, of course. I knew that." She took off her boots and handed them to him.

"I'll have them back to you as soon as possible," he said, shutting the door for her.

"No, problem. Just keep me updated on everything. I'll start making notes when I get home. We can compare them later."

They pulled away, and Jessie tried hard to ignore the smug look on Cora's face, until she finally relented. "Okay, what is it?"

Cora shrugged. "He's cute. Seems nice. And obviously he's smart and good at what he does."

"There's no way you could know all that."

Cora smiled. "I know it because you're still working with him after everything that went down. You like him, don't you?"

Jessie didn't say anything and hoped Cora couldn't see

the red creeping into her face. "It's not like that. He's a good man. He wants nothing but the best for this town. And it just feels like ever since I got here...it's been one nightmare after another."

Cora risked a quick glance at her friend. "And you think it's your fault? What's happening here?"

Jessie sighed and turned her face to the window. "Brody was one hundred percent my fault. And how do I know that the horror I just came from isn't related somehow?"

Cora breathed in deeply as she gripped the steering wheel tighter. "Jessie, speaking as a doctor, I have to tell you that it's essential to separate our feelings from objective facts. Feeling responsible doesn't mean you *are* responsible. Correlation doesn't imply causation." She glanced at her again and smiled. "And speaking as your friend, you've done incredible things and touched a lot of lives. Pine Lake's issues might have always been here, bubbling under the surface. If anything, you might be the one who helps bring them to light and resolve them."

Jessie didn't respond. Rationally, she understood what her friend was saying. She understood that while Cora was speaking as a trained psychiatrist, she was also speaking from the heart as someone with her best friend's interest in mind.

But for Jessie, her instincts, coupled with past experiences and trauma, told her a different story. All she could think about was what if her presence really was the catalyst for everything happening in Pine Haven? And even if it weren't her fault, she felt a responsibility to fix it. This town deserved peace and tranquility.

And no matter what it took, she was going to provide it.

9

Master of all he Surveys

The sun was just beginning to set, casting long strands of gold and orange across the water. The luxurious house that sat on its edge was magnificent, the epitome of modern elegance. The white facade gleamed in the sun's dimming embrace, contrasting brilliantly with the deep blues that came with the evening.

The back of the house was a testament to all that money could buy. Two stories of floor-to-ceiling windows commanded the view, capturing the lake's ever-changing moods and magnifying the beauty of sunset. An expansive deck of dark wood extended outward, offering an uninterrupted view of the water. The furniture, arranged perfectly around large planters and stone tables, suggested both comfort and luxury.

The back lawn was manicured to perfection. The bright green of the grass provided the perfect soft counterpoint to the house's contemporary lines. Mature trees lined the sides of the lawn, their gently swaying canopies providing relief from the sun and shade from any neighbors' prying eyes. He sighed as he looked over the excavation equipment that sat to one side. It was ugly; a pockmark on the beauty that was his landscape. Still, it was needed, and the last bit of construction to the house would be completed soon.

The owner of the property stood on the deck, a tumbler filled with ice and a clear liquid, balanced on the deck railing as he surveyed all that his hard work had afforded him. The ringing of his cell phone snapped him out of his reverie, and he looked at the screen annoyed. Taking a deep breath, he put it to his ear. "The office is closed now, you know that."

He was about to end the call when the voice on the other end rang out. "Someone else picked up the package."

The man froze, his heart started to pound in his chest. "Are you certain?"

"The reports just came in."

The man was silent for a few heartbeats as he looked out over the water. "Why wasn't the package picked up by our usual recipient?"

"The doc was late. When he arrived, others were already retrieving."

The little man sighed. "No names of any kind, please."

"How do we proceed?"

"Continue with next steps. We need to find our little birdie."

A pause let him know that his business partner still wasn't onboard with that plan. "Are you sure this is what you want to do?"

"Just handle it. Like we said." He disconnected the call, dropping the phone with a sigh. Tiny footsteps racing up behind him caught his attention and he turned just as the little girl threw herself into his arms.

"Daddy!" she screamed, letting out a chorus of giggles as her father lifted her, tickling her ribcage at the same time.

"How's my little troublemaker?" he asked, squeezing her tight, smothering his face in her tangle of blonde curls.

"Hey, I don't make trouble. You make trouble!"

He laughed as he sat her down. "Where's Mommy?"

"She's putting away the groceries and told me to come get you so you can help."

"Oh, she did, huh? Well, then I better get in there right away. Tell her I'll be there in a second."

He playfully pushed at her backside, shooing her back towards the house.

He turned, his face darkening as he surveyed the water and picked up his drink. His mind spun in a million different directions as he replayed everything. The body could potentially be a problem for them. He was confident the police wouldn't be able to identify her anytime soon. She wasn't in the system. Her fingerprints had never been recorded and her DNA would not show up in any database. He also wasn't worried about dental records. All his girls saw the same dentist, who didn't keep a database or record of their care. So he wasn't concerned about that.

But the drone.

That was a wrinkle outside of his control. What the hell was someone doing up there with a drone to begin with? Had they only been watching or was it recording as well?

The loud crack of the glass he was holding echoed over the lawn. He looked down and saw blood beginning to ooze from his palm.

"Fuck." He left the glass, holding his hand up to prevent blood from dripping across the deck as he made his way to the house. "Ellie! I seem to have had a little accident."

His wife appeared almost immediately, her eyes growing wide when she saw his hand. "What happened? Are you okay? Come into the bathroom."

"Ah, it's no big deal. But keep Sarah off the deck until I can clean up the glass I broke."

His wife smiled, wrapping his hand in a clean towel before removing some bandages and alcohol from the drawer beneath the sink.

The man watched his wife as she cleaned and bandaged his hand, his heart swelling as he looked at her.

Everything was going to be okay. His plan to find the drone owner would work. It had to. It meant inviting a new element of violence into his world. But he was okay with that.

Violence had become his specialty.

10

The Good with the Bad

"And you're sure you don't mind doing this?" Jessie asked. "I mean, I don't want it to feel like work for you."

"Don't worry about that at all," Cora said. "Trust me, this isn't work. Going by what you said, I'm really excited to see this."

They were in Jessie's jeep, Blizzard in the back seat, gleefully taking in all the scents Pine Haven threw at him as they made their way to the bed and breakfast.

"Mark and Eric are excited too. Nervous about what it might be, but excited, nonetheless. I think they want to make sure it's nothing that will get them...how did Mark put it...*cancelled*," Jessie added.

Cora stared at the scenery flashing by giving her a slight nod. "I can understand their fear. It's a touchy subject right now. And you're saying the home is on the historic registry?"

"From what I was told, yes. But does that impact anything found inside the house?"

"Normally, I wouldn't think so. But in a case like this, it might fall under the town council's discretion. But let's take a look and see if we can figure out what they're dealing with before worrying about that."

Jessie eased the jeep into the parking lot for the bed and breakfast, and they all climbed out, Blizzard running to the edge of the property to sniff around.

"Wow," Cora said, taking in the old Victorian and the breathtaking view it afforded. "This place is amazing. I can see why they would be so protective of it."

Mark and Eric were waiting for them on the porch as they approached. Jessie shook each one's hand and then introduced them to Cora.

"It's nice to meet you," Cora said. "You have a beautiful home and business here."

Blizzard ran up and sniffed the two men as well, lingering at Eric's side, his tail wagging happily. Eric reached down and ruffled the fur on his head.

Mark shook his head. "Before you ask, no, we still aren't getting a dog."

Eric looked up, winking in Jessie's direction. "Whatever you say, honey."

Mark playfully rolled his eyes, before stepping aside and ushering them inside. He gave Blizzard the side eye as the dog marched into the house as well.

"Oh, he'll be fine waiting in the Jeep," Jessie said.

"No, it's alright. There are only a couple of guests still in the house and they are not early risers," Mark said. He turned to face Cora, clasping his hands together. "First, thank you for taking time out of your busy day to assess this. It's just so horrible. It was the last thing we expected to find."

"Well, a lot of larger estates and homes in the south and parts of the north, utilized slave labor in an effort to save on the cost of farmhands and house servants. It's how a lot of families built their wealth. The fact that there might be a few remnants of that time hidden in homes isn't that surprising."

Eric shuffled his feet, visibly uneasy over the topic. "It's just so unbelievable what happened. I will never understand how someone treated another human being like that."

"Well, that's because you have empathy," said Cora. "Why don't you show me this room you found?"

Jessie didn't fully trust Blizzard not to run out the tunnel and disappear into the lake, so she took him to the foyer and told him to stay. The big shepherd promptly curled up on one of the large area rugs and began to doze off.

"If you don't mind, I'll stay up here and make sure Blizzard stays out of trouble," Mark said. "Plus, that place gives me the creeps."

Jessie understood exactly what he meant. Truth be told, she wasn't exactly thrilled with the idea of revisiting a place where so many had undoubtedly intentionally been harmed...and worse. She steeled her nerves as Eric led them through the house and out to the narrow stairwell that took them down to his recent discovery.

Without a word, Cora took in the place. Jessie could see the tension fueling her friend's body and instinctively took her hand, giving it a squeeze. Cora's jaw clenched when she saw the cages. She gave Jessie a quick, hard look, then headed over to inspect them.

She stooped down and peered into one of the smaller cages, looking all around the bars and the door before lying on her belly and inching into the cramped space. She lay there, her head moving from side to side for a few moments before she inched her way back out and moved on to one of the larger cages. Stepping inside, she again inspected the bars, the locks and the hinges on the door.

She walked out, letting go a deep sigh, before heading over to inspect the chains and restraints hanging from the walls. Jessie felt her heart break as she watched one of her closest friends tremble as she hefted the chains and pulled against one of them. She let it drop and it struck the wall with a heavy, clanking thud.

Jessie swallowed hard and watched as she made her way around the room. Occasionally Cora would stop, running her palm across something, and then resume her inspections. After what seemed like an eternity, during which neither Jessie nor Eric had spoken, Cora walked back over to her friend.

Eric was standing next to her, his arms wrapped around his torso in a way that made the short sleeves of his tee shirt strain to contain him. "So? How bad do you think it was? I mean...I know it was bad...but what's your opinion?"

Jessie didn't speak, just watched the emotions play out across her friend's face. She could only imagine what she was going through. Cora was one of the most empathetic people she knew. The weight that must have settled on her over the last hour was something Jessie would probably never know.

"Can you show me the opening to the tunnel you found?" Cora asked. Eric showed her and she peaked her head inside but didn't enter.

She turned back to them and took a deep breath, hands resting on her hips. "Well, the bad news is, this was definitely used to house slaves." She watched as Eric pinched the bridge of his nose between his thumb and forefinger. He squeezed his eyes tightly in a useless attempt to hold back tears. Cora moved to stand next to the man and placed her hand on his arm. "The good part about this is that this place wasn't created to hold and torture slaves. I'm pretty sure what you have here is a stop along the underground railroad."

Both Eric's and Jessie's mouths dropped open. The big man's eyes were as large as saucers as he stared at Cora.

"Are you sure? How can you tell something like that?" Eric asked.

She led him over to the cages first. "The wear and tear on the hinges of this door are all but nonexistent. You might expect that with the smaller ones, where children might have been held, but here" —she pointed to the larger cages— "where adult men would have been held, there is no way they would not have been shaking these bars and plying their strength against the doors. But the hinges show no sign of stress over time. And here" —she led them to the chains on the wall— "the same thing. These walls where the chains are anchored are little more than mud with an overlay of thin plaster and concrete. I'm pretty sure you would be able to yank one out of the wall. Let alone a man afraid for his life."

Jessie stared at the wall. "So, you're saying all of this is just for show?"

Cora nodded. "Exactly."

"But what purpose would that serve?" Eric asked.

"Because this is still considered part of the deep south. If there is even a hint of an underground railroad, not only would the property owner be in serious trouble, but so would his family. My guess is this was all set up in the event the house was ever raided or inspected by anyone from the militia. The owner could simply show him this dungeon and claim that this is where his slaves are kept or imprisoned when needed."

She motioned for them to follow her to the wall that she had been inspecting. "And look at this. There are tiny symbols carved into the wall. They're so small and blend in so well with the plasterwork that if you didn't know to look for them, you'd never see them." She pointed to a couple of places along the wall that Jessie had to squint and get right up on to see. "A hand—indicating that someone in this house was willing to reach out to help those in need. And here, the North Star. A symbol of guidance used to inspire strength by saying freedom is just a bit farther north."

Then she moved over to the tunnel. "But this is the big tale. If you were imprisoning your slaves here—for torture or whatever else—why would you have a tunnel that leads out to the water? If a slave were to break free of their binds, they'd have a good shot at escaping." She shook her head. "No, my guess is this was where they bought them in to hide them, feed them, maybe a change of clothes or a disguise, and then would use the tunnel to move back out at night and on to the next stop."

She saw the look of relief that flooded Eric's face.

"Now, that's just my assertion of the situation. You should probably have someone who is a true expert in the field go over this place with a fine-toothed comb. I can certainly provide you with a couple of names of people I'm sure would love the opportunity. But I think this place was a refuse for slaves. In a time of extreme ugliness, it was a safe house."

The man trembled as he reached for her, arms wide.

"Oh, okay," said Cora as he swept her into his embrace.

"I'm not much of a hugger, but I just really appreciate what you did here. And you have free room and board anytime you want to visit," he whispered.

"Well, thanks, but that isn't really necessary," Cora said, giving him an awkward pat on the back until he broke their embrace.

Jessie broke out in a smile just as her phone buzzed. She pulled it out, frowning as she read the message.

"What is it?" Cora asked.

"It's from Alex. He's at the coroner's office and there's something he needs me to see right away." She glanced at her watch. "I can drop you off at home and then—"

"Oh no, don't do that," Eric said. "You go take care of your business. I'll be more than happy to drive Cora back to your house. Plus, I have a new batch of blackberry jam I created, and you get your pick of the first pot."

Cora's eyes lit up. "Well, who am I to say no to some good jam?"

Jessie gave her friend a hug and headed for the stairs. "And don't worry. I'll take Blizzard. I'm sure he's driven Mark crazy by now."

At the top of the landing, she made her way to the small reception area where she found Mark on one knee enthusiastically rubbing Blizzard's sides and mumbling to him in a baby voice.

As soon as he saw Jessie standing there, his face went stern, and his voice deepened. "Uh, and that's why you don't slam your big, beautiful tail around like that in a house filled with antiques."

Jessie gave the man a half-smile. "Thank you, Mark. I'll take him from here, and I'm sorry about your... antiques."

He blushed slightly. "Well. I guess it will be okay. Hey, where's your friend? How bad is it?"

Jessie's smile broadened. "Eric is taking her home for me. I just got a call I need to respond to. But I think you're going to be very pleased with the outcome."

She patted her leg, letting Blizzard know it was time to leave. Together, they made their way out to the Jeep.

Jessie took a deep breath as she took to the road, heading for the coroner's office. She hoped she was wrong, but she was worried that the fact the medical examiner was calling them so early in his examination couldn't be a good thing.

11

That's Not Braille

W hen she arrived at the coroner's office, Alex was waiting for her at the door.

"That was quick," he said.

"We were at the bed and breakfast. Cora was able to give them some good news I think."

He pushed the door open for her then followed through. "Something tells me we aren't about to get the same."

"That's what I was afraid of." She looked down at Blizzard and held her palm up in the air and then turned her hand over, palm down. Immediately the dog moved to lie down by the wall, curling up into a large ball of white fur.

Alex gave her an appreciative look. "Impressive."

"We've been working on learning hand signals. He's scary smart and a fast learner."

Alex smiled. "I'm glad you took him in. He seems happy, and so do you, for that matter."

He was right. Blizzard played a crucial part in her life that she hadn't been aware was missing. Companionship.

They made their way through the sterile medical office until they found Dr. Lindquist's office near the back of the building. After stepping through a couple of swinging metal doors, they arrived in a tiny room where they were greeted with paper booties to cover their shoes, blue paper lab coats, and surgical masks.

Once they were properly covered, they rang a buzzer next to the only door that led into the coroner's lab. Dr. Lindquist appeared in the tiny window and buzzed them in.

"Morning, Doc. Have you already identified our victim?" Alex asked as they trailed him to the metal table in the center of the room where the body of the woman rested.

The doctor shook his head and looked at the officer. "Unless you have been able to find her identification, then no, we don't have her ID just yet. I'm fast, but not that fast."

Alex frowned. The Medical Examiner was a little crankier than usual. That only happened when he was particularly disturbed by something.

"I'm sorry," the doctor said, reading the look on Alex's face. "But I did find something I think the two of you should see."

There was a large rolling cart with a monitor and various trays and medical instruments arrayed that sat to the side of the exam table. Dr. Lindquist reached over and powered on the monitor. He navigated through a multitude of thumbnails until he found the picture he wanted and expanded it to fill the screen.

An area of skin appeared to have been zoomed in on. In the center of the photo, the skin bore a series of slight elevations and indentations in a linear pattern. Jessie squinted her eyes at the photo, making out a series of dots and dashes that made up the aberration on the otherwise smooth skin.

"Is that braille?" she asked.

Dr. Lindquist held up a finger. "That was what I thought as well. It was small, but palpable to the touch. When I ran my fingertips across it, it that was the first thing it made me think." He lifted one of the small, plastic containers from the table and held it out to them. Alex took it and held it up to the light so Jessie could see it as well.

Inside the container was a metallic, linear strip comprised of the dots and dashes they had seen in the photograph.

"Where was it on her body?" Alex asked.

The examiner led them to the woman's body and lowered the sheet that covered her to her waist. He grasped her right arm and rotated it outward enough for them to see the small incision on the upper, inner part of her arm, just below her bicep. "The inner arm. Here." He pointed to the area.

Jessie gave the doctor a hard look. "That can't be a coincidence."

Alex frowned. "What can't be a coincidence?"

"That was found in the same place that a lot of

contraceptive implants are placed in women," she said, her voice strained.

Questions were written across the officer's face and Dr. Lindquist turned to address him. "Birth control implants are often placed in this area because there is a layer of fibrous tissue found there that holds it securely in place, keeping it from moving or migrating to other parts of the body."

"It's also easily accessible but also hidden from view, for the most part," Jessie added.

"But why?" asked Alex, scratching his head. "What purpose does it serve? And you said it's *not* braille, Doc? Because it sure looks like it."

The doctor shook his head. "I immediately compared it to the braille alphabet, and it does not match it in the slightest. I'm not sure why she would have this."

Alex's brow furrowed. "Something familiar about it..."

Jessie's eyes widened. "That's because we've seen this before." She spun, heading quickly for the exit as she called over her shoulder. "Can you please send me some close-up pictures of that metal strip?"

She was out the door before the doctor could answer. Alex shrugged and gave the doctor a nod before racing after her.

"Jessie, what is it?"

She had already torn off her gown and was pulling the booties free when he entered the antechamber.

She looked up at him excitedly. "Alex, that pattern of dots and dashes, it's like the entries into the ledger that Jordan Myer was keeping. Everything in it was marked with them. This can't be a coincidence."

Realization settled across Alex's features as he sat down and quickly began removing his own protective wear. They headed for the door, Jessie giving a sharp command with her hand to Blizzard, and he immediately fell into step at her side.

"This could be our first break in this," she said as they stepped into the sunlight. "You go to the department and start going through the NamUs database. See if you can find any mention of more bodies with this particular type of branding."

"What about you?" he shouted as she and Blizzard climbed into her Jeep.

"I'm going to compare the patterns from that brand to the ones in the ledgers. See if I can find any similarities."

She pulled out, watching Alex fade in the background. This was what they were waiting for. She could feel it. A break in the case involving Jordan's murder and this ledger she had been keeping. Jordan's murder was a closed case. Brody, Jessie's own brother, had been responsible for it.

But the question as to *why* still lingered.

Obviously, they had both gotten themselves involved with some very dangerous people—Brody had used his dying breath to tell her as much—but who those players were remained a mystery. Every path they might have found since Brody's death had led them to a dead end.

But this one felt different. Jessie felt a chill race up her spine as she edged the Jeep a little harder than she normally would, taking the bend that led to her driveway a little sharper than she should have.

She parked the car next to Cora's Prius, and made her

way up the stairs to the porch. Instantly, she knew something was wrong. It was quiet.

Too quiet.

And then she saw the broken bit of wooden doorframe where the latch was. Panic flooded her as she threw open the door. "Cora!"

Only more quiet greeted her.

"Blizzard! Patrol!"

The shepherd tensed, reading his human's mood, and knowing this wasn't just a drill. The hair on his haunches stood stiff as he silently raced into the house, moving immediately to the back door, the sliding patio doors and lower level windows, sniffing for any sign of intruders.

Then, he traced up the stairs, repeating the same motions, checking for anything that could give away a stranger hiding in his home.

While he cleared the upstairs, Jessie took in the main living area. Her heart threatened to leap out of her chest it was beating so hard. The living room was in disarray. The first thing she saw was a gift basket lying on the floor, little jars of jellies and jams strewn across the room. The coffee table was overturned, its contents scattered haphazardly across the floor. The floor lamp that stood to one side of the sofa was lying broken on the floor. The couch cushions were thrown about the space, and the chair that sat next to the couch had been knocked around sideways.

The scent of violence lingered in the room.

She breathed the slightest bit of relief when she didn't see evidence of blood anywhere. Whatever happened here, Cora hadn't gone down without a fight.

Good for her.

Blizzard returned to her side, his tail wagging from side to side as she bent down to rub between his ears, whispering "Good boy," to him.

The world around her began to lose its focus and she felt the cold fingers of numbness reach for her. A knot formed in the pit of her stomach as she took out her phone and swiped at Alex's number. Her throat was coated in sand when he answered.

"They took her. They took Cora," was all she was able to get out before she receded into a void that turned her body into a cage.

12

Once More into the Void

It might have been twenty minutes. It might have been hours that she sat on the floor, her back against the wall, facing the mess that was once the center of her home. Blizzard never left her side, his head lying softly in her lap.

She felt him stiffen, his head lifting, his nose quivering as he sampled the air, a tiny whine leaving his throat.

Seconds later, Alex entered the room at a run, his gun drawn. Behind him, two more officers entered the house, weapons at the ready. Blizzard let out a low, rumbling growl, followed by a short bark.

"It's okay, boy," Alex said, holstering his weapon and holding out his hand for the dog to sniff. "You're being a good boy, and everything is going to be okay." He followed the shepherd's eyes as they landed on the two officers he didn't know. Alex waved them off. "It's okay.

Give us a minute. Check around back, see if you can find anything back there."

As soon as they retreated, Blizzard began to whimper and lick at Alex's hand.

"It's okay, I'm here," Alex said to Blizzard and Jessie. He tentatively took her hand and began to massage her fingers, then added the strumming she had shown him. His fingers played out the rhythm that he hoped would register in the back of her mind. "Jessie? Can you hear me?"

She didn't move, but he could see a slight change in her breathing as his presence began to pull her back from the cliff. Slowly, her fingers tightened around his and her eyes swept to his face.

"I'm going to get you some water, okay? I'm not going anywhere," he said softly. He felt her grip on his hand loosen as he slipped out of her vision and into the kitchen.

She swallowed, trying to regain control of her rapid breathing. She reminded herself that she was safe here. Blizzard had not left her side, and Alex was here now.

She was safe.

Alex returned and she felt the coolness of the glass pressed against her mouth. It was an effort, but she was able to part her lips just enough to take in a small sip. It was a balm to the rawness of her throat, and slowly, she felt her muscles begin to relax and come back under her own control. She looked around, her eyes blinking rapidly as they travelled from Alex to the officers who had returned and were staring at the two of them.

"Hey, is she okay? Do we need to call the medics?" one of them asked.

"No. She's fine. Probably just had the wind knocked out of her. Would one of you call the crime scene boys? We are going to need this place processed ASAP," Alex said. When they left the house again, he lowered his voice, turning back to Jessie. "Do you think you're ready to stand?"

She swallowed hard and nodded. He took her hand in his and slowly began lifting her to her feet. Her steps were small and shuffling as he guided her to the chair, easing her into it.

"Do you know what happened?" he asked.

She shook her head, trying to force her voice to obey her. Finally, she managed to coax her words out. "Cora. I came home and found the place like this. No sign of her."

She knew that he had assessed the scene as soon as he entered the house. The fact that he had called for the CSI team told her he had reached the same conclusion she had.

She tried to sit up and winced. Her muscles weren't quite back under her control. "We need to establish a timeline. Dust this place for prints. See what they might have—" She stopped mid-sentence and pointed at the piles of paper scattered across the living room floor. "Alex, the printouts from the ledger...they were on the table. Did they take those?"

He turned and made his way to the papers, dropping to his knees as he shuffled through them. "They're still here. Looks like they didn't get them."

Jessie frowned, sitting forward as she rolled her neck

from side to side, limbering up stiff muscles. "But that doesn't make sense. Why take Cora and leave the ledger?"

"Maybe it wasn't the ledger they were after?"

Placing her hands on the chair arms, Jessie forced herself to her feet. She shook her head as Alex rushed to her side. "I'm okay. It's passing. The shock of what happened, the sudden knowledge that Cora was taken in a violent attack…it was a bit much. Overwhelmed me for a moment and brought on an episode. But I'm okay now."

Alex nodded and stepped back, giving her room.

"How long for the crime scene guys to get here?" she asked. "I want them to go over this place with a fine-toothed comb; I don't care how long it takes. No way this kind of a struggle went down without some kind of DNA, or something being left behind."

She walked back to where she had sat against the wall when her catatonia struck her. She bent down and retrieved her phone, quickly placing a call and holding the cell out for Alex to listen in as well. After two rings, there was a connection made on the other end.

"Hello?" It was Eric.

"Eric? It's Jessie. What time did you drop Cora off at my house?" Her voice was rushed and her tone just a click away from panic.

"Jessie? We left here just after you did. I took her right home. What's wrong?"

"Did you see anyone around the house when you left her? Did you follow her into the house? Do you know if she locked the door behind her?" She was speaking so fast she could barely follow her own words.

Eric stammered a bit on the other end. "I— no, I

didn't go into the house with her. She said she was fine and thanked me for the jams and that was it. I pulled out after she opened the door and left." He was breathing hard now. "Jessie, what happened? Is she okay?"

She hesitated before answering. "No. She's missing. I'm going to have Alex send someone over to take your statement. Start writing down every little detail you remember about dropping her off...even if you think it isn't important."

"Of course. I'll do whatever is needed."

She could tell he was shaken up by the call, but she didn't have time to comfort him. Her friend was missing, and time was of the essence.

She stood in the middle of the floor, looking around, her eyes taking it in but not focusing on any one thing.

"...Jessie? Did you hear me?"

She looked up, realizing that Alex was talking to her. "What?"

"I said, we need to take your statement right away, and you need to step out of the house. The CSI team is on the way. You can't be in here while they are working."

She glared at him, her mind racing. "My statement is that I came home, found the door busted, and my closest friend taken." She headed for the door, motioning for Blizzard to follow.

"Where are you going?" Alex asked, trailing behind her.

On the porch, she wheeled on him. "Well, you said I shouldn't be here, so I'm leaving." She turned to step off the porch but stopped herself. "I'm sorry. I didn't mean to come off like that. But I can't stay here. I need to start looking for her."

"But where?" Alex asked.

"Well, it stands to reason that someone grabbed Cora because we were getting too close to whatever the hell is going on with this ledger, right?"

Alex nodded slowly. "I could see that."

"Well, my brother worked for whoever these people are. Jordan Myer also worked for them. These aren't the type of people to get their own hands dirty. So, who's to say they also didn't get someone else to grab Cora?"

"Okay. I follow. But where do we start looking?"

The fact that he said *we,* didn't escape her. "If you were going to recruit someone to pull off something illegal like this, where would you start looking?"

Her eyes narrowed to steel slits, her words more leading statement than question.

Alex's eyes widened. "Oh. The Gray Eagle."

She was nodding, already heading for her Jeep and motioning for Blizzard to jump into the back. It was time to pay her old pal John Bartley a visit.

And God help him if he was involved in kidnapping her friend.

13

A Notorious Hotspot

The Gray Eagle was a notorious hotspot for petty criminal types looking to get a foothold in the upper echelon of the big-boy crime world. From the outside, it appeared to be nothing more than an exclusive motorcycle club, but Jessie knew that on the inside you could pretty much find anything and everything for hire.

John Bartley owned the club, and he controlled everything that came in and went out of his bar. If there was action to be had, then he commanded a sizable cut. Jessie had crossed paths with him during the Jordan Myers investigation and had even saved the man's life. At the time, he had made it known that she, and by extension, Alex, were off limits to anyone looking for freelance work of any kind in Pine Haven.

He had been grateful not only for his life, but also the fact that Jessie and Alex had solved Jordan's murder. He had been in love with the woman, and her death had hit him hard. This was why Jessie had such a hard time believing he would be involved in anything like kidnapping Cora.

But she also knew that everyone had a price. She had seen that time and time again in the military. Everyone could be turned under the right circumstances.

The building itself was a sprawling structure that looked like a cross between a warehouse and a large barn. There was a large, billboard-sized sign at the entrance to the parking lot with a bald eagle, wings spread, welcoming bikers. The parking lot itself was surprisingly busy considering the time of day.

"Business must be booming," Jessie said to Blizzard as she slammed the Jeep in park.

Alex pulled up beside her and climbed out of his patrol car. "You sure you want to do this, Jessie? John's a reasonable guy. We could just...call him. Might be better than just bursting in and making accusations of kidnapping." His tone was only half serious until he saw the look on her face. "Jessie, this is crazy. We can't just—"

She cut him off. "No, *you* can't just go in there. But I'm not a cop, remember? I can do what I need to in order to get some answers." She turned to the white shepherd. "Heel." He fell into step beside her as they headed for the large, double doors that led to the club.

She strode past the knot of bikers gathered on the outside landing. They gave her a hard stare but quickly parted at the sight of the large dog stalking at her side.

"Shit," Alex mumbled as he started after her.

Stepping inside, Jessie clenched her jaw, channeling

the anger that had been rising within her into iron resolve. She looked around the room, ignoring the stares, and made her way through the cloying stench of booze, stale sweat, and lingering cigarettes. Josie was working at the bar, and she immediately made her way towards the big man. He stood at six feet five inches and easily had two hundred pounds on her.

He pulled himself to his full height, back stiffening, when he saw her approaching. He reached up, shoved a handful of unruly gray and black hair from his face, highlighting the scar that ran from his forehead, through one eye, and down to his cheek. When he spoke, his tone was little more than a snarl. "What can I do for you, *officer consultant*?"

His tone was both mocking and condescending. Jessie swept it aside effortlessly. "Save the pleasantries, Josie. I don't have time for it." She deliberately made her voice loud enough that it carried to many of the patrons enjoying an early beer at the tables that dotted the bar space. "I'm here to find out who knows what happened to my friend. She was kidnapped a little over an hour ago. From my house."

The hum of chatter that had saturated the air when she walked in died. Rowdy laughter and the clack of billiard balls thinned out until it was church-mouse quiet. She could feel eyes burning into her, but she refused to acknowledge anyone.

Josie frowned, his one good eye narrowing as a crimson blush made its way up his neck. "You know, you can't come in here just spouting accusations like that."

She leaned in, getting closer to his face. "I didn't

accuse anyone of anything. I said I had questions. Now, if you took that as an accusation, maybe it's because you feel guilty." Now she took the opportunity to sweep the crowd. "Or maybe someone else feels guilty and has something they would like to share with me." Her eyes cut to Josie's hand as it carefully slid beneath the counter. "I wouldn't."

He glared at her, and she could see him weighing the odds of getting to whatever was under the bar before she could get to him. Word had spread as to how well she could handle herself, and finally he moved his hand back to full view, lying it flat on the counter.

"So, as I was saying. My friend is about my height, maybe a little more curvaceous, African American. Someone grabbed her and I want to know who did it and where they took her." She turned her back on Josie, addressing the crowd that had gathered. She also saw Alex standing inside the doorway, watching carefully, hands on his hips. His right hand slid ever so closer to his gun. She gave him an almost imperceptible shake of her head.

"You know, John wouldn't like you just coming in here like this, thinking you own the place. Who do you think you are?"

She turned her head and saw the man who had spoken to her. He was in his forties, lean, wearing a black leather riding vest over a grungy short-sleeved white tee shirt. She squinted at him. "I don't think I know you, friend. Are you new in town?"

He spat onto the floor. "I ain't your friend, pig." He laughed, turning his nose up at her. "Yeah, I can smell your kind a mile away. And even if I knew who grabbed your friend, I wouldn't tell you."

"Ken...easy, man," said Josie, motioning for him to take a seat.

Jessie looked at Josie. "No, that's okay." She turned her attention back to the man known as Ken. "If you're new here, then you have no say in this matter. I know what goes on in this bar. Just like I know that there has been some messy business going on here in town lately. Some of you undoubtedly know what I mean. But I'm not here for that. At least not yet. For now, all I want is my friend."

Ken guffawed, swaggering closer to her. "Look, cop—"

"I'm not a cop." Her tone had turned to ice, and the two men standing next to Ken took a step back from him.

"Then you got no cause to even be in here asking us shit," the man growled. "Nobody knows who grabbed your friend, but maybe, whoever got her, is going to do something real fun with—"

That was all that he managed to get out. Jessie closed the gap between them and slammed the heel of her right hand into the center of his face. His head whipped back as blood spurted from his nose.

"Bitch!" he cried, reaching inside his vest to withdraw a six-inch knife.

Before he could raise the blade, Jessie locked on his wrist, wrenching violently, causing the blade to fly from his hand. Then, twisting her body and dropping her center of gravity, she sent him crashing into one of the tables in front of them.

There was stunned silence, followed by the unmistakable sound of a twelve-gauge shotgun being pumped.

Jessie turned to see Josie standing there, both hands on the weapon as he pointed it at the ceiling.

"Okay, enough of this," said Alex, pushing his way forward. "Josie, put it down." The man didn't take his eyes off Jessie and didn't relax his grip on the gun. "You know, how long has it been since this place was raided? How would your boss like it if that happened?"

"He wouldn't."

They turned to see John Bartley standing on the stairs behind the bar. All eyes followed him as he turned, motioning for Jessie and Alex to follow him back up the steps.

Ken drew himself to his feet. His face was red, covered with blood and embarrassment. He spat dark phlegm in Jessie's direction as she walked away. "You'll pay for that. Just you wait. They're gonna have so much fun with you." And then he staggered towards the exit, brushing aside any offers of help from other bikers.

Jessie smiled as she walked past Josie and up the stairs, Alex following close behind.

Upstairs, they followed John to an enclosed loft area, comfortably appointed with leather furniture, a bar, and an entertainment center. There was a mini bar attached to the entertainment center and John made his way over to the bottles and began filling a small tumbler. "Drink?"

"It's a bit early," said Alex.

John swirled his glass, clinking the ice. "It's also a bit early for you to be harassing my patrons. What was that about?"

"Someone kidnapped my friend," said Jessie. "I want to know who."

John regarded her for a moment, lifting the glass to his lips. "And you think someone here had something to do with that? That hurts, Jessie."

She narrowed her eyes. As much as she hated to admit it, something in his tone rang true.

He let out a deep breath. "I told you; no one is going to mess with you and yours. Nothing about that has changed." He sat his drink down, giving both of them a hard look. "And kidnapping? No way I'm okaying anything like that. After meeting Jordan...and everything that happened, my business model has changed. I'm not saying I don't dabble in certain types of...gray businesses, but nothing like that."

There was a time when Jessie had made a living by assessing whether someone was telling the truth or lying to her. John Bartley might have been many things, but he wasn't a liar. "What can you tell me about that guy Ken?"

John shrugged. "He's a newbie to the club. Trying hard to fit in."

"Maybe too hard," Jessie said. "As in he's trying to show he wants to be one of the big dogs, garner the right attention."

"Kenneth Blackburn," John said. "He's reached out to me a couple of times about joining the club. And now that you mention it, he said he could get us in on some interesting work happening around town. I never pushed...wasn't really that keen on working with an unknown."

"Did he ever say what kind of work?" asked Alex.

John shook his head. "Nah. I've let him hang around some, try to get a feel for what kind of man he might be.

See how he handles himself." He smiled in Jessie's direction. "And from what I just saw, not very well, I'd say. Maybe you could give me a few pointers sometime?"

Something in his tone gave Jessie pause, and she quickly looked away from his dark eyes.

Alex's brow was pinched as he began pacing. "You say he's a Blackburn? As in one of old Ollie Blackburn's kids?"

John gave him a shifty smile and nodded.

"What am I missing?" asked Jessie.

"I went to school with the oldest Blackburn, at least until Ollie pulled them out to work the farm," Alex said. "Two brothers. Each one meaner than the next. And as we grew older, one thing always stuck when it came to them. They'd do anything to make a quick buck. No questions asked."

Jessie's eyes flitted from one of the men to the other. "What I'm hearing is that we may have flushed out our man."

Alex's face grew dark, and his eyes shifted from Jessie to John. "There's something else. The Blackburn farm? It's a massive property that is pretty much the only bit of inhabited property up on Devil's Peak."

Jessie's eyes lit up. "The same place where the—it— was found."

Alex nodded. "Looks like I get to pay the Blackburn boys a visit."

"No," replied Jessie, her voice stern. "*We* get to pay them a visit."

14

The Clock Starts

After being assured by John that it would not suffer any damage, Jessie left her Jeep parked at the Gray Eagle and rode with Alex up the mountain. Blizzard was stretched out in the back seat, eyes closed, ears twitching in lazy contentment.

The afternoon sun was already low in the sky. Jessie watched as the landscape changed, the dense forest thinning to reveal expanses of untamed, overgrown fields.

"What kind of farm is this?" she asked.

"Mostly cold-hardy crops and a few livestock. Potatoes, kale, root vegetables, and for a time sheep and goats. Now...who knows. Rumors are that Ollie let parts of it be used for growing just about anything; so long as he got his cut, he didn't ask questions."

It was hard for Jessie to imagine the property being productive at any point. Driving along a long stretch of dirt road, she made note of the farm's dilapidated state. Rusty, unkempt fencing outlined the drive; it was bent and broken in places, no longer capable of holding in livestock. They drove past an abandoned tractor, faded and chipped, one large tire now flattened and sinking into the earth. Looking around, she noticed other pieces of broken-down, neglected machinery that had been overtaken by weeds and wildflowers.

Ahead of them, the farmhouse proper squatted. At one time it might have been a very quaint, sturdy home sitting on a picturesque plot of land. But now it was weather beaten and in desperate need of repairs. The paint had eroded, revealing splintering wood framing and a sagging porch that looked on the verge of collapse. The front yard had long since given in to overgrowth, with wild weeds and bare patches of earth surrounding the structure.

Alex came to a stop, just outside the house and peered through the front window at the edifice.

"Think they're in there?" asked Jessie.

"No place else for them to be."

They both climbed out of the car. Blizzard stood up on the seat, but Jessie motioned for him to lay back down. She left the back door open, just in case they needed him for reinforcements.

"I know you're not going to like this," said Alex, "but let me take the lead here. After what you did to Ken back at the bar, I don't think his father will want much to do with you. You'll probably just make him clam up."

Jessie held up both hands in silent agreement. He was right, she didn't like the thought of just standing back while he took the lead, but she also wasn't about to do anything that could ruin her chances of finding Cora. And as much as she relished the idea of letting Blizzard clamp down on someone's leg until they told her what she wanted to know, she knew that wasn't the right option either.

At least not yet.

Jessie took note of a couple of all-wheel drive vehicles parked not far from the house, along with two newer-looking motorcycles. She guessed that one must belong to Ken, but the other one appeared brand new as it gleamed in the late-day sun, the shiny, black tires looked like they had never seen the road before.

As they approached the front door, Jessie thought she saw the curtain flicker in one of the windows that looked out from the lower level. Alex's body stiffened and she knew he had seen it as well.

He stepped up and rapped on the door heavily. "Sheriff's office." His voice was loud and deep. Silence greeted him and he waited a moment. "Anyone home? We just want to talk."

There was a shuffling that came from the other side of the door, followed by a gruff voice. "Who's *we*?"

Alex frowned and glanced at Jessie. "I'm officer Alex Thomas with the Pine Haven Police Department. This is Jessie Night. She's a consultant with the department. We're just here to ask a few questions is all. Can you open the door?"

More silence followed by some shuffling. Finally, there was a series of clicks as locks were pulled back and bolts unlatched. The door opened a few inches, stopped by a chain from opening completely.

A rheumy eye, embedded in a grizzled face and covered with a matted beard, shoved through. "You got no business here, lawman. Get on off my property before I give you the business end of old Bessie here." This was followed by the sound of a rifle bolt sliding into place.

Alex held up a hand to show he wasn't a threat. "Ollie, be reasonable and put that thing away."

The man disappeared amidst some harsh whispering from multiple sources that filtered through the opening before Ollie's eye popped back into view. "That the gal that bloodied my Ken's nose?"

Alex cleared his throat before Jessie could say anything. "Trent, I was there and saw the whole thing. Ken was being a hot head and was clearly the aggressor. Jessie was defending herself."

The old man made a spitting noise and barked out a laugh. "Hell, I don't care. When he came limping back in here all bellyaching, I cuffed him one myself. Told him he ought to be ashamed getting clocked by a woman."

Jessie stiffened. She couldn't tell if it was a compliment or a challenge.

"I'll give you one minute to ask your questions," the old man said.

Alex nodded. "A young woman was kidnapped this morning. A friend of Jessie's. You or your boys heard anything about it?"

A split-second of silence before the gruffness returned. "No. Don't know nothing about a kidnapping. Now if you'll—"

"Where's Terry?" Alex interjected. "Ken was at the bar, but I haven't seen Terry in town in quite a while."

"He's busy. Now, like I said, since nobody here knows anything about a woman being kidnapped, you can go."

He started to close the door and Jessie stepped forward placing her foot between the door and the jam. "What about a body that showed up a couple miles south of your property? Know anything about that?"

His cloudy eye twitched for a split-second before narrowing. "Your one minute is up. Now unless you got a search warrant, you need to get off my property. Cause I'm pretty sure I have the right to defend myself if I feel threatened on my own land." He looked down at Jessie's boot. "And right now, I feel pretty threatened."

She locked eyes with the man, then slowly withdrew her foot to allow the door to close. Bolts and latches slammed into place, followed by angry whispers and shouts and what she was pretty sure was the sound of a fist striking flesh, followed by a whimper.

Alex winced as he stepped off the porch. "That was fun."

Jessie followed him. "That was useless is what it was. We needed to talk to Ken."

"Maybe. Or maybe I took a page out of your book. Ken is the older of the two brothers and easily rattled as you've seen. But Terry? He's the brains of this outfit. I'm betting he was in there taking it all in. He's the one we need to get to." They made it to his patrol car. "Word of advice. He's also the more unstable of the bunch. I wouldn't advise hitting him."

Jessie scuffed her feet. "Can we get a warrant? Come

back and check those barns and outbuildings?" She jutted her chin in the direction of the derelict-looking structures that dotted the landscape just beyond the house.

Alex chewed at his lower lip a bit. "Honestly, I doubt it. We have no basis for a warrant. There's no sign that Cora is here, and we have no evidence that says anyone on the premises was involved in her disappearance."

"Did you see the way he hesitated when I mentioned the body?"

Alex took a deep breath. "About that. You know you might have just compromised an investigation. You shouldn't have brought that up."

"But he didn't say no," Jessie continued. "He said our time was up with the questioning. Maybe he dodged it because he couldn't come up with a lie in time." She opened the passenger-side door and climbed in. "Maybe that body showing up and Cora's disappearance are linked somehow." She remembered the ledger. "The metallic implant possibly matching the code in the ledger. And now Cora's kidnapping? There has to be something connecting all this." She slammed the heel of her hand into the dashboard, causing Blizzard to jump to attention. She shook her head. "I'm sorry. I just...I can't let anything happen to her." She turned her head, staring out the window. "I can't lose anyone else close to me."

Alex looked over at her. "You're not going to lose her. I promise." His phone buzzed and he looked down at it with a frown. "It's from the CSI team. They're almost finished inside your place and are moving to the outside.

They are going to work around the clock on processing this one."

Jessie sighed, giving him a thankful nod. "Do you mind driving me back to Eric and Mark's? I can't take Blizzard back to the house until they've gotten everything they need. Hopefully I can leave him with them until both of us can be back at the house."

"Yeah, not a problem. Plus, it will be good to speak to Eric again in person. See if maybe he remembers anything at all out of the usual from this morning."

"Good idea," Jessie said. Her eyes drifted back to the worn-down farmhouse. What she really wanted was another run at Ken. He knew something, of that, she was sure. She just needed to get him alone long enough to convince him to talk.

A buzzing distracted them. This time it was Jessie's phone that demanded attention. She frowned at the screen when she saw 'unknown caller'. She sent it to voicemail, only to have it immediately begin ringing again.

"Hello?" She hoped the annoyance in her voice would let whatever telemarketer had gotten hold of her number know she was not the one to toy with.

Her body went rigid as she looked over at Alex, eyes wide, all the color draining from her features. With a trembling hand, she clicked the speaker option and held the phone aloft.

"I'm sorry, what?" she managed, her voice trembling almost uncontrollably.

The voice that filled the air was deep and masculine, but not digitally altered. The caller spoke in a cool, rational tone that said he was used to being in control and getting what he wanted.

"I have something that you want. And I'll return it, but you have to do something for me. Somewhere out there, in that little lakeside community of yours, is a drone. A drone that may have footage that could be very damaging for me and an associate. I want you to bring me the drone and the owner. That's it. Bring me what I'm asking for and you get your friend back."

Jessie's heart was jackhammering in her chest. Blood rushed through her head so hard she could barely hear her own words. "How...how am I supposed to do this? What am I looking for? Where am I supposed to make this exchange?"

"You're the investigator. You figure it out. You have forty-eight hours, and then I start sending you a piece of your friend for every hour after that. As for where..."

Her phone pinged again, and a pin appeared, hovering over a geographic point.

"Can't I just bring you the footage? Why do you need the person that captured it as well?" Jessie asked. Her brain was spinning and for some reason she felt like she needed to stall this conversation.

"The owner of the drone saw something they should not have. So, I'm going to need to torture them to tell me who else they may have shown it to, and then I'll kill them. Any other questions?"

She swallowed hard; her breath caught in her throat.

"I didn't think so," said the voice. "Forty-eight hours, at the location I provided; otherwise, you're going to start getting some very unpleasant packages left on your doorstep. Oh, and tell Alex that if he involves any of his cop buddies in this, I'll know. And that's when things will get very, very messy."

The line went dead, and Jessie could only stare at her phone.

15

Asking For Help

Alex was staring at her in silence as the line went dead. "Holy crap."

"Not how I would have put it, but okay," Jessie replied, finding her voice.

"You think that was legitimate?"

She nodded without hesitation. "Absolutely. Whoever that was, they aren't some minor criminal element here in town. He was too calm; too self-assured. They've done this before. Or something like it." She looked to her watch and flicked her finger across the face of it. "Forty-eight hours."

Alex scratched his head. "Okay. Forty-eight hours. Where do we start?"

"They said there was drone footage they need. Are there any kids in town who have drones that you know of?"

Alex's hand covered his mouth and pinched at his

lips. Slowly he shook his head. "Not that I recall. This is a small community, and I don't know a single kid with a drone."

Jessie frowned. Her heart was beating hard, creating its own countdown. "It's still the end of the tourist season. Maybe it belongs to one of the seasonal families. Or someone that was just in for the weekend." The thought of that scared her. Whoever the owner of this drone was could have already left town.

Alex started the car. "I was going to suggest we hang out here. Thinking was that if we rattled Ken again...or Terry, they might head out and we could tail them. But given the call—"

"I don't think they had anything to do with this. They're up to something I'm sure of it, just not this," Jessie finished.

"Okay, we go back to the station and rally—"

"No. Not the station," Jessie said. "You heard what he said. We can't involve the cops. After what happened with Todd, we still can't be sure everyone left on the force is clean."

Alex eased the car forward, heading for the main road. "Then what? Unless you want to go door to door in town, asking who has a drone, what do you think we should do next?"

Jessie was afraid to admit she had already thought of, and dismissed, that idea. They just didn't have the time. Plus, what if the person they were looking for got wind of them and bolted? While she didn't know what was on that footage, she had some ideas. Whoever had it was probably on edge as it was. An idea began forming in the back of her mind.

One that she was sure Alex would not be onboard with.

"Can you drop me off at my Jeep back at the Gray Eagle? Then, you find Will Mason and see if he can come up with something to maybe run in the paper that requests the aid of an experienced drone pilot. Maybe we can get lucky."

Alex thought for a second. "The Taste of the Pines festival starts today. Maybe he could take out an ad asking for someone to provide a drone to get some overhead shots."

That was actually an excellent idea, and Jessie nodded quickly. "Great thought. Not sure our pilot would fall for it, but it could get people talking and they might mention someone they know with a drone. It's a start at least."

"What are you going to do?" he asked.

"I'm going to swing by some of the shops on Main Street. The coffee shop in particular. Angela seems to know the comings and goings of everyone in the community. I want to see if there's been anyone in town lately that just didn't sit right with her."

Half an hour later and she was standing at her Jeep, Blizzard at her side, waving goodbye to Alex as he pulled out. She stood there, watching him disappear around the bend before she ushered the shepherd into the Jeep. "You stay here this time."

Then she turned, took a deep breath, and walked into the Gray Eagle.

Josie took one look at her and shook his massive head. "You've caused enough problems here for today. You need to—"

"Josie. Please. I need to see John. It's an emergency."

She wasn't sure if it was the look in her eyes or the pleading tone she had adopted, but the big man gave her a side-eyed glance and finally picked up a phone from under the desk and spoke quietly into it.

John appeared at the top of the stairs and motioned for her to come up.

He stood by the bar as she entered and pointed at a glass. This time she nodded. He poured two generous shots into tumblers and handed one to her. "To what do I owe two visits in one day?"

The glass trembled in her hand as she lifted it to her lips and downed the amber liquid in a single gulp. She sat the glass on the tiny side table and dropped down onto the leather couch, her face in her hands.

John watched her across the small distance that separated them. His arm was frozen in midair as he lifted his own drink, and his eyes were locked on Jessie. He placed his drink down and took a seat on the coffee table in front of her. "Hey, what's going on? Is this the same person who just bashed Ken Blackburn in the mouth? The same one who took out" —he paused, struggling with his next words— "a killer in hand-to-hand combat?"

She looked up, letting out a deep sigh. There was a small napkin on the coffee table next to where John sat, and she reached for it. As she began recounting what had happened that led her to return to the bar, she nervously shredded the paper into thin strips. When she finished telling him everything, she dropped the ribbons onto the table. "And that's everything."

The man looked at her and took a sip from his glass. "And now you're coming to me for...?"

"Help," she replied. She swallowed hard and hoped the word hadn't come out sounding like she was pleading.

John looked at her, compassion flooding his features. "Whatever you need. Consider this a thank you."

She was shaking her head. "I don't need to be thanked for doing the right thing." Even if that *right thing* had cost her more than she would ever be willing to admit.

"How's Alex feel about this? Me helping you, I mean," John asked.

For the first time, she couldn't meet his gaze. "He doesn't know I'm here."

John frowned. "I see." He stood and moved to pour another drink, lifting the bottle in her direction.

Jessie shook her head. "No thanks. And Alex is doing what he can to help, but there is only so much he can do as an officer of the law. This kidnapper specifically stated that he didn't want the cops involved. I've a feeling that whoever he is, he may have some kind of contact within the department. After what happened with Todd, I'm still learning who I can trust."

"Good instincts," John said, returning to his seat on the table. "They say I'm the shady one, but that department has been gray as long as I can remember." He gave her a serious stare. "Except for Alex. You don't have to worry about that one. Just don't tell him I said that."

This made her smile. "Your secret is safe with me. And I just can't risk anything happening to him. I'd never be able to forgive myself."

John arched an eyebrow in her direction. "Ah, I see. So, I'm expendable, huh?"

Her eyes immediately widened. "No. Not at all. That isn't what I meant. Alex stands out, and these guys obviously know who he is. But hopefully you won't be noticed. Plus, I'm pretty sure you have access to resources that the police do not. And I've a feeling I'm going to need that."

The corners of his lips drew down as he considered her words. "I like that. Sounds like a plan I can get behind." He made his way to a panel on the wall next to the entertainment center and pressed a button. After a moment, he spoke quickly into it, his voice too low for Jessie to make out.

"What was that?" she asked.

"I just had Josie send a couple of the guys out. One's going to keep an eye on the Blackburn farm. Any of them try sneaking off, at least we will know where they went. They don't have the skills to pull off what's happening now, but they're sketchy enough that they might know who did. Especially the younger brother, Terry. He's bad news, that one."

"You're not the first person to tell me that. When we were there, I did notice a couple of new toys in the driveway. Not cheap ones either. Made me wonder where they are getting the money from to buy them."

John scoffed. "Not from selling those run-down pigs they claim to be butchering, that's for sure."

"Interesting," said Jessie. "And where is the second person going?"

He held out his hand. "I need your phone for that. I'm dropping him the location of the exchange the kidnapper gave you. I want someone to scout it out...look for any hidden vantage points where someone could lie in wait to pick you off. Kidnappers are nasty creatures; they won't think twice about sniping you from a distance if you show up with what they want."

Jessie had been nodding as they spoke. Everything John said made perfect sense.

"You're good at this," she said.

He moved to retrieve his leather vest that had been thrown across the back of a chair. "Years of practice. Always needing to stay one step ahead of everyone else." He swung the vest on and headed down the stairs. At the bar, he turned to Jessie again. "One more thing. Do you want me to have someone watch Alex's back? He won't even know they are there."

Jessie hesitated, trying to think how Alex might take the news. Not telling him wasn't an option. There was no way she was going to have someone follow him around without his knowledge; no matter how good the intentions were. "No. Let's not go that far. Right now, whoever is behind this wants me to be able to focus on finding this drone owner. I don't see them doing anything to distract me from that."

John shrugged. "Whatever you say." He walked over and took something from behind the bar, shoving it into the backside of his jeans, then leaned over to Josie, gave him some instructions and headed back Jessie's way.

"What was that?" she asked, nodding in the direction of the bar.

"Well, protection for one thing. Never leave home without it. You need one?"

Nothing about his tone made her think he was joking, and she just shook her head.

"Suit yourself. I told Josie to keep an eye out for anyone we don't know coming in here," he continued. "Also, I wanted him to ask a few of the more loose-lipped members here if they've heard that anyone in our circle is freelancing. Like I said earlier, this isn't something my team would ever touch. But it can't hurt to be sure."

Together, they walked out into the setting sun.

"So, where to first?" John asked.

"Well, I understand the big festival started today. I'd like to go there. Not that I expect there will be any drones flying, but if whoever is behind this is keeping an eye on me, maybe you'll be able to spot a tail that I can't."

He was nodding appreciatively. "Good plan."

"But first, I need to swing by my house so I can feed and drop off Blizzard." She motioned to the Jeep. "Not afraid of a little old dog, are you?"

John looked at the hundred pounds of claw and fang watching him intently from the back seat.

"Nah," he said reluctantly. "He looks friendly enough."

Jessie climbed behind the wheel and headed out. She tried not to think about the fact that she was bringing a stranger—*this* stranger—into her life. But in that moment, she would have made a deal with the Devil himself if it meant bringing Cora home safely.

16
———

Pain is Good

Pain was a good thing.

That was what Cora had convinced herself. It meant she was still alive. And as long as she was alive, she had a fighting chance of getting out of the hell in which she now found herself chained.

She jerked at the metal cuffs, scraping already raw skin. The small motion sent spikes of pain through her body. How long had she been bound like this? She searched her memories. What did she remember prior to waking up slumped against a wall, her wrists chained at face level?

Eric had dropped her off just outside of Jessie's house. She heard him pull away just as she was walking into the house and closing the door behind her. She remembered putting the basket of jams on the coffee table...and then there was someone behind her. Where had they come from? Had she left the door open? No. She was sure she hadn't.

They were already in the house, lying in wait for her.

She wasn't a fighter, yet she had fought. For her life. She was missing a fingernail and remembered gouging the man's forearm. She had wanted to leave some type of DNA evidence for Jessie. Hopefully it had worked. And even if she hadn't managed to leave something tangible behind, she hoped the attacker would have a scar for life.

Again, she rattled the manacles. Nothing.

These weren't lodged in mud and dirt like the ones below the bed and breakfast. No. This was the real thing. These restraints weren't budging.

Blinking away blurry vision, Cora tried to look around the dimly lit room. Movement to her left caught her attention, but before she could swivel her head that way, she heard a door shutting and heavy footsteps coming her way. Letting her head sag against her chest, she closed her eyes.

The heavy musk of the man who had attacked her assaulted her nostrils, followed by the sharp scent of his breath on her face.

"You can stop pretending. I saw you looking around. I know you're awake," said the man.

Cora tucked that bit of knowledge away. Wherever she was, there were cameras on her.

She opened her eyes, looking into the face of the man who attacked her. He was crouched down, studying her face, before standing up and placing his fists on his hips. He towered over her, and his eyes burned with hatred. He was wearing a short-sleeved tee shirt, the gauze that was haphazardly wrapped around his arm made Cora smile.

"Nice tape job." She smirked.

His upper lip quivered, and she could feel the increased heat roiling from him. She braced for the slap she sensed was coming. But somehow, the big man suppressed his rage, choking on it as he studied her.

"You're going to wish all you had was a similar scratch when this is over," he breathed into her face. "You best believe I will make sure of that."

"Why am I here? What is this about?" She fought to control the tremble in her voice.

The man huffed. "We need your friend to do something for us. And you're the whip that will ensure she does it."

Cora's mind was racing. This wasn't about her. They were after Jessie. She tried to laugh but ended up wincing from the pain in her shoulder blades. "You're crazy if you think you can use me to *make* Jessie do anything."

"Well, for your sake, you better hope that isn't true." He turned his back and walked away, taking a cell phone out of his pocket and raising it to his ear as he left her.

It gave Cora a chance to survey her surroundings. From her position, she had no idea how large the space was that held her. The unrelenting cold that seeped into her from the concrete floor told her she was most likely underground. Her fingers brushed the rough, damp stone walls, tracing a path to the iron anchor driven deep into the rock that held her manacles.

Yeah, these weren't for show.

The light around her was dim, coming from overhead fixtures that cast a faint, flickering glow into the chamber. She strained her ears, but could only make out the faint, electric hum of the overhead lights and her own heartbeat thundering in her chest. More likely than not, the room was soundproof, so screaming would do her no good. The fact that the attacker had not bothered to gag her also said he wasn't afraid of her attracting attention from the outside world.

The thought made her freeze in place. It wasn't just that he hadn't gagged her; he also hadn't bothered to blindfold her. Or wear anything over his face.

He didn't care that she knew what he looked like.

Cora pushed that thought to the back of her mind. Since the chains weren't coming out of the wall anytime soon, she began scouring the floor, looking for anything that might come in handy.

Either as a weapon or a tool.

A slight scuffling sound caught her attention. It came from the far corner of the room, where there was very little light. Squinting her eyes, she held perfectly still as the outline of a structure slowly came into focus. She realized what she was seeing was the outline of a large cell, the bars barely glinting in the dim light. Shadows moved within. She blinked, waiting for her eyes to adjust even more.

Then she realized they weren't shadows. They were people. Women.

They seemed huddled together in the center of the cell. Long, loose clothing flowed from them, and judging from the sound their feet made, Cora was pretty sure they were all barefoot.

She looked around, her ears desperately trying to pinpoint the man's whereabouts. No sounds. He had taken his call and left them.

"Hey!" Her voice carried across the space in a harsh whisper. "Hey! Can you hear me? Who are you? Where are we?" Her voice sounded desperate, even to her own ears.

But the women only shifted their position slightly, their silence louder than any words they might have uttered.

Heavy footfalls approached and the women stiffened. Cora looked up to see her captor standing over her again.

"They ain't gonna say shit to you. They know what will happen if they do. And while I might not be able to take it out on you" —he gave her a nasty smile— "yet. I promise I will make them suffer greatly if you do get one of them to talk to you."

Cruel. She added that to the growing mental list she was creating about her kidnapper. She wasn't yet sure what she was going to do with the knowledge base she was building, but she had to believe it would come in handy. Her body was restrained, and even if it weren't she knew it wouldn't be much use against a giant like this. Even back at Jessie's house, she had the feeling he was just toying with her as he chased her around the room, relishing the screams he was getting out of her. Even when she scratched him, she had a feeling he liked it.

Physically, she might be restrained and outmatched. But mentally? That was a completely different ballgame.

"I bet you'd like that, huh?" she said. "Something tells me it wouldn't be the first time you've hurt a woman."

His upper lip drew back. "Only when they deserved it. You women are no different from men in my book. Everyone has their place in the pecking order of life. Don't step out of line and everything is fine."

Cora squinted. Interesting. She took note of the way he expanded his chest and flexed his biceps as he spoke. "So, you're the muscle of the bunch, huh?"

Her words made him wince. She had struck a nerve.

"What I bring to the table balances out our partnership. I'm not just muscle."

Cora sank back against the wall. She had everything she needed for now. This wasn't a one-time kidnapping. Muscle Head wasn't working on his own, and he certainly wasn't in charge. "What are you going to do with me once Jessie does what you want?"

He looked at her and smiled. "That's not up to me. I know what I'd like to do to you, but we have a deal with your friend. Behave and do as you're told. You'll be set free at that point. As agreed."

A lie. A good one, but a lie, nonetheless. When he spoke, he looked up and to the right, ever so briefly. At least she now knew his tell.

"You just keep quiet, don't cause waves, and you'll be home in a couple of days." He turned his back, walking out once again.

Cora frowned. So, there was a time clock. She had less than forty-eight hours to find a way out of this hell. She glanced over at the cage holding a group of silent women.

Only now, she wasn't the only one counting on her

finding a way. Her mind raced as she took in the space around her. Then, her mind and her eyes settled. There was something on the ground to her right. Something that blended perfectly with the flooring.

A long, concrete nail lay covered in dust and was only a couple of feet away.

17

Hunting at the Festival

The swath of green space comprised of interconnecting squares of manicured lawn that swept through the center of town was an ocean of green, where couples and families picnicked, children flew kites, and dogs chased frisbees. The Great Lawn, as it was named, flowed between the sidewalks of Main Street, flanked by all the mom-and-pop shops, professional businesses that had taken over the quaint cottages, and free-standing ice cream and soda carts.

A single-lane road ran in each direction, with parking spaces splitting off and leading to the sidewalks where people could stroll and window shop to their hearts' content. At one end of the Great Lawn sat Town Hall, while the other was open to the network of roads from around town that poured into the business center of Pine Haven.

But during the Taste of the Pines Festival, the Great

Lawn was a sea of tents, booths, carnival rides, and petting zoos. The air was thick with the smell of cotton candy, grilled meats, apples, fried dough and the metallic tint of machine oil and diesel pumps to power the rides. People came from two counties over to enjoy the festival, laughing, screaming and pumping their dollars into the town's coffers.

Jessie and John stood to one side of the stairs leading up to Town Hall and surveyed the crowd entering the festival proper.

"Okay," began John, "down the center row are the tents housing most of your carnie attractions. To the left of those is where you'll find the local artisans selling their wares, and to the right will be the food venues. Basic layout for a festival I suppose." He turned and looked at Jessie. "You know, if someone is following you, they'll be doing their best to blend in."

"And that's where you come in," she replied. "Hopefully, you'll be able to spot them."

He huffed playfully. "Yeah, all my years of working and living in the crime-infested underworld will come in handy, right?"

She glanced over at him and saw that he wasn't meeting her gaze. His tone was sarcastic but tinged with something else as well. Jessie didn't have time to analyze the man. She looked down at her watch. Cora was running out of time. She hoped someone was keeping tabs on her and that they could flush that someone out. Then, it would just be a matter of making that person talk.

And he would do whatever it might take to get them to sing.

They took a step forward and Jessie stopped, reaching for John's arm. "Remember, we need to stay within signaling distance of one another. If you see someone, don't approach them. Just let me know. And...thank you, John."

He turned away from her quickly. "You're welcome. Let's do this."

They separated and headed into the festival. The distant sounds of a folk band mixed with children's squeals greeted Jessie's ears. The sounds of the little voices reminded her that this would not be the ideal place for a confrontation of any type. If she were lucky, John would spot a tail and they'd be able to lure them away from the festival.

But Jessie didn't believe in luck. She believed in opportunities and strategy.

She made her way down the middle of the fairway, assessing where someone would have the best vantage point, and yet remain unseen, if they were surveilling another. She dismissed the food vendors. There were too many long lines and nowhere to duck for cover if spotted. Likewise for the main tent attractions. Going inside to see the exhibits left one too exposed with only one way in and out.

That left the artisan vendor booths. They were open, with people milling in and out simultaneously. Tables and booths with plenty of mirrored surfaces hanging about would provide an excellent way to keep an eye on a person without having to look directly at them. She made her way to the line of vendors and began slowly walking from booth to booth, examining table after table of homemade trinkets and artifacts.

Had she not felt the weight of a ticking clock bearing down on her, she might have enjoyed what she was seeing. There were some true artists and crafters on display, and she made a mental note that when all of this was over, she was going to start supporting the local artists in her new community. There were traditions on display here that deserved to go on, and she would do what she could to ensure that happened.

She chanced a quick, innocuous glance in John's direction. He was meandering through the booths as well, keeping his distance, but always within earshot. He was engrossed in looking at some pieces of leather that had been stretched, cured and dyed. But she could tell from his body language that he was every bit as attuned to his surroundings as she was.

They moved through the festival in this manner—apart but also attached. A silent duo on the hunt.

Thirty minutes of browsing and they had nearly reached the end of the festival. Jessie chanced another look at John. He wasn't looking at her but gave a subtle shake of his head.

Nothing.

She wasn't being followed. There were no eyes on her. Jessie took a deep breath, steadying her nerves. She refused to panic. This was always going to be a long shot. But at the moment it was all they had. Unless Alex could find some recent complaints of someone possibly creating a disturbance with a drone.

No. She refused to think in possibilities. If this didn't work, then they would resort to going door to door down by the lake. Drones weren't cheap. Someone there had to know which of their neighbors were flying them. She had entered the last vendor booth and stopped in her tracks, eyes wide.

"John!" She looked to her side and motioned to the man.

He hurried to her side, looking frantically around. "What? Did you spot someone?"

Her eyes were fixed on something in front of her, and she pointed. John looked up and saw several framed, black-and-white portraits of the Blue Ridge Mountain range, as well as Pine Lake and other well-known landmarks around town. They were stunning pictures, capturing the majestic beauty of the lake and the surrounding landscape in all its glory. The expansive shots of the mountain range, complete with waterfalls, flowing rivers, and hiking trails were surreal in their beauty.

And all the photographs were aerial shots.

"Excuse me," Jessie said, pushing her way past a small crowd admiring the works. She made her way to the table where the vendor sat, an open cash box in front of her. "Ma'am, are these yours?" She gestured to the pictures on display.

"Well, yes, these are the most recent paintings from my gallery." She nodded to the easels opposite the photographs filled with still life paintings and lake view panoramas.

"No, not the paintings, the black and white photographs of Pine Haven."

The vendor smiled. "Oh, those. No, I did not capture those. That is the work of a very talented young artist." She frowned. "He was supposed to be here tonight to help me set up the booth and never showed. Good thing he had already dropped off his photographs at my barn, or he wouldn't be getting the sales he has. Even so I'm tempted to dock him for ditching me last minute like this—"

Jessie held up a hand, trying not to be rude. "So, you know him? The photographer?"

The woman nodded. "Of course. His name is Kevin Hicks. He lives up in the Narrows."

Jessie took a deep breath. "I don't suppose you have Kevin's contact information, do you? I'd love to talk to him about his work."

The woman looked a little leery as she turned her face away. "I don't know about that. That boy likes his privacy, and...I'm just not sure how he'd feel about me giving out his information like that."

Jessie reached into her pocket and took out one of her business cards. She was about to hand it over when John gently placed his hand on hers.

"Ma'am, this young lady and I represent an art dealer from New York City...and we think he would be interested in buying all of this young man's works. It's just what our buyer has been looking for."

The woman's eyes grew large as she stared at them. "New York City? Well, why didn't you say so?" She reached under the table and took out a notebook. She tore out a page, folded it, and handed it to John. "This is his address. He doesn't have a phone, but you can find him here."

Jessie nodded to the woman. "Thank you so much. Our...buyer will be very grateful. And one other thing. You wouldn't happen to know how he took these shots would you?"

"Why yes. He has one of those fancy flying camera things. Saved up a couple summers' worth of his jobs to get it from what he says. Flies it all around the mountains taking pictures. Pretty nice, huh?"

Jessie smiled as they backed away. "Pretty nice, indeed."

They hurried away from the booth, John already unfolding the piece of paper the woman had given him.

"Do you know where these Narrows are that she mentioned?"

John nodded as he studied the address. "It's a mobile home park just across the tracks on the other side of town. From what I've heard, a bunch of the rich, season-types took to calling it the Narrows many years ago, making fun of how skinny the homes were that people had to live in. The name stuck, and the park has been called the Narrows ever since."

"Christ." Just hearing that made Jessie feel sick to her stomach. But it also made her feel guilty. While she knew she would never disparage anyone because of their living conditions, she also had to admit she was the first to assume that anyone flying a drone had to come from the rich side of town. She gave John a half-smile. "That was good thinking...the art buyer thing back there."

"Well, if you had whipped out your official police consultant business card, I guarantee she would have clammed up. This is a very tight-knit community. You're making inroads, but you're still an outsider. And an outsider flashing her association with the law will stay an outsider."

Jessie understood what he meant. She didn't like it, but she understood. The sense of community was one of the things she had loved best about military life. If you were born into it, you were in. Doors opened. Opportunities presented themselves.

Of course, when those doors closed, you became an exile. A pariah.

Things weren't so different here in Pine Haven. She would have to prove herself if she wanted to truly be accepted here. She'd taken a big first step in helping to bring down her brother. But she knew she was still a long way away from being seen as a true member of the community.

But none of that mattered right now. She had a lead. A huge one. One that could mean the difference between Cora's living and dying.

"Alright, what now? Do we head over to the Narrows and pay Kevin a visit?" John asked.

Those were exactly the thoughts that had been flashing through Jessie's mind from the moment she saw the photographs. "I don't think this part is something I can involve you in. Whoever is behind this is very dangerous. And now, there are potentially two lives at risk here. Alex is probably my best bet for bringing this kid in alive and protecting him." She saw the brief look of hurt that passed across his face before he could turn away. "But thank you. So much. I wouldn't have this chance without you. I won't forget it."

He turned back to face her, and she could tell he liked the compliment.

"I'll be a phone call away if you need something. You know that, right?"

She hesitated briefly before nodding. She walked away; her mind already focused on what lay ahead. She frowned to herself. Even if Kevin hadn't bolted out of town, bringing him in was only the first part of the equation. Handing him over to a bunch of kidnappers and murderers wasn't an option.

She had a plan, or course. One that Alex would not like and probably forbid her to enact. But it was her friend whose life was in the balance. If Alex wasn't going to be onboard, then she would have to do things the hard way.

18

A Way Too Personal Ad

Even though it was later in the evening, the police station was a beehive of activity. Big events, like the Taste of the Pines Festival, were great for drawing bodies and dollars to Pine haven, but it also brought a lot of nuisances with it as well. Nothing serious, just petty mischief mostly that kept officers out on calls and caused the switchboard to be a little busier than your typical Pine Haven evening. Alex sat at his cubicle, serenaded by the tapping of keyboards around the room and the muffled chatter of voices on their phones.

The smell of coffee was overpowering as the department was quickly burning through pot after pot. A second cup sat on Alex's desk as he nervously tapped at his own keyboard, running through any noise or disturbing-the-peace calls that had been reported in the last couple of months. But all of them were dead ends. Not one mention of a drone being the cause. His frustration was growing as he reached for the coffee and then decided against it. He was jittery enough; no need to fuel that fire even more.

A chorus of boisterous laughter jolted him into looking up. A couple of officers were congregating at one of their desks, laughing at who-knew-what. He saw Chief Walker among them, and the big man glanced his way, giving him a small nod. Alex tilted his head back in acknowledgment and returned his attention to his monitor.

He checked his watch. Where the hell was Will? Why hadn't he called him back? Will was the editor and reporter for the town's only paper. He was also the personal photographer and public relations specialist for Maggie Beaumont, Pine Haven's mayor. He began to fret, tapping a pen on his desk. What if Will was tied up doing something for the mayor? Maybe he hadn't even picked up Alex's message.

The officer's mind was a maelstrom. Caught between his desire to perform the duties of his job to the best of his abilities, and his conflicting emotions involving Jessie. He could see her face; so determined and capable, yet broken and afraid after what she had just experienced with her friend. She had asked him for his help, and circumstances had dictated they act in secrecy.

He was torn between his desire to do the right thing and his need to keep Jessie's confidence. He owed her. If it weren't for her, he probably wouldn't be alive. She was so strong and capable. Yet, the look on her face earlier had been one of vulnerability. And all Alex wanted to do was take that away from her.

He knew that shared traumatic experiences could create bonds between people that might not otherwise exist. Is this what had happened with them? Lately, he found himself thinking more and more about her when they were apart. But was that because he admired her so much? That he looked forward to having discussions with her because there was so much he was learning? Or was it something else?

He sighed, rubbing his temples. He had never felt so alone in a room full of people in his life.

"Headache?"

He looked up to see Chief Walker standing next to his cubicle.

"Chief Walker. Sorry, no. Just...a few things on my mind," he answered.

The chief nodded, narrowing his gaze at the officer. "Not interested in some pizza? I can bring some over if you want."

"No. Thank you, but I'm not really hungry."

The chief nodded, clearing his throat, his eyes looking around Alex's desk and then back in the direction of the congregation of officers chatting loudly and shoveling pizza into their mouths. Alex bit at his lower lip, returning his attention back to his monitor. He was well aware of the tension that had crept into his relationship with Chief Walker. The events that transpired earlier in the year had permanently altered their dynamic.

He still respected the chief, looked up to him, but something had changed. He respected the chief for the position he held, because it was something he had to do. But he had lost his respect for him as a man.

And Chief Walker knew it as well. Alex had watched him become a little more withdrawn, keeping to himself in the office, interacting as needed with the department. But his heart was no longer in it, and everyone knew that the sooner he found a replacement, the better it would be for everyone.

The chief cleared his throat, hooked his thumbs in his belt and rocked back on his heels. "So, um, if you need anything. Or need to talk...just let me know."

Alex's phone rang and rescued him from having to answer. He looked at the screen, his eyes widening. "Hey, thanks, Chief, but I really need to take this..." He punched at the screen and lifted the phone to his ear.

Chief Walker nodded and backed away, heading for his office.

"Will, about time you called me back," Alex said in a loud whisper.

"Oh, I'm sorry, I'm only overseeing the printing of the town's only newspaper...by myself...oh, and I'm also at the twenty-four-seven beck and call of the town's mayor. I didn't realize I'm also at your beck and call as well."

Alex flinched at his tone, and immediately softened. "Will...I'm sorry. That came out harsh and I apologize. Are you alright?"

There was a deep exhalation on the other end. "I'm fine, Alex. It's just been a day. And I apologize as well. I had no right to take my bad day out on you. How can I help you?"

Alex hesitated before diving right in with his request.

"I need you to run an ad for me. I'm looking for someone with access to a drone who lives locally. You can say it's for a project or something like that. Be creative but say that the need is urgent and I am willing to pay top rates." He could hear Will scribbling furiously on something.

"And when do you want this run?"

"Immediately. Like, I need it in the paper in the morning," Alex responded.

Will sighed. "Of course. I can make that happen. What's one more rushed classified ad..."

"Wait. Was there another one?"

"Well, yeah. Some kid called with a cryptic ad he said was life or death and needed run immediately as well."

Alex's spine went stiff, and something began to buzz in the back of his mind. "Will, what exactly was the ad he wanted run?"

"Hold on, I have it right here..." there was a pause as he ruffled through some paper. "It reads, 'I have something you don't want getting out. Let's make a deal and settle on a price. Then it's all yours'. Weird, but hey, who am I to judge?"

A shiver of excitement passed though Alex. "Will, has that ad run?"

"Yes. It was in today's paper."

A knot was forming in Alex's stomach, and he swallowed hard. "Can you email me the ad? And I also need the contact information for the person who placed it."

"Alex, I don't know about that. Is that legal?"

Alex could hear the hesitation in Will's voice and immediately pressed him. "Will, this is a matter of life and death. Literally. I can't give you the details, but I need you to trust me on this." Silence from the other end. "Please. It's important."

"Fine," Will sighed. "But you did not get this from me. These ads are called classified and personals for a reason."

Alex closed his eyes, breathing a sigh of relief. "Thank you, Will. I owe you. One last question; has anyone replied to the ad?"

"That I can't see. The original poster provided an email address for responses. And that I can't see."

Alex's mind raced. His phone dinged and he moved it away from his face to see Will's message notification. He'd emailed him the information. Now, Alex just had to hope the kid who placed the ad wasn't already dead. He needed to speak with Jessie.

"Thank you, Will. I promise you I would never ask this if it wasn't important. I gotta run." He stood, pushing the chair back from his desk.

"Wait, do you still want your ad run?" Will asked.

Alex contemplated his question for a moment. His gut told him he had the information he was after. "No. Let's hold off on that. I think you've given me everything I need."

He disconnected the call and immediately pulled up Jessie's number. The ringing in his ear was echoed by a cell ringing down the hall. He looked up to see Jessie walking towards him, her boots creating a rapid fire, staccato rhythm on the polished floors.

"Jessie, I was just calling you," Alex said, his breath catching in his throat.

She held up her phone. "So, I see."

He tried and failed to contain his excitement. "I think I got a lead."

"Me too." She looked around at the room full of officers. "But not here."

Alex grabbed his coat and followed her away from his desk. He glanced the chief's way and saw the big man watching the two of them. With a nod, he led Jessie outside of the precinct to the stairs that led into the building. "I think I got a lead on who owns the drone." He held up his phone, pulling up the information Will had emailed him.

Jessie frowned. "I was coming to tell you the same thing. I think I have a lead as well." She took out the piece of paper the photography vendor had handed over.

When they each saw the name the other presented, they exchanged wide-eyed stares.

"No such thing as coincidence," said Alex.

Jessie nodded. "Time to go pay Kevin Hicks a visit. And hope we get to him before anyone else."

19

Into the Narrows

The ride to the Narrows took them just outside of the town limits and into an incorporated area of Pine Haven that Jessie was not familiar with. As they took the roads that led to the outskirts of town, the ambience shifted noticeably. The beauty of the lake outlined with majestic, breathtaking homes, gave way to the well-lit splendor of downtown Pine Haven with its tidy homes and manicured lawns, which in turn transitioned to the rougher roads and darker, more forlorn stretches leading to the railroad tracks that divided the town.

Increasingly sporadic streetlights gave off a glow that barely pierced the darkness in places, creating deep pockets of shadows that played with Jessie's imagination. After they crossed the railroad tracks, the feeling that they were entering another world became even more apparent. The smooth roads gave way to more potholes that hinted at years of neglect. On either side of them, the distance between houses grew farther apart, and the dwellings themselves became more and more overgrown and dilapidated.

Alex made a couple of turns and headed down a tight road barely wide enough for one car at a time. Jessie saw a sign that read 'Nair's Mobile Court' in peeling yellow lettering.

"I've never seen this part of town, even as a child," she said.

Alex gripped the steering wheel. "You wouldn't have. Your aunt wouldn't have any reason to bring you over here."

Something in his eyes, the way he stared straight ahead, told Jessie there was more that he wasn't saying. But she wasn't about to pry.

They turned into the mobile court, and onto a gravel drive that separated the homes. The trailers were of varying age and conditions. Some were older, with paint and siding showing signs of wear, while others appeared newer with small plots of grass and flowers in front of them, defiant against both judgement and the passage of time.

As they made their way slowly through the court, Jessie could see people dotting the stoops of a few of the trailers, their eyes following the cop car with distrust. Often, they would stop what they were doing and nudge one another, their chin jutting in Alex and Jessie's direction, before returning to their smokes, or simply heading indoors, slamming their doors behind them.

Alex navigated the gravel roads until he reached the

end of the park, where only a few trailers were parked. There weren't any signs to denote the name of the makeshift roads around the court, yet Jessie noticed the officer had no problem following them to their destination.

He rolled the car to a stop. "This is it." He pointed ahead at a brown and white trailer with a blue tarp covering parts of the roof at the very end of the drive. It was dark, no outside lights to illuminate the surroundings or the inside of the trailer. Either no one was home, or whoever lived there was in hiding.

Jessie hoped for the latter.

She climbed out of the car and opened the back door to let Blizzard out. They didn't dare involve the other police officers, but Alex had agreed that having a large German Shepherd at their back could come in handy. Jessie took in a deep breath, noting the air was a mixture of cigarette and marijuana with a faint overlay of diesel.

The nearest trailer was a hundred feet away, the lone lamp post behind it cast lonely shadows in their direction. Jessie stood there, listening for signs of movement both inside and outside the trailer. Nothing caught her attention, and she could tell from the relaxed body posture of the canine at her side that Blizzard wasn't picking up anything either.

She glanced at Alex and saw the muscles of his jaw tightening as he looked at the trailer. "Ready?"

He nodded in return, and they headed for the cement blocks that acted as steps leading to the front door. Jessie motioned for Blizzard to sit at the base of the steps as she ascended, Alex close behind her.

"Maybe I should knock first?" Alex said.

She shook her head. "If he sees you in uniform first, he may panic and try to make a run for it. Do you know if there is a back door?"

"Most mobiles are required to have a second door," he whispered. "Safety. So yeah, if he spooks, he may run out the back."

"Then let's not spook him."

She knocked, pressing her ear to the door. "Kevin? Kevin Hicks?"

No answer. She glanced down at Blizzard. The dog's ears were twitching slightly and focused on the door. Someone was on the other side.

She knocked again; this time lighter. "Kevin, I know you're in there. My name is Jessie Night and I'm here with Alex Thomas. He's an officer with the Pine Haven police department. You're not in any trouble, but I believe you might be in danger. We're here to help you, Kevin."

There was a shuffling on the other side of the door that was almost imperceptible. Jessie looked at Blizzard and noticed his tail start to wag slightly as he leaned forward, his eyes focused on the door.

"Kevin," she continued, "we know about the drone. We also know that the men you are trying to make a deal with are very dangerous. You don't want them finding you first."

More movement, this time accompanied by the sound of a lock retracting. Slowly, the door cracked open, stopped by a thin, gold chain that stretched to keep the door from opening completely. Jessie was pretty sure she could pop the chain off the fixture it was attached to by throwing her shoulder at it, but that would do nothing to convince Kevin they weren't a threat to him.

"Show me some identification." The young man's voice trembled as he spoke through the narrow opening.

Jessie glanced over at Alex and nodded. She took one of the business cards out of her jacket pocket and Alex produced his badge. Together, they held them up enough that the young man could see them.

The door closed, followed by the rattle of the chain, before swinging wide to let them enter.

"Your card says consultant," he said, stepping back. "You're not a cop?"

Jessie shook her head. "No, I just work with the police on a case-by-case basis as needed."

Once they were inside, Jessie could see why the trailer appeared so dark from the outside. Kevin had taped black trash bags over all the windows, preventing any light from leaking out, and ensuring that no prying eyes could see in.

The man himself was barely out of his teens. Kevin Hicks was tall and gangly, wearing gray jeans that were faded from age, not by design, with a black belt cinched tightly around his waist to hold them up. He wore a black tee shirt with a white silhouette of a crow emblazoned on the front and a pair of heavy-duty Doc Martens. His face was angular, with pale blue eyes, set off by a shock of auburn hair.

His eyes narrowed, locking in on Alex.

"It's okay, Kevin. You can trust him," Jessie said.

"Hmph," the young man replied. "Haven't met one of his kind yet that can be trusted." He watched as Blizzard made his way in behind Alex, his large tail wagging side to side.

Jessie held out a hand as Kevin started to back away from the shepherd. "It's okay. He's friendly."

Kevin gave the dog the side eye, not completely convinced. "If you say so."

Alex let out a breath. "I know you have probably not seen the best of the police department before, but all that's changing. I promise." He kept his voice soft and soothing, trying to get the young man to relax.

"Are you here to arrest me? Because of the whole drone thing?" Kevin said. His blue eyes seemed to swell with barely held back tears.

Alex took a deep breath, staring at the young man. This was something he and Jessie had spoken about on the drive over. Technically, what the man had done, withholding a piece of evidence in a murder investigation, would be grounds for arrest. But right now, they need him to find Cora. After that, decisions would have to be made. "I'm not here to arrest you. Jessie was telling the truth when she said we were here to help you. You have to trust us."

Kevin plopped down on the worn sofa with a sigh of relief. His unshaven face showed signs of stress as his eyes darted nervously around the room, finally landing on a makeshift wooden table where his camera and drone rested. The very thing that had pulled him into this dangerous game.

Jessie followed his gaze to the gear laid out on the table. "Kevin, what exactly is on that footage?"

His eyes dropped to his hands which were drumming

against his thighs. He shook his head. "I...it's awful." He stood and moved to the table, snatching up the handheld control for the drone. He keyed a couple of switches across the top, bringing it to life. A few more swipes and he handed it to Jessie, unable to meet her eyes as the screen played out what had given him nightmares the first time he saw it.

Alex peered over Jessie's shoulder, watching along as the horror unfolded onscreen. Jessie's hand was shaking as she handed it back to Kevin once the scene was over.

"Kevin, why didn't you turn this in as soon as you realized what it was?" she asked.

He shrugged, his eyes wide. Jessie wanted to shake him, make him realize just what was at stake.

"I don't know. I panicked. At first, I thought it wasn't real. I mean, I hoped it wasn't."

Alex shifted in place, crossing his arms over his chest. "Oh, it is real alright. And we have the body in the morgue downtown to prove it."

Kevin flinched as if the officer had struck him. "I'm sorry, okay. But I had no idea what to do. I've never seen anything like that. I thought about going to the police, but...every instinct I had told me not to; that they would somehow find a way to pin this on me." He looked up at Jessie with panicked eyes. "I even thought about giving it to you. I had heard good things about you. That day at Angela's Bakery I almost approached you. But I was scared."

Jessie's mind snapped back to the young man who had been sitting in the corner of the bakery. She cursed herself for going soft and not trusting her instincts in the moment. Back in her military days, she would have approached the man and questioned him. But this was Pine Haven. Maybe it was good that those other instincts were waning.

Alex was shaking his head at the young man. "Kevin, did you place an ad in the town paper about this?"

He looked up at them, his face going red. "Is that how you found me?"

"That's how *I* found you," Alex said.

"I tracked you through the photographs for sale at the festival," Jessie said. Her tone softened. "You really do beautiful work."

Kevin slammed the palm of his hand against his forehead. "The festival. I forgot all about it. I bet Ms. Houston was really pissed I didn't show to help set up."

Jessie gave him a slight smile. "She wasn't the happiest at doing all the work herself. but I've a feeling she will forgive you." She studied his face, clenching her jaw as she considered her next words carefully. "Kevin. You have to come with us. It's not safe here."

Panic began to wash over him once again. "Go with you where? And yeah, I know it's not safe here. That's why I just wanted to score enough money off this to get out of town once and for all."

Alex and Jessie exchanged a worried look.

"Kevin, these people are very dangerous. They kidnapped my friend and are threatening to kill her if I don't get this footage and turn it over to them." She wasn't about to let him know that they were asking for him as well. That would serve no purpose at this point.

Kevin's eyes brimmed with tears again. His hand went

to his head, grasping at his hair. "No, no, no—that isn't my fault."

Jessie started to speak but then noticed the large duffel bag sitting next to the trailer door. There was a second, smaller bag with a set of bungee cords atop it next to the duffel bag. "Kevin, were you planning to go somewhere? To run?"

"Run? No. I just wanted the money. For a clean start."

Jessie's eyes widened. "Tell me you didn't already make contact with those killers?"

He gave her a pleading look, biting at his lower lip. At the same time, a car engine could be heard outside the trailer and the sound of tires rolling slowly over gravel. Blizzard's ears flattened against his head, and he let out a low, rumbling growl.

Alex crossed the room and pulled aside a small corner of the trash bag to see out the front window. He immediately drew his gun. "Heads up. We got company."

20

A Dirty Escape

"You carrying?" Alex asked Jessie. She shook her head and the officer frowned. He bent down and retrieved a second, smaller gun from a holster around his ankle. He handed it to her, before returning to peek out the window. "Dark green sedan. Looks like only two men. They're just sitting in the car for now."

"I'm sure they weren't expecting to pull up and see a police cruiser," Jessie added. She shoved the gun into the back of her waistband and looked around. "Kevin, is there another way out of here?"

He pointed to a white door at the far end of the living room. "That leads out back." He headed for the door, but Jessie stopped him.

"No, too dangerous. If that's the only other exit they will be expecting that. We won't get far." She looked at Blizzard, and the dog sat at attention, reading her body language. She moved to the back door and motioned for Blizzard. "Patrol." She opened the back door quickly and the shepherd darted out. She quickly closed the door behind him and turned to Kevin. "What about a window in the bathroom or bedroom?"

He shook his head. "Too small to get through." He thought for a second and then his eyes lit up. "There is another way, but it won't be fun."

Jessie looked at Alex. "Cover us if anyone comes through that door. Then follow." She turned to Kevin. "Let's go."

Kevin started forward but then ran back to the coffee table to retrieve the handheld control panel for the drone. He gave the only place he had ever known as home one last look around before heading down the tight hallway that led to the back of the trailer. Jessie was on his heels as he reached the end of the hall. There was a place mat on the floor that didn't match the rest of the carpet and Kevin bent down, yanking it aside. Beneath it was a loose piece of plyboard.

"One of the many things my dad started over the year and never finished," he said, lifting the board. Beneath it was a square cutout in the floor with blackness beneath it. "He was going to install central air, so he cut the vent that leads to the crawlspace under the trailer."

There was a jangling at the back door of the trailer that caught Jessie's attention. There was a third person with the kidnappers, and he had made his way around the back, attempting to gain entry that way. A deep bark and snarl echoed through the thin walls followed by the sharp exclamation of surprise from whoever was attempting to enter the space.

Jessie swallowed, trying not to think of the danger Blizzard could be in. "Does this lead out?"

Kevin nodded, his brow breaking out in perspiration. "Yes, there is a utility door at the back of the trailer that not many people would even know about."

Jessie cleared her mind, focusing on the task at hand. "Stay behind me." She risked a glance towards the other end of the hall and saw Alex standing with his back to them, gun trained on the door. His head turned briefly in the direction of the back door where Blizzard's snarls were punctuated with the sound of yells and a body slamming against the side of the trailer.

Jessie tried to drown out the sounds as she slipped into the opening, dropping down a few feet into the darkness. She felt something slippery beneath her feet and her nose was immediately assaulted by a foul stench that nearly made her gag. The crawlspace beneath the trailer was so tight that the only way for her to move forward was on all fours. She tried not to think about what she was putting her hands in as they sunk into the foul, soft mud beneath her. "Okay, Kevin, get down here."

She heard him drop behind her as he landed in the mud as well. "Just go straight as far as you can. Then there's a little latch door that will open to the outside." He gagged, trying not to retch. "Sorry about this. The plumbing for the bathroom is not the best. Another thing Dad said he was going to fix years ago."

Jessie tried not to think about that as she made her way through the muck, one hand always sweeping the air until she felt the solidness of a wall ahead of her. She ran her hand along the wall until she felt the door Kevin had mentioned. She groped for the latch and turned it, pushing the door outward until she could fit her upper body through. She gulped a lungful of fresh air and crawled out into the night.

Once clear, she crouched with her back against the trailer, letting her eyes adjust to the dimness of the night. She breathed a sigh of relief when she felt Blizzard nuzzle against her leg. She dropped an arm around the big dog's neck hugging him to her as Kevin crawled out to squat beside her. They stood, backs pressed against the trailer.

Jessie leaned in close to Kevin, her lips nearly touching his ear as she whispered. "Stay here and wait for Alex to come out."

She signaled for Blizzard to stick to her side as she inched towards the corner of the trailer, sliding carefully around the corner towards the front of the mobile home.

Instantly, two hands grabbed her by the front of her jacket. Blizzard shot past her, leaping in a flurry of white fur and fangs at a second man who had been waiting on them. Jessie raised her arm and brought it smashing down on the man's forearm, breaking his hold on her. Before he could recover, she cocked her elbow and delivered a smash to his face with the butt of her gun.

He sputtered blood and reached for his broken nose with both hands. Jessie took advantage and reached forward to grab him by his shirt. Throwing her hip into his pelvis, she turned and jerked, throwing him to the ground over her shoulder. As soon as he hit the ground she followed up with another smash from the butt of the gun to his temple, knocking him unconscious.

A yelping caught her attention, and she looked up to see Blizzard rolling across the ground, then quickly making his way to his feet. The man he had attacked had a torn sleeve with blood flowing copiously down his arm. Jessie knew from the bite marks on his pants that he had to be the same guy Blizzard had attacked behind the trailer. To her horror, she watched as the man took a gun from somewhere in his jacket and leveled it at the white shepherd.

She didn't think, didn't hesitate. She dropped to one knee, bringing the barrel of her own weapon up, and squeezed off a shot, clipping the man in the shoulder. His gun flew out of his hand, and he staggered backwards, heading for the car idling next to Alex's patrol car.

A noise behind her caught her attention and she wheeled, gun up.

"It's me!" Alex shouted, raising his hands.

Immediately Jessie lowered her weapon, letting out a deep sigh as Blizzard once again returned to her side. "Where's Kevin?" Her voice ballooned in panic.

Together, they rushed to the end of the trailer and then around to the back where they found Kevin in a deep crouch, eyes closed, his hands covering his ears. He was shaking violently and jerked away from Jessie when she reached for him.

She dropped to one knee, gently resting a hand on one of his arms until he opened his eyes. "Kevin, it's alright. You're safe."

His trembles stopped and he lifted his eyes to meet

hers. "I'm so stupid. I can't believe I was going to make a deal with them. I'd...I'd be dead now."

Jessie looked at the boy and felt what little patience she had remaining flee. "Yeah, well you didn't die. As a matter of fact, *we* were nearly killed protecting you. Yes, you did something stupid, and hopefully you'll think twice before you decide to extort killers. But sitting here feeling scared and wallowing in self-pity isn't going to help get my friend back. If anything, you just moved the clock ahead for her." He looked up at her, his mouth hanging open. "So, what we're going to do, is get up and get the hell out of here. For all we know they've already called for more help and are on their way back."

She stood and extended a hand. Kevin reached up, taking it, and she hauled him to his feet. Alex was staring at her appreciatively.

"Come on. Let's grab the guy who attacked me and get out of here. Maybe he can tell us something useful," she said.

They returned to the front of the trailer, only to find a patch of blood where the man she had incapacitated had been. But that was all.

"Damnit!" she said. "Okay, everybody in the car. We need to get out of here. By now the neighbors will have reported my gunshot and someone from the department could be on their way."

They headed for the squad car and Kevin was shaking his head. "No one will report anything. And even if they did, the cops might show up sometime tomorrow." He gave Alex a look. "Maybe."

They piled in, Kevin and Blizzard in the backseat, and Alex hastily pulled away from the trailer.

"Where to?" he said.

"We can't go back to my place," Jessie said. "They know where I live and by now, they may already be waiting on us there."

Kevin became visibly upset, his leg beginning to tremble. His grip on the drone controller tightened as his hands shook.

"We can go to my place," Alex said.

Jessie was shaking her head. "They know about you. That's the next place they'll look, and something tells me they don't care in the least that you're a cop." She frowned, deep in thought, before turning to look at Alex. "I know a place."

He looked at her, seemingly reading her mind.

Thirty minutes later, they pulled into the parking lot of the Gray Eagle motorcycle club.

21

An Uneasy Alliance

Despite the hour, the bar was busier than Jessie had ever seen. The cloak of darkness that settled over the bar seemed to bring with it a life all its own. The conversations were loud, and the drinks were flowing. Every table was taken by groups of people holding court and the bar itself was three people deep.

"I had no idea there were even this many people in Pine Haven," Jessie said, leaning over to Alex as they stood just inside the doorway.

"They aren't all from Pine Haven," he said. "The Gray Eagle attracts clientele from counties away. Good to see membership is booming for John." His sarcasm wasn't lost on Jessie, and she took a deep breath as they pushed their way into the crowd.

There were also a lot more women in the bar than

Jessie was used to seeing. The late hour seemed to bring out a subset of the working class that were draped over whichever man they found themselves near. They laughed raucously, tossing back shot after shot, seeming to encourage crass remarks and roaming hands. Some of them gave Jessie a downright evil look as she passed. She ignored the hard eyes, instead heading for the bar, dragging Kevin along with her. Alex had zipped up his jacket to hide his badge, yet still attracted more than a few unwanted stares.

Shouldering her way through the crowd, Jessie headed for the bar and Josie. The big bartender saw her coming and frowned. She could tell he didn't want her approaching the bar and was relieved when he gave her a deliberate stare, then glanced over his shoulder to the right. Following his eyes, she saw John Bartley sitting in the last corner booth before the stairs that led to his personal loft area. He was shoved into the corner and appeared to be deep in serious conversation with three other men.

He looked up as they approached. If he was surprised to see the trio, he didn't let on. "Gentleman, can you give us a minute? Or three?" His voice was calm and conveyed a level of authority that Jessie hadn't experienced before.

The three men sitting with him slid out of the booth, picked up their glasses, and headed for the bar. They barely gave Jessie a second glance, but focused heavily on Alex as they walked past the officer. To his credit, Alex mustered a smile and nod for the men.

John motioned for them to have a seat across from him, and then gestured towards the bottle of Johnny

Walker Gold sitting on the table. Jessie shook her head but was surprised when Kevin nodded. A signal from John and two clean glasses were dropped off at the booth. He poured a generous tumble for Kevin, filling the booth with the sweet aroma of alcohol. It was like fresh fruit with just the right amount of honey drizzled over it, and for a moment Jessie nearly succumbed to having a glass as well. But she needed her mind clear and focused.

Kevin lifted the glass and gave it a sniff before downing nearly the entire amount in a single gulp. The burn caused him to cough uncontrollably for a moment, much to John's amusement.

"Are you sure you're old enough to drink?" asked the bar owner.

"Shouldn't you have asked that before you served him?" interjected Alex. The two men exchanged hard looks. Jessie broke the tension by clearing her throat.

"We have a problem," she said.

"And your first thought was to bring it to my steps?" said John. He waved a hand in Kevin's direction. "Let me guess; this has to be Kevin Hicks."

Alex's eyes widened. "How do you know him? I thought you had nothing to do with this?"

John took a swig of his drink. "Easy there. I know his name because I was with Jessie when we came across his work at the festival." He narrowed his eyes as he glanced from one of them to the other. "Wait. She didn't tell you?" He sat back in the booth, pushing against the soft leather, a look of satisfaction crossing his features.

Jessie turned to Alex and saw the muscles of his jaw clenching and unclenching. "It wasn't a big deal. I thought maybe someone was watching me; maybe one of the kidnappers. I figured they knew you but might not know John. If I was being tailed, he might have been able to flush them out. But that never happened."

Alex nodded slowly. "Makes sense. It would have been nice to know what you were up to though."

John smiled. "So. What's your problem? Other than the obvious, that is." Again, his eyes drifted to Kevin. The young man pointed towards the bottle in the center of the table and John shook his head, reaching out and pulling the Johnny Walker closer.

"We weren't the only ones who discovered his address," Jessie said. "Kevin's home was hit by the kidnappers. We managed to get away, but it was close."

John exhaled sharply, puffing his cheeks out. He leaned back and interlaced his fingers behind his head. "And let me guess. You can't stash him at your place."

"You know I can't," said Jessie.

Kevin's spine stiffened and his eyes moved from Jessie to John and back again. "Wait. Are you pawning me off on him? I thought you were going to protect me." His voice was rising in panic.

"And I will. By stopping these people and getting my friend back. But I can't do that and watch you too. I need to know that you are somewhere safe." She glanced at Alex. "And right now, that can't be at my house. Or Alex's, for that matter."

"So, you want me to stay here?" He looked around the bar with wide eyes. "How do you know that the kidnappers aren't one of these patrons? Everyone knows what kind of element hangs out here." He quickly cast an apologetic look at John. "No offense."

John shrugged. "None taken, because you're not wrong. However, none of my people had anything to do with this." He made the sign of a cross over his heart. "Scout's honor."

"Not sure that's how that works," said Alex, "but whatever."

John looked around the bar and leaned forward, resting his arms on the table. He spoke in a tone that was little more than a whisper. "I did manage to get a potential lead for you. Those men I was speaking with when you interrupted? They are my most trusted lieutenants." He looked over at Jessie. "One of them was just back from staking out the drop site your kidnapper gave you. He's going to organize a few men to go back there and watch over the pinch points where you could be ambushed. They didn't have to do it, but they did it for me. You're welcome."

Alex couldn't help but scoff. "What is this? Your own little army now?" Jessie gave him a look and he felt the top of his ears grow hot.

John focused on Alex, interlacing his fingers. "If you really want to know, I have been considering opening more chapters of the Gray Eagle in a couple of adjoining states. So yes, you might say that I am building my own army." He sat back, letting out a breath. "But back to what I was saying, these men are my eyes and ears when it comes to the comings and goings of not only Pine Haven, but the greater Blue Ridge as well. And what I've heard is that there is another faction brewing. Seems that someone wants to use Pine Haven as a gateway for certain... off-the-grid activities."

Alex glanced at Jessie. "You mean because we are so centrally located to so many roadway systems?"

"That, and the relative isolation here in the mountains. Plus, the fact that we rely so heavily on traffic coming into and out of town seasonally. It makes it easy to blend in with tourists when you're moving certain types of shipments," John added.

Jessie was nodding along with him. "And the fact that the town is so divided between the haves and the have-nots. The homeowners around the lake aren't really going to get involved in whatever happens across the tracks; and those residents don't trust the cops enough to report any illegal activity they might see."

Kevin gave a loud snort and crossed his arms. "Are you kidding? Illegal shit happens all the time there. Hell, it pays better than cleaning some lake house pool or mowing some lawn. People aren't going to report it because it's a nice side gig for them."

John made it a point to gesture in Kevin's direction with an open palm. "Exactly. The economic divide here in Pine Haven has grown to the point that people turn a blind eye to what their neighbor is doing to make ends meet, because they never know when they might have to do the same thing."

"We've seen some of this already," said Jessie. "We just aren't sure how it all fits together. Yet."

"Did your men say who is behind this new faction looking to muscle in?" asked Alex.

John hesitated, glancing around again. "That's just it.

Whoever it is, they are staying out of the spotlight. Keeping a very low profile. However, one name did keep popping up." He turned his attention to Alex. "Your old pal, Terry Blackburn."

Alex frowned. "He ain't my pal."

John arched an eyebrow. "Really? Because the way I hear it, the two of you used to be thick as thieves back in the day."

Alex gave Jessie a nervous look. "That was a long time ago. We've both changed since then."

John studied the policeman, pursing his lips together. "One of you changed for the worse from what I hear." He took a last draw from his glass, glancing at Jessie. "I'll let you guess as to which one."

"Then it sounds like Terry Blackburn might know something about the kidnapping," said Jessie. She nodded to Alex. "Your instincts were right about him being the one that might know something."

"We don't even know where he is," said Alex. "And even if we find him, chances are he won't talk. At least not in the time we have remaining." He glanced at his watch.

Jessie's eyes narrowed, her gaze growing hard. "Maybe *you* can't make him talk. But trust me, *I* can."

"I can't help with making him talk," said John. "I still don't know what kind of faction he might have already built up, and until then, I can't hurt him. But I can help you with finding him. As a matter of fact, I can tell you where he's going to be at noon tomorrow." He sat back, resting his hands behind his head.

Jessie huffed. "You just going to leave us hanging like that?"

John gave her a smile that would have rivaled the Cheshire cat's. "He's coming here. I've arranged for him to meet with my three lieutenants. It's under the guise of bringing him and his idiot brother into my little family."

"He would never go for that," said Alex.

"Of course not. But it brings him here into the open. And if you just happen to be here at the same time..." He gestured to Jessie.

Alex sat bolt upright. "I don't think that's a good idea."

"But do you have a better one?" Jessie asked, her voice quiet, almost devoid of energy. "Because Cora only has a few hours left. If she's even still—" She stopped. Unable —or unwilling—to finish that sentence.

Alex reached over and gave her arm a squeeze. "It's not time to think like that. You haven't received another phone call, so chances are we still have some time on our side."

Jessie nodded, patting his hand. What she didn't want to say was that the kidnappers probably now knew that she and Alex had Kevin. They were most likely regrouping and deciding on the next, possibly bloodier, course of action.

"And you're sure noon will work? We won't be disturbed?" she asked.

"High noon," John reiterated. "The bar will be closed to everyone with the exception of the invitees."

"That just leaves Kevin," Alex said.

"John, I hate to ask. You've done so much already, but can he stay here?" Jessie asked.

Kevin shook his head in panic. "No way. I don't care what you say, for all you know one of your own men could be in on this. I wouldn't feel safe here. I'll take my chances back home. What's the likelihood they'll go back to the Narrows looking for me?"

"There's every chance they will look there," Jessie said. "So, absolutely not."

"Don't worry," said John. "I wasn't planning on leaving the kid here. I have a place not far from here that no one —and I mean no one—knows about. It's off the beaten trail and he'll be perfectly safe there. I'll stay with him and make sure not a hair on his head is harmed. We can meet back here at noon tomorrow." He looked over at Jessie and gave her a smirk. "You're welcome to stay there as well. It's two bedrooms and I'll sleep on the sofa. Better than you going home. Especially if you've pissed off some really bad men. And I've a feeling you've really pissed some people off tonight."

She tried to ignore the hopeful look in Kevin's eyes, and the disdainful one coming from Alex. The truth was, John was right. Going home wasn't an option, and she wasn't entirely comfortable leaving Kevin solely with John. While she trusted him far more than she did a week ago, he wasn't trained for certain situations the way she was.

"I'll stay with you until tomorrow. Hopefully, Terry Blackburn will shed some light on what is going on and where Cora is," she said.

"Then it's settled," said John. He slid out of the booth and motioned for them to follow. "Let me just get something from my office and we can head out." He turned awkwardly to Alex as well. "You know, you're welcome as well. There's a recliner next to the sofa. We can make it a slumber party."

Just as they reached John's office, Jessie's phone buzzed, and they all froze. She took it out of her pocket and stared at the screen. "Unknown caller. It's them."

22

The Terms Change

They hurried into the office and John closed the door, shutting out the raucous noise from the bar. Jessie took a deep breath, tapped the screen of her phone, and sat it in the corner of John's desk.

"Hello?" she said.

"What the hell, Jessie? I thought we had an understanding." The voice was calm and even. Deep in timber with measured tones. Jessie thought it sounded like the same one she had spoken with before, but she couldn't be certain.

She swallowed a lump in her throat. "Did we? Because I thought you wanted me to retrieve something for you. I was doing my job. Your guys crashed the party."

"And had you let them do their job you and your friend would be sitting in front of your fireplace sipping wine right now."

"Where is she? I swear, if you've hurt her in any way, I will hunt you down and I promise you will beg me to end you by the time I finish with you." Heat colored her face and her tone.

"It's not too late to save her. Honor the deal and bring the boy to us," the man said.

She knew he was lying, but also realized there wasn't much she could do about it.

Kevin's eyes widened as he stared at Jessie. Slowly, he backed away from her until his back hit the office door.

"Bringing him to you won't do any good, because he doesn't have the drone." She looked at Kevin and held her finger up to her lips. The panic in the boy's eyes told her he was close to bolting. "You should be thanking me."

There was a pause before the man spoke again. "And why is that?"

"Because your goons would have killed him, and you still would not have had the drone. We found him first, but he had already hidden the drone and whatever is on it. Of course, that doesn't mean there aren't copies floating around somewhere." She let that hang in the air. "He's a lot smarter than he looks." She locked eyes with Kevin, pleading with him to trust her.

"Assuming you're telling the truth, what are you doing to find it?" the man asked.

Jessie let her voice drop in tone. "Oh, he'll talk. I'll get it out of him."

Silence again. "And why should I believe you?"

"Because you still have my friend," she said. "And I care a hell of a lot more about her than I do some kid I just met."

"Tell you what. Why don't we still make the exchange. Bring the boy to us at the agreed upon time and site and I'll let you have your friend. I have a feeling I can make this kid talk faster than you can."

Jessie huffed at the phone. "No way. You think I'm stupid? I hand him over and then you'll kill him and my friend. I'll get the drone for you. That gives me something concrete to trade."

"And what's to stop you from blackmailing us?"

"Because you only have one thing I want. I couldn't care less about anything else."

She paused, holding her breath as she waited for a response.

"I will honor our original timeline. But if you miss that...by even a minute, I'll send you two of your friend's fingers."

Jessie swallowed hard, letting out a breath. "Is...is she okay?"

"For now." The line went dead, and Jessie felt like the room was spinning around her. She placed her hands on the desk for support, letting her head sag.

"You...you were going to turn me over to them?" Kevin said, his voice shaking.

Jessie's head snapped up. "Don't be ridiculous. That was never a consideration for me. But I need to get my friend back, so I tell them what they need to hear."

"Do you think they bought that?" asked Alex.

Jessie raised her shoulders. "I hope so. It brought us some time, and that's what matters right now." She turned to John. "And you're sure Terry will show tomorrow?"

The bar owner puffed out his cheeks, exhaling hard. "It's not exactly a RSVP situation. But yeah, I'm pretty sure he'll show. How he responds to you being there is anybody's guess."

"I don't care what he might think," Jessie said. "We are against a ticking clock, and I don't have time for subtleties."

John gave her a serious look. "Just remember, I'm setting this bar up as neutral territory for this meeting. Don't go breaking any arms or doing something that drags us into some kind of turf war."

Jessie gave him an equally hard look. "My best friend's life is at stake. I'm going to do what I must in order to save her. So, you can either help me, or step aside." Her tone was harsher than she meant it to be, and she looked away at the pained expression John gave her.

Alex nodded to John. "I'm taking you up on your offer to stay at your place. Right now, we need to stick together. Send me your address. I need to go home and change out of my uniform." John gave him a questioning look and Alex sighed. "Unless you want me to show up at your bar tomorrow wearing this." He gestured to his uniform and badge.

"Fine," replied John before squinting his eyes at the officer. "But if it gets out where I live, then I'll know where it came from."

Jessie rolled her eyes at the two men. This was going to be a fun night.

John made his way to a drawer behind the desk and placed several folders from the desktop into them before locking the drawers and pocketing the key. He then moved to his computer and keyed in a few details before shutting it down as well. He turned to face the room. "Okay. Let's go."

He led the way out of the office with Kevin close on his heels. Jessie grabbed Alex by the arm as he started to follow them out of the room. He turned to face her.

"I want you at my side when we meet with Terry tomorrow. I'm hoping your presence will rattle him enough that he lets something slip."

"You aren't worried about my past with him, as John would put it?"

"Not at all. Hopefully it will work to our advantage. Also, stay close to Kevin. Don't let him out of your sight. No matter what."

Alex nodded. "Do you trust John?"

She hesitated, then nodded. "I do. But I can't say the same for everyone else in this club."

Together, they left the office and followed John and Kevin out of the club. Jessie retrieved Blizzard from the back of the patrol car and climbed into the back of John's oversized SUV.

She took a deep breath and tried to settle her nerves. She was telling the truth. She trusted John but couldn't shake the feeling that she was running out of options. If they didn't get something out of Terry Blackburn tomorrow, she would be down to one last card to play.

She stroked Blizzard's neck as she stared at the back of Kevin's head. The problem with playing that last card was that she might end up with the blood of an innocent on her hands yet again.

Unexpected Refuge

Nestled amidst the dense canopy of the mountains, John's house stood in stark contrast to the roar of motorcycles and the rowdy bar he helmed.

It had taken them forty-five minutes to make their way up a winding road to arrive at his sanctuary. Jessie had no idea where they were. For the entire drive she hadn't seen signs of any other homes, and for a split-second she wondered if she had made a mistake in venturing up the mountain without Alex.

But as they rounded a final bend, she could make out the dim glimmer of a porch light reflecting off the shimmering creek that ran beside the home. The house itself was a modest, wooden structure with deep-brown panels and a high-pitched, slanted roof. Jessie would have never guessed such an elegant, yet simple structure would have belonged to someone with John's reputation. They climbed out of the SUV and were greeted by the rhythmic babbling of the creek and the muted croaking of frogs in the distance. The only other sound that disturbed the serenity of the night was the hum of the sturdy generator that sat to one side of the house. A stack of firewood was laid out beside it, loosely covered with a dark blue tarp.

Jessie glanced at the steep roof and saw an array of solar panels arranged along both slopes to capture the sun's energy when it crested the tree-covered peaks. Her eyes trailed down to the water pump that the panels tied into as it drew from the natural spring nearby. She could see that the spring not only provided fresh drinking water, but also ran through a series of ingeniously designed pipes to feed a rustic outdoor water heater.

She glanced at John. "Are you completely off grid up here?" She couldn't mask the admiration in her voice. "I wasn't expecting that."

He led them to the creaky porch and took out his keys, slipping one into the lock and pushing the door open. "Down there...the bar, the motorcycles...all of it is just so frantic, so kinetic all the time. It's just motion, motion and more motion. Here, I feel grounded. When I come here, all the excess is stripped away and made unnecessary. It makes me appreciate the basics."

She didn't respond as he entered the space, followed by Kevin and Blizzard. Jessie took one last look back at the car and the winding road behind it, searching for any signs of lights or disturbance that might indicate they were followed. Satisfied, she stepped into the home, locking the door behind her.

The living room was dominated by a stone fireplace, and John immediately set about starting a fire to warm the space. Kevin made his way over to a large bookcase behind a comfortable-looking sofa and began to run his fingers along the spines of the tomes. In the other hand, he gripped the drone controller, hugging it to his body.

Jessie looked around the room, taking it in at a glance. The sudden crackle of flames caught her attention as John coaxed the fire to life, casting orange shadows on the wall. Above the fireplace, a picture of a much younger John sat on the mantle, his arms around a woman.

The living room emptied into a small kitchen with a large steel refrigerator on one wall, and a matching steel farmhouse-style sink sitting under a window. A dining table sat to one side, and in the corner was a wood-burning stove with a kettle and cast-iron pot sitting atop it.

Jessie looked up to a high ceiling to a loft area that disappeared behind a wooden railing. The stairs leading to the second floor ran along the wall as you entered the front door.

"Any other entrances or exits?" she asked.

John gave her a look and nodded. "Mudroom off the back corner of the kitchen. I bring the wood in that way for the stove."

Jessie nodded her head towards the loft. "And up there?"

"Two bedrooms off to either side of the loft. Mine is to the left, guest is to the right. One full bathroom off my room and a half bath in the hall for the guests. Windows are high on the backside of the house, and not reachable unless you're Spiderman. And yes, they are locked."

Jessie nodded appreciatively, glancing towards the kitchen. "What kind of door coming into the mudroom?"

John smiled. "A solid one. No glass to break, and it's got a deadbolt on it as well. No one's getting in through it." He could see his words only eased her mind a little, so he motioned to the grandfather clock in the corner of the living room. "See that clock? It's an antique I got from a flea market a couple of years ago. It doesn't work. Something must be blocking it from behind." He then motioned to the bookshelf Kevin was perusing. "And on the third shelf you'll find 'War and Peace'. Not exactly light reading." He pointed to the kitchen. "The second cabinet from the left, above the kettle? That's where the coffee grinder is kept. If you ever need a quick pick me up, it's worth a shot." He smiled at her. "Everything you might need is closer than you think."

Jessie found her appreciation for the man growing. Even though he valued the solitude and peace that came with his little hideaway, he wasn't stupid. It also reminded her that potential violence always hung over his head. Still, she felt more comfortable knowing that if something happened, there was protection only a few feet away no matter where she might be on the first floor. And that led her to decide that she would stay downstairs with Alex, while John and Kevin slept upstairs in the two bedrooms.

If trouble presented itself, it would have to go through her first in order to get to Kevin.

She told John her idea about the sleeping arrangements, and he didn't argue. He told her that while he doubted anyone would make it past her, he assured her that if that were to happen, he had the means at his disposal to defend Kevin as well. She nodded, understanding completely what he meant.

Seemed like the entire house masked an armory, and that thought brought her a strange amount of comfort.

John told Kevin which room upstairs was his then turned to Jessie. "Do you want me to stay up with you? Just until Alex arrives?"

Jessie thanked him for the offer but declined. She knew Alex well enough to know he wouldn't be happy with the course she had put them on, and she wanted the chance to let him voice his opinion. She hated the fact that she had involved him to this degree but was also grateful he was at her side. She felt the need to tell him just that.

That he mattered and that she saw him as more than a partner. He had her complete trust and coming from the life she had lived before moving to Pine Haven, that spoke volumes about the kind of man he was.

Headlights flashed through the living room window, followed by the crunch of gravel under tires. She carefully peeked out the window, making sure it was Alex before she opened the front door.

He wiped his boots on the coarse mat outside the door and then stepped in, nodding to Jessie. He was wearing a blue, fleece vest that he removed and hung on a freestanding coat rack just before the stairs began. Jessie's eyes swept over the form-fitting, white long-sleeved tee shirt that he wore tucked into his jeans.

Without the bulky, bulletproof vest he often wore under his uniform, he was leaner than she remembered. She quickly averted her eyes as she led him into the house.

"Kevin and John are already upstairs. I told him I wanted to stay down here." She glanced his way as she sat on the couch. "If that's okay with you, I mean."

He gave her a nervous smile. "Sure, John won't have something to say about that?"

Jessie flinched involuntarily. "If he did, it wouldn't matter to me in the least."

Alex sighed. "I'm sorry. Didn't mean anything by that. It's just...why didn't you tell me you needed help at the festival? That you thought maybe you were being followed?"

"Because they—whoever the hell they are—know you. They know the police. I needed someone who blended in with the locals that could watch my back and maybe spot someone that you wouldn't be able to. Besides, you needed to go through the police records regarding possible drone sightings. We had to split up and double our efforts. And look, we both hit pay dirt."

He dropped into the recliner that was angled next to the sofa. "I know. You're right, of course. It's just...John can come with problems. I know he says he changed, but who knows if that's true."

"Believe me, I know better than most that some people are incapable of change. They will always be who they are. They might be able to change masks when needed, but there will come a time when they'll show you their true face. If John is wearing a mask, it will slip at some point. But until then, we need his help."

Begrudgingly, Alex agreed. "Fine. but I'll be watching very closely for that mask to slip."

Jessie smiled. "I wouldn't expect anything less from you."

He took a breath, his body stiffening. "But you do have to trust me on this one. Terry Blackburn is a very dangerous man. Don't trust him, don't give him any information you might later regret, and don't turn your back on him. My gut tells me that if anyone from town is involved in this kidnapping mess, he is."

"Thank you. I appreciate that. I also get the feeling that John doesn't trust him either. I can't imagine why he's even entertaining the idea of getting into bed with him."

Alex was shaking his head. "John is testing the waters with Terry I'm betting. You know what they say about keeping your enemies close."

"Makes sense. It's what I'd do. Still, if he has no clue about who may have kidnapped Cora, then we're back to square one. Only we'll be out of time."

Alex looked away, scanning his surroundings until he spun back to look at her, concern etched across his face. "If that happens, I'm betting you have a backup plan. Care to let me in on it?"

She should have known this was coming. Alex was always thinking ahead; just like she was. "I might have one last trick up my sleeve."

She was hesitant to tell him because she knew how it would sound. But sitting there, alone in the dim light of John Bartley's home, she told him her last ditch, hail-

Mary of a plan. He nodded stiffly as she laid it out, and more than once she heard him let out a breath.

She whispered, aware of how voices could sometimes carry inside certain structures, and she didn't want anyone else—especially Kevin—hearing what she was saying.

When she finished, she looked at Alex. "What do you think?"

His eyes glinted in the near darkness as he stared at her. "I think we better hope Terry comes through with something solid tomorrow. Because plan-B sounds like a lot of people are going to get hurt."

She could only nod in response. "I think we should sleep in shifts. You want to stay up first or get some shut eye?"

He shrugged. "Somehow, I doubt either of us will be sleeping easy tonight. You go first, I'll keep watch out the window."

Jessie smiled, grabbed a blanket from the back of the sofa, and pulled it over herself. She was on high alert and knew Alex was right. Sleep would never come to her as she struggled to turn off images of Cora and body parts in boxes that played through her mind.

In minutes, however, she was deep in sleep. Exhaustion won out and thankfully, she fell into a dreamless slumber.

24

The Devil You Know

The sound of bacon crackling and the smell of fresh roasted coffee roused her from slumber.

She bolted upright, throwing the blanket back and looking around. Alex and Kevin were in the kitchen and were responsible for the aromas causing Jessie's stomach to growl loudly. She stood up, stretching a kink out of her neck, and made her way to the iron stove.

"Alex, what happened? Why didn't you wake me?" she demanded.

He grinned at her, flipping a couple of pancakes on a flat griddle placed near the back of the stove. "I tried. You were out cold. When I realized how tired you must have been, I just let you sleep."

She frowned at the man. "But you must be exhausted."

"Not really. My shifts alter so much lately that I adjust

easily. Besides, I told you I wouldn't be able to sleep last night, so staying up was pretty easy. I'm glad that one of us was able to recharge at least." He nodded to the pot of coffee on the counter. "Besides, I don't know what John puts in his coffee, but it is lethal. One more cup and I'll be ready to stay up another night."

Jessie looked around. "Where is John?"

"He's getting more wood," said Kevin. "Hey, did you know this stove runs entirely off wood? No electricity needed. That's amazing. John said just about everything in this house runs off grid. He said if I'm interested in that, he'll show me how to do it. Talk about a blessing, not having to worry about figuring out how to pay the next electric bill." He turned back to the stove, pushing some bacon around and then cracking a few eggs next to it.

Despite the severity of the situation, Jessie couldn't help but smile at the young man's enthusiasm. Then she remembered what was at stake and her smile faded.

Cora. That was who—not what—was at stake.

The back door slammed as John entered with an armful of cut wood. He placed it on the tile in the mudroom and brought a couple of pieces into the kitchen. Using a mitt, he opened the door to the stove and shoved a couple of pieces in before reaching for a poker and adjusting their location. He nodded at Kevin. "You don't want to put them directly under where you're cooking on the stove. That would create flareups and hot spots you can't control. Always shove them to the side and back."

The young man nodded like he had just been shown

the secrets to the universe. Alex looked at Jessie and playfully rolled his eyes.

In twenty minutes, they were seated at a small table in the kitchen and enjoying a full breakfast of pancakes, eggs, bacon, grits, and a new pot of coffee. John apologized profusely for not having fresh oranges to make juice, and Alex said that with the feast he was providing there wouldn't be room for juice anyway. Jessie tossed back her coffee and nodded approvingly to John. Alex was right...whatever he used, it hit like a freight train.

For the most part, they ate in silence. Occasionally, there was a request to have something passed, or a refill of coffee, but mostly, no one spoke.

Finally, Kevin cleared his throat. "It feels like this is the last supper." He tried to crack a smile but couldn't quite force it. Then, to everyone's surprise, he burst into tears. Everyone stopped mid-chew to stare at him. Then, even more surprising, it was John who pushed back from his chair, walked around to the young man, and placed an arm around him, pulling him in tight.

"It's alright. Everything is going to be okay," John said softly.

Kevin was sobbing and shaking his head in the man's arms. "No. No, it's not. This is all my fault. Jessie's friend is probably going to be killed. All of us might die as well. And why? All because I was greedy and could only think about me."

John let out a sigh. "You know whose fault this really is? The men who killed that young woman and took Cora hostage. They are responsible for their horrible behavior and no one else. Don't you go blaming yourself for the deeds of evil men. Trust me, that isn't a path you want to start down."

Kevin collected himself, and after several deep breaths, was able to nod and make an attempt at returning to his meal.

Jessie looked at him and leaned in. "Kevin, I know you don't need to hear this, but I need you to pull yourself together. The man we are going to speak with may or may not be involved in Cora's kidnapping or the murder of that young woman. But either way, I don't want him seeing you as someone he can zero in on."

Kevin nodded, unconvincingly. Jessie was tempted to suggest leaving him at John's house while they went back to the club, but she knew instinctively that she wouldn't be able to do that. They would have no choice but to take him with them. She just hoped the kid could hold it together long enough for her and Alex to find out what Terry might know.

Alex tried to fill the room with small talk and bits of laughter to ease the tension, and while Jessie appreciated the effort, she found herself unable to take part. Finally, John looked at his watch and indicated it was time to go. He needed to get to the bar early to open.

"Who else will be there for you?" Jessie asked as they headed out the door.

John gave her a mischievous smile. "Aw, are you worried about me?" He laughed at the look she gave him. "My three lieutenants and Josie. And of course, you guys. Why?"

Jessie didn't look back at him as she headed for Alex's car. "Just need to know who not to shoot if it comes down to it." She smiled to herself as she opened the back door of the car for Blizzard to climb in. It pleased her that John didn't know if she was serious or not.

They made the drive back into town, Jessie and Blizzard with Alex, Kevin with John. Jessie wasn't thrilled not having Kevin in the car with her, but Alex assured her there was nothing that could happen to him in the half-hour or so drive back into town. Plus, for whatever reason, the young man seemed comfortable around John, and that meant he might be a bit more at ease once they stepped into the Gray Eagle.

Pulling into the empty parking lot, the motorcycle club loomed ahead of them, and Jessie found herself gripping the worn leather of her seat as Alex pulled to a stop. He backed into a spot as close to the entrance as possible. It would make for a quick and efficient exit if need be. As they climbed out of the car, Jessie's eyes swept the parking lot and the tree line beyond.

She felt a chill race up her spine as she realized she didn't know what was behind the building. Another road? More parking? Out buildings and sheds? Not knowing made her nervous and she made a mental note to ask John.

With Blizzard at her side, she waited until John and Kevin had joined them under the peaked entryway that led to the club entrance.

"John, what's behind the club?" she asked.

He explained that it was a building, not much bigger than a standard barn, that housed mechanic and repair equipment. Club members could use it as necessary to rebuild engines and perform general upkeep on their bikes. He assured her there were no roads or parking that one could access. The only way to get to the repair shed was through a gated entrance on the far side of the Gray Eagle.

She nodded, satisfied with what he told her. John and Alex headed into the club, but Jessie grabbed Kevin by the arm and pulled him close to her. "If things go south in here, I want you to run. Don't wait for me, don't wait for Alex. You see that line of trees directly ahead—where the two big pines come together?" She waited for him to acknowledge that he saw. "Head straight for the path between them. Don't stop till you've hit one hundred paces, then I want you to drop into the thickest part of the undergrowth you find there. Flat on your stomach, and don't move until you hear me or Alex come for you. And no one else. Deal?" He nodded, swallowing hard. Jessie looked at him, puzzled. "Where's the drone controller with the footage on it?"

"I left it at Johns. He thought it best I not attract attention. Don't worry. I emailed the footage to myself, so it's on my phone."

Jessie took a deep breath, trying to hide her annoyance. Then she took out her phone and handed it to him. "Send it to my inbox, now."

As soon as he did what she asked, she forwarded the video to Alex's personal number as well.

"Don't mention a word about having that. As a matter of fact, don't say anything at all. From this point on, you don't speak."

Before he could protest, she tugged at his arm and dragged him into the bar. It was the first time she had seen inside when it was empty. The cleanliness impressed her. The wooden tables were clean, the floor was mopped, and every surface appeared to have been wiped down. The wood of the long bar top practically shined from the deep polish it had received at some point overnight.

"Where are we doing this?" Alex asked.

John pointed to an area in the back of the bar where two large tables had been pushed together. "It's one of a couple of areas of the bar where the surveillance cameras don't reach. There are certain topics in business that you don't want records of."

Jessie looked at her watch just as John's three lieu-tenants walked in. They didn't speak but moved to take up space on one side of the table. Kevin and Jessie sat at the farthest end of the table, with Alex pulling up a chair to sit just behind them.

John didn't offer to introduce the three men sitting across from them, and the men didn't volunteer who they were.

They heard the main doors open and then two sets of heavy footsteps across the concrete flooring. They looked up to see Josie escorting another man to the table. Jessie had wondered where the big bartender had been hiding and felt a bit of relief at the sight of him. He gave her a small nod and then moved to stand next to the bar, keeping a watchful eye on the table.

John stood and nodded to the man Josie had escorted. He shook his hand and motioned to the table. "Terry. So glad you could make it. You know my associates" —he indicated the three men sitting across from him before motioning in Jessie's direction— "and this is—"

Terry Blackburn interrupted him, tossing a smile in Jessie's direction. "Jessie Night. It's very nice to meet you in person."

Jessie frowned. "I guess it really is a small town."

Terry laughed, shaking his head. "I knew your brother. He told me all about you."

25

Can't Trust Family

And just like that, everything Jessie had planned, everything she thought she had prepared for...was out the window.

The moment Terry had muttered those words, it felt like her body was in freefall. Of all the scenarios she had mentally prepared for, this was not one of them.

Her brother?

Memories flooded her mind. Christmas laughter. Bike rides. Scraped knees. Him choking on his own blood after she plunged a shard of glass into his neck.

Her initial shock was quickly engulfed in a flood of questions. How could this man—a burgeoning crime boss wannabe—have known her brother? What exactly had been shared about her? Was there a connection between the most recent, horrible events in Pine Haven and her brother? Or was this just a calculated move on Terry's part to throw her off her game?

She clenched her jaw tightly. For Cora's sake, she refused to let this distract her. She needed a way to get back on the offensive; to feel like she was still in control of her own thoughts. "Funny. He never mentioned you." She tried to keep her tone playful, but underneath, she felt rage beginning to simmer. How dare this man use her brother like this?

But was her anger truly directed at Terry, or did it belong to her brother for daring to put her in this position? Every defense mechanism she had honed over the years threatened to collapse, replaced by a vulnerability she hadn't felt in years.

Terry laughed, his eyes twinkling as he turned away from her, focusing on John. "You didn't tell me this was an open meeting."

John smiled. "What can I say? Something unexpected came up."

Terry's eyes moved from the club owner to Alex, hardening as they fell on the police officer. "And let me guess. You're part of the unexpected something that came up?" He glanced back at John. "I don't know what you're up to, but I'm not feeling this." He turned to leave without sitting down.

"Wait," said John. "The reason they are here has nothing to do with our business. Pine Haven has always been a gold mine for the right type of business. And I'm willing to step aside and let you have your piece. For the right price."

Terry stopped mid-stride, his back stiff. Slowly, he turned to face the table. "What good would such an offer be if it is discussed in front of" —he glanced at Alex—"an officer of the law?"

"Alex was just about to step out," Jessie spoke up, staring intently at Terry.

Alex appeared startled as he looked at her. "I was?"

Jessie nodded, not taking her eyes off Terry. "And take the kid with you as well. This doesn't concern him." She turned her head and stared hard at Kevin. "Remember what I said."

Alex seemed perplexed as he stood. "You sure about this?"

Jessie nodded, her eyes going back to Terry's. "Don't let him out of your sight."

The officer looked around nervously, before motioning for Kevin to follow him. They left the bar, heading for the main entrance without looking back.

"Whoa," said Terry, his voice rising in pitch.

Blizzard had walked up to the man and was sniffing at his hand. Jessie watched the dog, taking in his body language. He was indifferent to the man. His tail stayed down, and his ears flattened before perking back up. He dipped his nose and took a sniff of Terry's trousers and shoes, then trotted over to sit next to Jessie.

She dropped her arm to scratch his back. "He's harmless. Well, to me at least."

"Gentlemen," said John to the three men that sat across from him, "could you give us a minute alone, please?"

Unlike Alex, the three lieutenants stood and left the table immediately, and moved to the bar to join Josie. They were far enough away that they would not be within earshot, but not so far that they couldn't respond in an instant to any perceived threat.

Terry's eyes narrowed as he studied Jessie. "And now there are three. Tell me, John, what is it you think I need from you?"

John extended a hand, gesturing towards the seat across from him. "I don't think it, I know it. I have contacts. People who can...facilitate certain endeavors."

Terry pulled the chair back from the table and took a seat. He threw one leg over the other and looked from John to Jessie and back again. "I'm listening."

John clasped his fingers together, throwing a quick glance at Jessie. "Look, the truth is, I'm making some fundamental changes to my business structure. I've operated for so long in certain gray areas that I've forgotten the reason I created this club in the first place. I wanted this to be a hub; a place where those of us who march to a different beat could get together and build our own community. Someplace where certain establishments wouldn't hound us. Gradually, over time, I watched as Pine Haven changed. It became a place where, if you had a lot, you iced well. If you didn't, then it became harder and harder to eke out a living. And I thought that maybe, by bending a few laws here and there, I could give the have-nots a chance to provide for their own. But along the way, that vision changed. I changed. I got involved in things I shouldn't have; spent time playing in mud that left permanent stains on me." He swallowed, taking a deep breath before continuing. "But I'm done with that now. I'm looking at opening a couple more chapters of the Gray Eagle in different states. Taking it back to what it was meant to be; a social club for others."

Jessie listened intently, trying not to react. John was talking to Terry, but she had a feeling that he was also speaking directly to her.

"And what does your change of heart mean for me?" Terry asked, a sly smile creeping across his features.

John's features grew hard, and for a second, Jessie saw the man who had earned the reputation he had. "Times are changing, Terry. The days of the police in Pine Haven turning their head to certain activities in exchange for a little off the top are limited. Leadership has changed. A lot of the old guard have moved on" —he glanced at Jessie— "one way or the other. You may not like Alex, but you know he can't be bought. Little by little, whatever stranglehold you're trying to establish in this town is getting shut off."

Terry dropped his smile and leaned forward. "Yeah, you're right. Things are changing. And disruption is the best time to create a new status quo." He turned towards Jessie. "Your brother taught us that."

A flash of red clouded Jessie's vision and she fought to bat it away. "My brother died messing around with the same people you're now working for. Are you that eager to follow him?"

Terry leaned back, sucking loudly at his teeth. "Way I hear it is your brother died...messing around with you."

Her eye twitched in response and she could picture herself leaping over the table and planting the heel of her boot squarely in his face. If she caught it just right, she could drive a shard of bone from his nose deep into his brain. He would be dead before his body hit the floor.

John must have sensed her feelings and slid forward in his chair, leaning further onto the table. "Exactly, Terry. This woman did what she had to do. And she didn't even have a connection to the crime she was solving. Now imagine what she might do if someone threatened a person she loved?"

He frowned, looking from one to the other. "What are you implying?"

Jessie snapped at the man. "He's implying that you are involved in the kidnapping of a woman from my house yesterday, or you know something. Either way, it's in your best interest to be truthful with me about it." A low growl rumbling from Blizzard emphasized her tone, and it made her happy to see Terry swallow in discomfort.

"There was also an attempt on the young man's life that was here with Alex," John said. "Related to a body that was found up the mountain."

Jessie leaned in, speaking quickly. "And that was related to my friend's kidnapping."

John jumped in, speaking just as quickly. "I know nothing about these events. Didn't involve any of my men. So, guess what? That leaves you."

Jessie made a point of reaching down to pet Blizzard, holding the big dog by his leash as she stared at Terry.

"And here I thought we were about to do some serious business," Terry said, regaining his composure. He leaned back, crossing his arms over his chest. "I might have heard something about a disturbance going down in the Narrows last night." He narrowed his gaze at John. "But info isn't cheap." He looked Jessie's way. "And I don't respond well to threats."

Jessie sneered at the man and was about to give him the snidest of replies when John spoke up.

"I'm prepared to give you a list of fencers that will come in handy. Pawnshop owners, art dealers and jewelers who are adept at turning certain goods into cash. No questions asked."

Terry arched an eyebrow, slowly nodding his head. "Interesting. Yes, I can see how that could come in very handy. But there is something else I want in addition." He gave John a leering smile and leaned in. "I want your documents guy."

Jessie watched as John drew back from the table, the two men eyeing one another. "What's a document guy?"

See could see John's jaw clenching as he stared at the man sitting across from him.

His discomfort made Terry even more gleeful. "It's a guy that John has in his pocket who can create all kinds of fun things. Like a new driver's license, passports, identities. Hell, I've even heard he can make passable counterfeit money. Right, John?"

Jessie was shocked. She could't believe what this man was comfortable saying in front of her, knowing show she was. The fact he was willing to discuss such matters told her he was testing her; trying to see how she might respond. That, or he was bringing up things that could potentially drive a wedge between her and John. Her eyes widened as she looked to John. In her time in the military, she had come across her fair share of forgers, and she knew how valued they were and just how dangerous their abilities could be. It was bad enough that John was connected to someone like that, and she knew it was a bridge they would have to cross at some point. She shuddered to think what Terry might accomplish with someone like that in his back pocket. "No deal." She turned to John, giving him a look that let him know she was ready to go back to physical intimidation.

"Hey, no sweat off my back," said Terry, standing up to leave.

"Wait," said John, his teeth clenched. "Fine. I'll give you his name and I'll let him know that you'll be doing business with him moving forward, not me." Jessie opened her mouth to protest, but he waved her off. "But for that, I need you to keep your business out of Pine Haven proper. Next county over is wide open for business. And...you are not to recruit any of my men for your start up. Deal?"

Terry pretended to consider the offer, but everyone at the table knew he would take the deal. After a moment, he held his hand to John. "Tell you what. Since I have my own teams I'm putting together, I won't be needing any of your men. And if any of them come my way looking for work, I'll politely send them on their way." He leaned close as he clasped John's hand. "But as far as territories go...I ain't making no promises. Could be that I might be the lesser of two evils heading this town's way."

Jessie had had enough of the man's vagueness and rolled her eyes. "You got what you wanted. Now tell us, what do you know? The murder of a young woman? The kidnapping of my friend? Are they connected?"

Terry gave her a long look before standing and shoving his hands in the pockets of his coat. "I honestly do not know about any kidnapping. But I have heard whispers of women's bodies showing up in the same area where you found the one earlier. Apparently, they are dropped there, and then they're gone. Into thin air."

Jessie gave him a dubious look. "You just happened to hear about this, huh?"

He pursed his lips and let out a loud sigh. "I heard about it because your brother was in charge of...clean up, shall we say."

Again, she felt like the man had punched her in the gut. For a moment, the pounding of her heart and the rush of blood through her head were all she could hear. Taking a deep breath, she forced herself to focus on what came next.

Terry looked at her with mock concern. She knew he knew full well the effect his words were having on her. "He was helping to set up a potential new syndicate of some sort in Pine Haven. It was all hush-hush, and he really didn't trust anyone with the details of who he worked for or what exactly he was doing. But there was a lot of money being thrown around, that much I know. But I know he dealt with the bodies."

Jessie watched him closely. The way the vein on the side of his forehead pulsed when he spoke. The way he briefly looked up and to his left when he recited certain facts. She stood up abruptly. "There has to be more. You know who he was working for."

He shook his head waving a hand at her. "No. I'm sorry. I don't—"

Before he could finish his sentence, she bolted at him. In a matter of seconds, she had him in an arm bar, his right arm locked painfully behind him as she smashed his face to the table. She pinned his wrist up awkwardly behind his back.

"I'm not asking again. Answer me right now or I'm going to break your wrist in a way that you'll never be able to fully use your hand again." For emphasis, she twisted his wrist slightly, causing him to yelp in pain.

"Alright! I swear I don't know who he worked for, but there was a guy he brought in."

"What guy?" Jessie asked. "The next crack you hear is going to be the tearing of the palmer and dorsal ligaments. Once that happens, I'll rearrange the bones in your wrist permanently."

He stiffened in her grasp but was helpless against the leverage she had. "Wait! It's a doctor. Or a medic or someone like that. Someone medical. Your brother was setting them up to be the go-to for any of his people who needed medical attention. The big wigs even set up a makeshift clinic for the guy to work out of so none of their people would ever have to set foot in town for an injury."

John leaned down, his face inches from Terry's. "Where's this clinic?"

"A farm. One that borders my dad's land. There's an old milk house they converted into the clinic. It's the only structure still standing on the land. But I swear my family had nothing to do with this. They don't even know it's there." Terry was grimacing in pain and spoke through gritted teeth. "This guy will know about the bodies and can probably lead you to whoever has your friend."

Jessie looked up at John, and he nodded at her. She released Terry, and he bolted upright, stepping back from her as he shook his stinging wrist.

"Christ. Your brother was right about you," he said. "You are something else. So, I've got one more surprise for you." He reached into his pocket again. When he withdrew his hand, it was closed into a fist. "Your brother left a gift for you; something he said to give you if he... weren't around anymore."

Jessie reached for his closed hand, and he jumped back, keeping his distance.

"Nope," he said. "Come any closer and I'll break it." He tightened his fist for emphasis. "I'll hand this over to you, but I want something from you in exchange. A favor."

She eyed him suspiciously. "What kind of favor?"

He shrugged and offered her a dark smile. "Who knows? But at some point, in the future, I'm going to ask for one. And when I do, you can't say no. Deal?"

She looked at him, her mind racing. She had the lead she needed to help Cora. Whatever he was holding in his hand most likely would not add any more information. She knew it was a bad deal. She shouldn't even consider agreeing.

And yet.

"Agreed." She held out her hand.

Terry smiled and reached forward, placing something small and metallic in her palm. "Nice doing business with you." He nodded at her and then at John. "Both of you." And with that, he was gone, making his way out of the bar.

"You shouldn't have done that," said John, watching the man leave.

Jessie sighed. "And you shouldn't have given him access to a forger."

"Hopefully, the information he provided will help save your friend. Then maybe it will have been worth it. What did he give you?"

Jessie looked down and opened her fist. In her hand was a silver thumb drive. She turned it over and squinted at markings scratched onto one side.

JN. Her initials.

26

All in the Open

essie stood in front of the bar, addressing John. "Keep an eye on him. He doesn't step foot outside of your office, understand?"

John nodded, looking over at Kevin. "We will stay upstairs. I've got some of my best men watching every way in and out of this place. No one that doesn't belong gets in today. I'll keep him safe until you get back."

As worried as she was, Jessie felt some relief knowing John was going to keep a close eye on Kevin. The two of them had bonded and instinct told her John would do everything in his power to keep Kevin safe.

Alex stood next to Jessie and John addressed them both. "Are you sure you don't want a couple of my men to go with you?"

Alex shook his head. "You've done more than enough." It came out harsher than he meant. "I mean, thank you. But if this turns bad, and I have to explain to my department what went down, it will probably be better if it doesn't blow back on you in any way."

Whether John believed him, Jessie couldn't decide. But she was happy when John nodded and shook the officer's hand.

"You know what kind of man Terry is," John said. "Don't underestimate him. For all you know, he's playing both sides and is on his way to this farm to warn whoever that you're coming."

This was something Jessie had already considered, but there wasn't time to come up with alternate plans. And she certainly wasn't about to risk Cora's life by having a bunch of yahoo police officers show up, weapons hot. No. This was something she would handle. She had Alex by her side, and the two of them would be enough.

They had to be.

Once they were in the car and on the road, Jessie turned to Alex. "I can see you're not happy about something. Spill it. We can't go into this distracted."

Alex twisted his hands on the steering wheel, readjusting his grip. "Honestly, I understand why we have to do this the way we are, but I'm just not sure I'm comfortable with just the two of us going into a potentially dangerous situation blind."

"You know why we can't involve the police. You heard what would happen if we did. Plus, we still aren't sure we can trust everyone in the department." She saw his face tighten as he squirmed against the back of the seat. "What?"

"You mean you don't know who to trust. At least not when it comes to the people I work with."

She steeled herself. Even though she knew this was coming, it was still not a conversation she looked forward to. Yet now was as good a time as any to get it out. "Why do I get the feeling this isn't about the officers in your department?"

He shifted uncomfortably again. "Well, since you mention it... I don't see how you can be so worried about working with a possible dirty cop when we're literally collaborating with a known criminal. And you don't seem to have a problem with that."

Even though she was ready for it, the rawness in his voice still shook her, and she took a moment to find her words "Alex, it's not about choosing him over your team. This is an extremely complicated situation. John can go places you can't, and he has his own network, resources that even the police might not have access to. Terry Blackburn being one of them." She hesitated, glancing at him. "Is this just about John? Or is there something else?"

Alex gripped the steering wheel tighter. "It's hard, Jessie. Watching you wade into waters with people I've spent my career watching, knowing the things they are into, and realizing their moral compass might not align with ours. I...I want you to be safe and understand who you're putting your trust in."

She stared at him. "Alex, I told you before, I put my trust in you. And your instincts. But this is my friend whose life is on the line. And while I know you would do whatever is needed to help her, I don't know that about anyone else. I also know how things work when bound by the letter of the law. It's slow and designed to protect everyone involved. Moving like that would get Cora killed. Time is literally of the essence here."

"John will want something out of this as well. Trust me when I say that. He may not be as blatant as Terry, but he isn't doing this out of the kindness of his heart."

Jessie said nothing, just turned her face back to the scenery flying by. There was bitterness in Alex's voice, tinged with something else she hadn't heard in his tone before. "And we will deal with that when and if the time comes. But for right now, I need his help. But more importantly, I need your help. I need to know that whatever we are about to walk into, you're here one hundred percent."

He gave her a quick look. "Always."

She settled back into her seat. "Good. Now what do we know about this farm?"

As soon as Terry had given them the lead, Alex had wasted no time researching the area.

"I accessed the Geographic Information System, and according to that, it shows farmland of roughly one hundred and twenty acres bordering the Blackburns. There is one main entrance off the road, but there seem to be a couple of smaller, herding trails scattered off-road. Those are the ones we will access. I've downloaded all of that to your phone. The northern one is what we will use, as it puts us closest to the only structure that shows on the map." He paused while Jessie pulled out her phone and began flicking through the information Alex had shared.

"Got it," she said, closing her phone.

"I also scanned the property records. The land is registered to a Logan Marshall. I ran him through the system and guess what? He passed away three years ago. No known relatives have claimed the property, and it's fallen into Probate. The state has been trying to identify any heirs to distribute it to, but no luck so far." He glanced over at her. "The interesting thing is, there is a listing agent and realtor who was working with the courts to determine value and property assessments. Three guesses as to who that was."

Jessie let out a breath. "Jordan Myers."

"When she was alive, it looks like she had her fingers in everything. My guess is she arranged for it to be used by your brother and whoever it is he's working for."

Jessie turned her face to the window. Everything came back to the brother she had been forced to kill. Without realizing it, she felt for the thumb drive resting in the inside pocket of her jacket. She shouldn't dwell on what could be on it but couldn't help herself. Terry had said her brother wanted her to have it in the event something happened to him. Did it contain information about who he was working for in Pine Haven? Did it detail what type of criminal activities he had set in place?

She wanted to tell Alex about it, but knew the timing was wrong. With what they were about to walk into, the last thing either of them needed was another distraction. Whatever was on that drive could wait until her friend was safe and sound. Right now, that was all that mattered.

They made the drive up the mountain in silence. Jessie made a mental note of how close they were to the Blackburn family which they had visited earlier. Despite

Terry's assurances that his family wasn't involved, she wasn't sure she believed that. Maybe this clinic setup just happened to border the Blackburn farm. Maybe the fact that they were both located within close proximity to the location of a dumped body was also happenstance.

But her instincts told her that wasn't the case.

They passed the entrance to the Blackburn's, heading north of their property, and drove until Alex made a right turn into what looked like an open pasture. The hard jarring of the car as it crossed over grass and dirt made Jessie wish they had taken her Jeep.

They jostled to a stop, and Alex pointed to a break in the tall grass in front of them. "That's the herd trail. It's a little grown over...hasn't been used in a while, but it should still be passable. That's our way in."

Jessie stepped out of the car and opened the back door to let Blizzard out. Together, they joined Alex in heading for the trail through the woods.

"Blizzard, track," Jessie said in a whisper. Immediately, the shepherd's nose went down, and he began sniffing at the broken grass.

"What's he doing?" Alex asked.

"Taking in the scents. I want him to familiarize any smells we might run into later."

Together, they marched through the thickets until the path broke into an open field. Rather than the tall, green grasses of summer, yellow and brown thatches crept into view, crunching underfoot. The expanse of the farmland stretched out before them, with a single outbuilding the only structure to be seen.

The building was made of corrugated metal and

gleamed oddly in the late autumn sky. The metal was far too shiny to be old, and Jessie had a feeling the building hadn't been there very long. The surrounding field was devoid of grass, having been flattened by whatever equipment was used to haul in the materials used in the construction of the building.

Alex picked up on that as well. "The reports refer to this as an old milk barn. Looks like someone has upgraded it." He thrust his chin in its direction. "I see two cameras on the front corners of the building. No way to approach it without being seen."

Jessie stared at the structure. "Good. We don't have time to sneak around. I need answers. Now." She started walking towards the building, Alex and Blizzard on her heels.

She gave a deliberate look up at the cameras as they approached. The only opening to the structure was two sliding metal doors centered in the building's framework. Jessie raised her fist and pounded.

There was no reply from the other side, and she worried maybe she had acted too hastily. They hadn't bothered to check around back. For all she knew, there was another entrance and whoever was inside could be making a run for it at that very moment.

On impulse, she grabbed the large handle on one door and pulled it to her right. To their surprise, it slid open effortlessly.

The smell of industrial-strength disinfectant burned their noses and caused their eyes to water. The scent of ammonia was cloying, threatening to clog their lungs; but underneath was something else. Something sweet and disgusting.

Blizzard's ears flattened, and he gave a tiny growl. Jessie gave Alex a determined look and a nod. Pushing the door open further, they stepped into darkness.

27

Hog Tied

Stepping inside the door, they gave their eyes a moment to adjust to the darkness. There were no windows and the light coming from behind them, through the open door, only projected so far. Reaching into her pocket, Jessie took out her phone and turned on the flashlight feature before heading into the space. She gave a silent hand signal to Blizzard, and he fell into silent step at her side. Alex took out his own phone to add to the illumination and followed close behind.

The inside of the building seemed to be one large, open space that spread out as far as their light could penetrate. As they took cautious steps forward, the only sound was their own footsteps echoing off the concrete floor.

Their phones revealed a pristine cleanliness that felt out of place in the surroundings. As they walked towards the back of the building, the smell of bleach and chlorine grew stronger. But so too did the sweetness that hinted at something horrific. Again, Blizzard growled, his nostrils flaring. This time, Jessie caught a new scent. Something smelled like wet earth and clay.

Their light bounced off a plaster partition to Jessie's left. It was a makeshift wall that had been erected and she and Alex inched their way around, shining their cell phones ahead of them. On the other side, they could make out a medical exam table with a leather cushion atop it, taking up the majority of the cordoned-off space. Behind the table was a bank of files and drawers of all sizes, along with a row of cabinets attached to the wall.

"Looks like terry was right about this place operating as a clinic," Alex said.

A shuffling noise, followed by a muffled grunt, caused the two of them to whirl around. The noise came from the other side of the partition, along the far wall.

Jessie placed a hand on Blizzard's back, letting him know to stay at her side as they left the makeshift medical room. She glanced at Alex and saw his gun in his hands as she aimed the light from her phone at the far end of the space.

A large stainless-steel table that reminded Jessie of the autopsy table in Dr. Lindquist's office was positioned against the back wall. Movement in the shadows next to it caught her attention, and she shined the light in its direction.

She and Alex gasped simultaneously at what they saw. There, chained to the floor, was a large pig that was easily three times the size of Blizzard. It looked at them, black, hooded eyes roving from one to the other as it grunted again, bobbing its head and shifting its massive weight from side to side.

"What the hell?" asked Jessie.

Alex pointed to another piece of equipment that squatted on the floor between the pig and the steel table. It was a large, industrial-sized meat grinder.

Alex frowned at the sight. "There were no kinds of permits for farm animal harvesting attached to this place. Even before it fell out of ownership. I don't think I want to know what is happening here..."

Jessie stared in horror at what she was seeing. She shined her light at the ceiling above the pig and the meat grinder and saw several black faucets and hoses attached to the ceiling on pulleys.

No. Please, not that.

The sounds of a large vehicle interrupted them. An engine ground to a stop and, for the first time, Jessie noticed the backside of the building where they stood had a large metallic door operated by a garage opener. The hum of electricity waking up, and the grinding of the chain echoed in the space as the door slowly rose.

Jessie quickly shut down her phone and shoved it into her pocket. Alex followed her as they dove for cover behind the wall that partitioned off the exam room. She flattened her palm, holding her hand parallel to the floor, and Blizzard instantly lay flat, his eyes locked on Jessie.

As the door opened, they heard two car doors slam and two male voices reached their ears. Their words became clearer as they entered the building. They weren't arguing, but they didn't sound like the best of friends either.

"...Because that's how it's set up, that's why. We don't question it," one of them was saying.

There was a loud click as one of them threw a switch and light flooded the room.

"Yeah, well, if you'd let me come in when it happened, I wouldn't have had to deal with all the pain I've been in," came the reply.

Jessie froze, her heart pounding. She knew the second man's voice. It was Ken Blackburn. The weasel she had tangled with at the Gray Eagle. She glanced at Alex and could tell by his body language that he recognized him as well.

"Honestly, the way you were carrying on, I was expecting your arm to be snapped in two," said the first man. "Do I need to remind you about the process the boss set up for requesting my services?"

"Maybe not him, but we would like to hear the process," Alex said, as he and Jessie stepped from around the wall.

Ken Blackburn froze as his eyes locked on Jessie. He was wearing the same clothes and leather jacket that he wore at the motorcycle club, only he held his arm close to his body, nestled in a sling.

"Hey, Ken. How'd I guess we'd be seeing each other again?" Jessie said. At her side, Blizzard growled at the startled man.

His mouth hung open, but he didn't speak. Jessie swept her eyes from him to the man standing to his left. He had a wiry build and was maybe a couple of inches taller than Alex. He wore a pair of navy-blue chinos and a white, long-sleeved tee shirt. A shock of blond hair stuck out at wild angles from beneath a black baseball cap, and his eyes were narrow slits as he returned Jessie's stare.

He raised both arms, giving them the universal sign of surrender. "Did you remember to lock the front doors when we left?" He leaned slightly towards Ken as he spoke.

"I thought you did," came the reply.

Alex pointed towards Ken with his gun and motioned for him to take a few steps away from his friend. He did as he was told, taking two steps to the side.

"Now you," Alex said to the man in the chinos, "get down on your knees and place your hands on top of your head."

The man looked at Alex with steely eyes, possibly gauging whether he would shoot. Whatever he saw in the officer's eyes convinced him to drop to his knees and follow directions.

Jessie walked over to Ken. This was a different man than she had me in the bar. There was no one for him to showboat for; no one to impress. All his false bravado was now laid bare. "You even blink an eye at me wrong and I'll have Blizzard take off one of your legs, understand?"

Ken's eyes widened, and he nodded his head violently. His good arm was shaking as he held it out in front of him. "Don't hurt me. I swear I have done nothing wrong."

"We'll see about that," Jessie said. "Who's this boss you and your friend over there were talking about?"

Ken looked at the man on his knees. He opened his mouth, but some message must have passed between them as he shook his head, squeezing his eyes shut. "I can't say. I mean...I don't know. But if I did, I couldn't say. They'd kill me for sure."

Jessie let out a loud sigh. "Well, I won't kill you, so you're in luck." She clenched her fists a couple of times, rolling her wrists. "But I will maim you."

Ken's eyes grew large, and a tear formed. "No...wait. The only thing I know is—"

A sudden burst of action choked off his words as the man Alex was watching dropped to all fours and struck out with his right leg, catching Alex in the side of his knee. Alex grunted and fell away from the man. Before he could regain his balance, a swift blow to the back of his head caused him to see stars. He pitched forward, his gun falling from his hand.

Diving forward, the man launched himself at the firearm. Coming up from his roll, gun in hand, the man aimed it at Ken.

Jessie reacted instinctively, pushing Ken hard one way while throwing herself the other. Ken slammed into the pig and fell to the floor, startling the pig into a series of squeals and snorts as it tried to get away from the man.

The man squeezed the trigger, only for nothing to happen. He looked at the gun, trying to work out where the safety was, just as Jessie closed the distance between them. "Cover!" At her command, Blizzard was on Ken, making sure he didn't try to get up as his jaws snapped inches from the terrified man's face. A growl told Ken what would happen if he so much as flinched.

Judging from the way the other man moved, Jessie knew he had military training. He didn't have time to slide the safety off, and she expected his next move would be to brandish the gun at her in a melee-style attack.

That was exactly what he did. As she reached him, he swung the gun at her in a manner meant to strike her thigh. She stepped aside, dodging the attack, and dropped forward with an elbow hit that connected solidly with the side of his head.

The man was braced for the blow, but still let out a grunt as it hit home. He raised the gun once again, and this time Jessie grabbed it in both hands, attempting to get a lock on his wrist. Too late, she realized her mistake.

He had deliberately drawn her in close so that both of her hands were effectively tied while grappling with the gun. He brought his free arm around in a roundhouse punch that connected with her side. Luckily, her straightened arm took the majority of the blow, rather than the kidney he was undoubtedly aiming for.

As she grappled with his arm, twisting the wrist enough to get him to release the gun, she was simultaneously aware of his leg. A skilled fighter would use the back leg to try and trip or sweep her. By leaning into his body, placing the outside of her knee against him, she limited his range and mobility.

As with most military fighters she had met, he was used to striking while standing, employing lightning-fast strikes against his opponent. Jessie moved to employ an arm bar, hoping to force him to the ground, neutralizing his striking abilities.

He seemed to sense what she was doing and brought up his free hand between them, seeking to drive his fist into her midsection, breaking the stalemate.

She pivoted slightly away from him, turning his thumb up as she stepped back and down. There was a loud snap as the bones on the outside of his wrist cracked.

His eyes squeezed shut in pain and that was when she finished him off. Hooking the back of her knee over his arm she let go of his wrist with one hand and placed it on the back of his head. Dropping her full weight on his, she drove him face first into the concrete.

His teeth shattered as he hit the pavement, and the tendons along his biceps tore with a resounding snap. He lay there, not moving as she rolled off him, breathing hard.

She looked to her right and saw Alex slowly rolling onto his side, rubbing at the back of his head. She rushed over, bending to examine him.

"Hey, take it easy," she said, trying to steady her own ragged breathing. "You just took a nasty hit to the head."

He winced as he probed at the back of his head. "What...what happened?" He squinted up at her. "Damn. That guy was fast."

"It's alright. He's subdued."

Jessie helped him to his feet and then looked over at Ken, who was lying on his back, cowering from Blizzard's sharp fangs.

Alex looked over at the second man, lying motionless in a puddle of blood. "Is he...?"

"No. But he won't be able to answer questions for a few months." Jessie looked over at Ken. "But *he* can still talk. For now."

28

A Connection to Jane Doe

"Blizzard, heel."

The white shepherd moved to sit at Jessie's side, his eyes still locked on Ken Blackburn. The man sat up slowly. Sweat poured from him as he looked from the dog to Jessie and finally over to the man he had walked in with.

"I'm not in any mood to play twenty questions," Jessie said, her eyes hard. Ken sent a pleading glance in Alex's direction. Jessie snapped her fingers at him. "Look at me, not him. He's off duty and can't help you now."

Ken swallowed hard, pressing his lips together.

Jessie shrugged. "Have it your way. I was kind of hoping it would go like this." She half turned to Alex. "Why don't you wait in the car..."

Ken jumped as the officer turned to leave. "No, wait." He looked up at the two of them, fear clouding his features. "If I tell you what I know, do I get some kind of police detail for protection? Or relocation assistance, or something like that?"

Jessie rolled her eyes. "No. But here's what I can promise you. I'm going to spread it around town that you were such a big help to us in our ongoing investigations, and that we couldn't do our job without you. How long do you think it will take for your boss to get wind of that? We are going to find out who's behind all this one way or another. The only question is, will we be able to do that before they find you?"

Ken's eyes flitted back and forth between them, and finally he gave in. "I don't know any names, and that's the truth. All I know is that there are two guys running an import-export business and they are making a lot of money. They are setting up Pine Haven as the hub for the business."

Jessie frowned. "Drugs? Is that the business?"

Ken hesitated, but then shook his head. "No. No way they could get this kind of money from running drugs."

"I'm losing my patience. What are they running?"

"It's not a what...but a who." He dropped his eyes, his shoulders slumping.

Jessie looked at Alex, her mind spinning. "Traffickers. Are you telling me there are human traffickers operating out of Pine Haven?"

His face contorted as he lifted his shoulders. "I mean...I don't know the specifics. And maybe that's not the right word for it." He was interrupted by a moan from the man lying face down in his own blood. "He knew a lot more than me. Ask him what's going on."

"He's not going to be talking for a while," said Jessie.

She looked at Alex, motioning with her head in the man's direction.

The officer left her side, made his way over to the still-unconscious man, and rolled him over to rifle through his pockets.

Jessie turned her attention back to Ken. "What is this place used for? Your brother said it's a clinic for treating the employees of whomever it is you're working for. Is that correct?"

A look of confusion crossed his face. "Terry? Oh, Christ, you brought him into this? He's going to kill me." He began to whine at this point.

"Is Terry involved?" Jessie asked.

Ken shook his head violently. "No. He doesn't know about this. I just wanted to make a name for myself; to get out from under him and show him that he's not the only one in the family with great ideas. He will kill me for real if he finds out I'm working with someone behind his back and cutting him out of any deals."

Jessie contemplated what he said for a moment, then shook her head. "You know what? I don't care. I'm not interested in your messed-up family dynamics. What goes on in this building?"

"He works on the women. They get brought here and he does something for the bosses. But I don't know what. That part is above my pay grade."

Jessie pointed to the large pig that had resigned itself to lying stretched out on the floor a few feet from them. "And that? What do you do with it?"

For the first time, Ken's face grew red, and he averted his eyes. "I've never actually seen it done. I swear."

Jessie's upper lip drew back in rage. "Seen what? Say it."

"Doc over there—that's all I know him as—says they use the pigs to get rid of the bodies."

Jessie was filled with disgust. "You feed him the bodies of the women they get rid of? Was that young woman who was killed meant to be taken care of this way?"

Ken's eyes bulged, and he looked at her in disgust. "What? No, the pigs don't eat the bodies. Doc said that pig DNA and human DNA is so closely related that they can be hard to tell them apart sometimes…"

Jessie felt anger unlike any she had ever known flood her body.

"Hey, found his phone," Alex called out.

Jessie stepped back from Ken, her arms shaking with rage. She struck out with a right hook, catching him across the cheek.

He buckled back, clutching at his face with his good hand. "What was that for?"

She tried to control the shaking in her voice. "One, to remind you not to try and move; and two, for being such a terrible human being." She turned to Blizzard. "Cover." As the white shepherd took up position standing guard over the whining Ken Blackburn, Jessie turned and walked over to Alex.

He frowned as she approached. "Get anything helpful out of him?"

She took a deep breath. "In the military, a place like this would be called a dump site, or a cleaning room. It's where bodies are disposed of."

Alex looked at her, then glanced around the room, his eyes landing on the pig. He swallowed hard, a look of disgust creeping into his features.

Jessie shook her head. "No. They weren't doing that. Humans and pigs share about ninety-eight percent of the same DNA. One way to dispose of human remains is to use the meat grinder. Pass their remains through it, but then pass the remains of a pig through it a couple times. Then clean the grinder. Any forensic team that comes across the grinder and tests it for evidence of human remains...won't be able to tell with any certainty what's human and what's porcine. It's an almost fool-proof way to dispose of bodies and not leave a trace." She looked at the large grinder. "Who knows how many bodies have passed through it. No lab will ever be able to tell us."

Alex held up the cell phone he had removed from the unconscious man. "Maybe this can help us." He swiped at the screen before looking at Jessie, exasperated. "Locked, of course."

"Let's try something." She stood over the prone form of the doctor and reached down to grab a handful of hair. He groaned when she pulled his head up. "See if you can unlock it with his face."

Alex squatted in front of the man, holding the phone up. "Not working. I think his face is too busted up. Maybe it can't recognize him."

Jessie eyes lit up as another thought hit her. She reached around with her free hand and used her forefinger and middle finger to pull up the man's eyelids. "Try now."

The phone dinged as it unlocked, and Alex gave Jessie

a smile. She let the man's head drop with another groan as she went to stand by Alex.

"Change the passcode lock on it to all zeros so we can get into it at any time," she said.

"Good idea." His fingers flew over the screen as he made the adjustments.

"Do you have cuffs on you?" Jessie asked. When Alex nodded, she held out her hand for them, and then placed them on the unconscious man, pulling his arms behind his back. "Not that he's going anywhere anytime soon, but better safe than sorry." She stood to walk back into the room that doubled as a medical bay. "Look through his contacts. See if there's anyone he's receiving a lot of calls from."

Alex did as she asked while following her behind the partition. "Looks like he's been deleting his history and call logs as they've been coming in. We'll probably need forensics to go through this and see what they can recover."

Jessie was shaking her head as she began going through drawers and cabinets. "We don't have time for that. Ken said whoever these two have been working for is trafficking women. If that's who has Cora, she might have even less time than I thought." Just thinking about her friend in the hands of people who had no regard for human life terrified her. She pushed the thought aside as she rattled through drawers.

Alex came to a sudden stop, his eyes locked on the phone.

"What is it?" asked Jessie.

He walked over to where she stood, holding out the phone. "Look familiar?"

She focused on the screen and couldn't believe what she was seeing. Alex had been going through the photos section of the phone, and the picture he showed her was one of a small group of metal strips laid out on a piece of white cloth. The strips were of various lengths, and all comprised of small metallic beads and dashes strung together.

"These are the same as what Dr. Lindquist pulled out of our Jane Doe," Jessie breathed. She reached for the phone and began flicking through photos.

There were more pictures of the little markers, all in various lengths with different configurations of beads and markers. Her finger froze against the screen as she came to the next set of photos. They were still the same lengths of markers, but this time they were photographed against the backdrop of flesh. On every picture, the camera was zoomed in on the strip.

"These could be the upper arm, where Dr. Lindquist pulled the one from on our victim," Jessie said. "Maybe he is measuring the length?"

Now it was Alex who looked around the room as Jessie continued to thumb through the photos. "Jessie, come take a look." He had moved over to a small medical stand on the far side of the exam table. It had been covered by a piece of blue cloth that he removed.

Jessie looked down at it and caught her breath. On the tray were the same metal strips they had seen in the pictures.

"He was using this place to implant them. He knows

who these women are," Jessie said. That meant that he probably knew where Cora was.

He was their biggest lead, and thanks to Jessie, he wouldn't be able to speak for months.

But she had known men like him before. He wasn't like Ken Blackburn. Even if he were able, he would not have given them anything.

"There has to be something in this phone we can use," Jessie said. "A way to—" Her voice choked off and she stopped moving.

Alex approached and looked over her shoulder. "What is it?"

She held out the phone to him. There was another photograph of a marker against flesh. Only this bit of flesh was darker in tone, with a lighter, jagged scar running across it.

One of Jessie's hands covered her mouth, and she felt a wave of nausea hit her. "I know that scar. That's Cora. She got it as a child when she and her brother were horsing around at their home, and she fell onto a glass table, shattering it. A piece of glass cut her inner arm. She used to joke to me that it was her first battle scar." Her body shook as she turned to face Alex. "They have no intention of returning her. They're going to traffic Cora."

29

Considering a Last Resort

"And you're sure you can trust them?" Jessie asked.

She was outside the property where they had discovered the makeshift lab and disposal site.

"One hundred percent," Alex replied. "Ever since the whole Todd incident, I've been working to vet the new candidates on the side. These two are solid. They'll process Ken and our mystery doctor and make sure nothing leaks outside precinct. As far as even the Chief knows, these are just two suspects arrested on the suspicion of running a meth lab up here. It will be enough to hold them until we can find Cora." He placed a hand on Jessie's arm. "And we will find her."

Jessie looked back at the foul structure. They had left the doctor handcuffed while waiting for the officers Alex had called to arrive. While she was pretty sure Ken Blackburn wasn't going anywhere, they had still zip-tied him to the medical table, despite his assurances he wasn't going to run. He was genuinely terrified of whoever they had been working for and promised to cooperate with the investigation as long as no one found out.

She bit her lip as another thought intruded. "What about the pig? I know it seems trivial at this point, but...I feel bad for it. What they had planned for that poor animal."

Alex gave her a tight smile. "I'm going to make a few calls. There's a lady two counties over in Kent who runs a non-profit for all kinds of rescue animals. Not sure if she has ever taken in a pig—but there's a first time for every-thing." He shook his head. "I just can't face turning him over to one of the farms around here, knowing how he'll end up."

It was a small thing, but Jessie liked the thought of the poor thing not ending up on someone's plate. It had undoubtedly been through enough.

"Do you think some of your new CSIs can pull anything off that phone that might give us a clue as to where Cora might be held?" Jessie asked.

"It's the only shot we have right now. That or maybe recover the contact list or phone logs from it. Maybe tell us who the bastard has been talking to."

Jessie frowned. "Let me see the phone." He handed it over and she opened it once again, scrolling through the phone's apps, before opening one. "That guy was military trained. And if there is one thing that all military personnel are fanatics about, it's money. And like a lot of military men who are into shady stuff, they don't use banks. This app is called PayBack, and it's popular with people who like moving their money into offshore accounts and dark web holding sites." Her eyes zipped through what she was seeing. "There are a lot of large deposits here. I can see the accounts they are going to but not where they came from. Get your CSI guys to focus on this. Maybe we can follow the money back to...whoever is behind this."

Alex was nodding his head and already making the call. They waited until the two officers Alex had reached out to showed up and went through the building.

They were both young, and obviously looked up to Alex as he gave them instructions. He handed the phone over to one of the officers and informed him who to give it to on the CSI team.

"And no one else," he emphasized. "The perp with the messed-up face...get him the medical attention he needs, but don't leave his side and don't let anyone speak to him. Do what you have to in order to make it happen. Is anyone at the precinct?" Without saying the chief's name, the officers seemed to understand exactly who he meant.

"No. The place is quiet and secure," one of them replied.

"Good," said Alex. "Contact Dr. Lindquist, have him look him over and patch him up. But no one else."

Both officers nodded and began hauling the offenders into the respective vehicles.

"They trust and look up to you," Jessie said. "You're in a position to really guide the direction of the department."

His face reddened. "I'm just trying to lead by example.

The new ones are eager to please and they're good people. I trust them. A couple more years and the Pine Haven Police Department will be what it used to be; something this community can be proud of and believe in."

Jessie eyed him. "Spoken like a true chief."

He gave her a waning glance but didn't acknowledge the remark. Instead, he changed the subject. "I need to go to the station. I think it will go a long way with these two if I show them everything we're doing is above board...for the most part." He shuffled his feet, breaking his stare with her. "But I feel like I need to be with you."

She shook her head. There was something she needed to do, and she didn't want Alex with her when she did it. The comments he had just made cemented in her mind that, while what he was doing to help her was crucial, he had a larger role to play in Pine Haven's future. A role she would not jeopardize. She knew he was already playing fast and loose with the rules. She didn't like that he was involving new recruits, and she told herself she wouldn't let him do it again. He was too important to this town to risk his career for her. Or for someone she cared about.

For a moment, she thought of John. Is that why she had relied on him so heavily in recent times? Did she view him as somehow less than Alex? Did she view his role in Pine Haven as being expendable? Hadn't he proven himself to her as of late? If not proven himself, his stock had certainly risen in her eyes.

She turned to Alex. "Can you do me a favor? Check in on Kevin? Make sure he's still safe. And see if John has heard anything else that might help us out. Now that we know there's a human trafficking ring using Pine Haven as its hub, it might spark something with him we could use."

He was hesitant but agreed. "What are you going to do?"

"I need you to drop me off to get my car and then I'll head over to the bed and breakfast. I'm still not ready to go home just yet, so I think I'll crash there for a few hours. Clear my head, figure out next steps. I don't think Mark and Eric will mind."

Alex's brow dipped together, but he didn't argue. They made their way back to his car and headed out. "You know, you and Blizzard are perfectly welcome to stay at my place. It's small, but it's secure."

"Thank you, Alex. That means a lot. But I need to be close to town. Just in case there's a break. I want to be able to act as soon as possible."

Everything she said was true. Technically. A lie by omission was still a lie, but if it kept him safe, then so be it.

She and Blizzard climbed out of the car at the police station and into her Jeep. She sat there, head resting against the headrest, trying to focus her thoughts. She could feel the start of a headache coming on, and realized it was her body's way of telling her she had been pushing it too hard over the last few days.

Right now, that didn't matter. She would continue to push herself until she broke if needed. They were finally getting somewhere. A break in the storm in the form of a confiscated cell phone would have to be enough.

She sighed and started the Jeep, easing out of the parking lot and pointing it in the direction of the bed and breakfast. She needed to refocus. Trust her mind to work out the details of what they had learned and how best to proceed.

The fact that they were dealing with human trafficking had added a particularly terrifying layer to Cora's kidnapping. She thought back to her time as a military investigator. She knew the mindset of men who saw women as commodities. Men like that lacked empathy. They saw other people as something to be exchanged for something bigger and better.

While trafficking had cast its dark shadow to almost every corner of the world, it was a particularly booming industry in certain regions. The things she had seen still haunted her dreams.

She refused to consider the fact that her friend could become part of that nightmarish hellscape she visited in her sleep.

No. That wasn't something she was allowed to consider.

She forced herself to think positively. The CSI team would be able to pull metadata that could leave a trail or restore contacts and communication logs that could provide valuable information. She also considered that they could go to the carrier for the phone number and get the records that way. But there was a huge problem with that.

Time.

She was running out of it. As it was, any information the CSI officers could get might be too late. Her grip on the steering wheel tightened until her fingers ached.

If she was to save Cora's life, she was running out of options. The fact that there was a picture of one of those strips against Cora's arm told her these men were not looking to exchange Cora for the incriminating video footage. They were planning to make her part of their trade.

But why? What had changed? Maybe it was the fact that they had nearly gotten to Kevin themselves. Perhaps they thought they didn't need Jessie after all. And if they didn't need her, then they no longer needed Cora. But they wouldn't kill her. That would be a waste of potential goods. If they didn't kill her, that might buy a little more time to find her.

The clock was still ticking but now the penalty for missing the deadline had most likely changed. Only, the traffickers didn't know that Jessie knew what they were planning. In their minds they were still hoping Jessie would come through and deliver them Kevin.

Kevin.

He was her last resort. The one thing she had that they wanted. Turning him over to them was out of the question. But he was her only bargaining chip. Using him meant putting him in harm's way.

At this point, she wasn't sure that offering to turn over the drone footage would be enough. Surely, they realized how easily that footage could be copied and emailed to a thousand different places.

Or did they?

She began to think about everything that had

happened. The lengths they had gone to in order to get that footage and Kevin. The sloppy way they had tried taking Kevin out at his trailer after learning his address.

They weren't acting like professionals. At least not the kind she had dealt with in the past. There was no surgical precision to their actions. It was sloppy work; the work of someone who hadn't had to deal with things that didn't go their way.

Also, she had seen the amounts paid to that military doctor they had up their sleeve. Those weren't small amounts. Add to that the cost of setting up that disposal and treatment facility, which meant there was some serious money being dumped into this operation.

Why would someone with that kind of money be so sloppy?

Unless the real players weren't aware of what was happening on the ground level. That might explain why the kidnappers were acting so rashly. They were acting out of desperation.

Everyone has a boss. That was something she had always heard in the military. That and shit rolls downhill. Maybe these guys were desperate to get out of the way of what they knew would be rolling their way if they didn't get this mess cleaned up. The thought didn't make her feel any better. Desperate people do desperate things.

Like kidnapping the best friend of an ex-military investigator and using her as a bargaining chip.

Maybe they panicked and decided killing Kevin and getting their hands on his footage wasn't enough. More likely than not, they wanted to erase any and all evidence tied to them. And that meant not only taking out Kevin, but Jessie and Alex as well.

And anyone she might have come into contact with.

She couldn't allow that to happen. One way or the other, she had to end this. And if that meant using Kevin as bait to draw out a murderer, then so be it.

30

Conceding Defeat

"Great news!"

It was the big one again. He clapped his massive hands together and the sound echoed like an angry thunderhead rolling across the plains. He stormed past Cora and made his way to the cell containing the cowering women. Cora watched the way he walked, the way he carried himself.

Something had happened.

What it was, she couldn't tell, but she doubted it would be good for the women or her.

The man loudly trailed his hand along the bars until coming to a stop in front of the women. He pointed, excitedly. "You there. Coal Eyes. Your buyer is here. I can't tell you how happy it makes me to not see your scheming face anymore."

The young woman he was pointing to separated

herself from the rest of the ladies and stepped forward, her chin high. "I have a name."

A mean chuckle escaped the man. "Not for long you don't. Your new owner already has one picked out for you. Who you were before doesn't matter because she no longer exists." He gave her an evil look and blew her a kiss as he stepped up to the cell door, placing his thumb on the electronic lock pad causing the door to click. He tugged it open. "Now get out here and let's go meet your new keeper."

Cora watched as he turned his back on the women, taking a few steps away from the cage as he waited. He was big, but there was also a half-dozen women in that cage. Why didn't they rush him? At least try to fight back. Instead, they shrank away from the woman who had been singled out and watched as she shuffled through the door.

"Don't forget to close it behind you," the man said, turning to face her.

The cell door clicked shut and the whir of the electronic lock engaging filled the air. She stared defiantly at the giant of a man.

"You know, I really hope he sends you back. We're skipping the three strikes rule for you. You come back, and I'm going to personally put that bullet in your head. After a bit, I mean…"

Her face darkened to match her narrowed eyes and she drew in a deep breath before spitting into the giant's face. "Despite what you would have everyone else believe, you are a small man. And no amount of weightlifting will ever change that."

His upper lip drew back in a sneer, quivering in anger as he looked at her. His right arm drew back, but the girl didn't flinch. His bunched muscles twitched with the anticipation of the blow that would land her on her backside. Slowly, he lowered his hand to his side and gave her a tight smile. "You're lucky your sale is going through today. I can't tarnish the merchandise. But you better hope you and I never meet again."

He reached out, wrapping one massive hand around her arm and dragging her through the room. As they passed Cora, the man scowled at her. "And don't think I've forgotten about you. We have something very special in mind for you."

The look he gave her was no doubt meant to strike fear in her, but all he succeeded in doing was angering her further. "She's right, you know, you're such a small man." Her voice came out as little more than a snarl. "Keeping women in cages and chained to walls."

He stopped in his tracks. "You know, I don't think anyone will miss you. Your friend hasn't come through, and at this point, she's causing us more trouble than she's worth. Certainly more trouble than you're worth. Still… we'll at least get something for you on the market. For once, I'm not going to be picky and haggle prices. I'm practically going to give you away for free."

With that, he turned and dragged his captive away. The woman gave Cora one last look over her shoulder before disappearing out of the room. It wasn't a look of fear. It was one of someone who had conceded defeat. Hopelessness in the face of an adversary who couldn't be defeated. It was a look Cora feared would haunt her for the rest of her days.

And she was determined to make sure she would not suffer the same fate.

As soon as the large door was closed, she rolled the tiny nail she had managed to snag from between her cheeks and gums. She bit down, holding it firmly between her teeth and bent forward, trying to fit it into the keyhole of her manacles.

31

Trusted Friends

Jessie apologized profusely for ringing the doorbell of the bed and breakfast at such a late hour.

Eric opened the door and ushered her inside. Mark was standing well back from his husband, a baseball bat in his hands. He breathed a sigh of relief when Eric stepped aside, and Jessie and Blizzard walked through the door. Jessie gave the bat a curious glance.

Mark rolled his eyes as he put it aside. "It is after midnight, and someone comes knocking on the door? My motto is stay ready, so you don't have to get ready."

Eric ushered her into the sitting area and motioned for her to take a seat on the couch. "Is everything okay? Did you find Cora?"

Jessie breathed out in frustration. "Not yet. But we have a couple of leads."

Eric looked distraught. "I was hoping you were here with good news."

"Actually, I'm here to ask a favor. I'm headed home to crash for a few hours, but I need you to do something for me."

Mark eyed her suspiciously. "What is it?"

Eric leaned forward, giving his husband a sideways glance. "Of course, whatever it is. How can we help?"

Reaching into her pocket, Jessie took out the tiny thumb drive and held it up for them to see. "I need you to put this someplace safe until I come back for it." She saw the fear in Mark's eyes as he stared at the device. "You can say no. I wouldn't blame you."

"What's on it?" Mark asked, moving closer.

"Honestly, I don't know. I only just came into possession of it. But I can tell you that it is personal. It doesn't have anything to do with what happened to Cora or the case we are working on." I hope.

Eric reached for it but stopped when Mark spoke up again.

"Why don't you give it to Alex? Seems like the two of you have gotten close."

Jessie smiled at him. "Because our...relationship is based on work. And this isn't that. Like I said, it's personal."

Eric reached out and took it from her. "We'll keep it safe for you."

She bit her lip and took a deep breath. "One other thing. If I don't come back for it; if something happens to me...then destroy it. Don't give it to anyone else."

Mark's eyebrows shot up. "Oh. It's one of those, huh?"

Jessie felt her cheeks redden. "Like I said, I don't know what's on it." She mulled her next words carefully but decided to take a chance. "It was left for me by Brody. My brother."

Both Eric and Mark looked from her to the drive and nodded.

"We'll put it in our personal lock box, which we keep in the safe," Eric said. He gave her a stern nod. "We'll keep it safe for you until you come back for it." His tone left no room for any other possibility.

Blizzard had been napping on a rug near the big fireplace, and jumped to his feet when she stood up.

"You know, if you need us to watch Blizzard for you, we can do that," said Mark, softly.

"Thank you, but I think I'll keep him with me tonight. It might do us both some good to relax in our own space for a bit." She saw the fleeting disappointment in the man's eyes. "But, moving forward, I may take you up on that if there are times when I need to go out of town or something."

They made their way to the door, and she stepped out onto the porch before turning to face the two men again. "Thank you both for this. I definitely owe you."

"I'm sure we'll find a way to collect," Mark said playfully.

Eric's face was stern as he looked at her. "Be careful. And let us know as soon as you find her."

She nodded, swallowing hard, before making her way to the Jeep and leaving the parking lot.

After pulling the Jeep up to the house, Jessie cut the engine and paused, her gaze fixed on the house looming before her. Bathed in shadows, it stood silent and unlit against the encroaching night. A monolith shrouded in darkness, its stillness an imposing presence.

She watched the windows carefully. The blinds didn't part, the curtains never fluttered; there were no shadows moving behind them. The house was empty as far as she could tell.

She exited the car and motioned for Blizzard to follow. Every sense was attuned to the foliage around her as she walked up the steps to the front door. The door jam and frame had yet to be repaired. She was unsure if it had been tampered with as she pushed it open to the silence that greeted her.

"Patrol," she whispered to the shepherd.

The dog padded softly into the house, checking for signs of intruders on the ground floor before hurrying upstairs. He returned, tail wagging and sat at Jessie's feet staring up at her.

"Good, good, boy. Let's get you some food." She made her way through the living room, careful of overturned furniture and broken knick-knacks that reminded her of the violence that had befallen her friend.

Once in the kitchen, she made her way to the mudroom and retrieved a cup of Blizzard's food and poured it into his dish. She watched as he greedily gulped at his kibble before turning her attention to the living room.

She still had not gone over the CSI report regarding the break-in and kidnapping. There really wasn't a need as she doubted there was anything they had found that would help her find her friend. But at least it was all documented. If—no, when—they caught these guys, they could at least corroborate evidence.

She exhaled deeply as she went to the small pantry closet to retrieve a broom and dust pain. She set about righting furniture and brushing up bits of broken bulbs and bits of wood. She hoped the work would momentarily take her mind off what she had been through. But in her mind's eye, all she could see was Cora fighting for her life against an assailant who had violated Jessie's home.

She plopped down on the sofa, leaning her head back. The fact that she was running out of time weighed heavy on her. She told herself she could do it, that she'd be able to keep Kevin safe and get Cora back.

They wanted Kevin, and she would be forced to use him as bait to draw them out of hiding. That was all she needed. If she could get one of them in the open, take him down...she knew she could make him talk.

But what if her instincts were right? What if they were spooked and had decided to cut their losses? They were already ghosts...she had no clue who they were. Maybe they would kill Cora and run.

Or worse, sell her to God knows who.

She closed her eyes, trying to stave off a headache. Just a few minutes of rest then she'd text John. Have him bring the boy to her. What would she tell him? He was so afraid, and he trusted her.

Self-hatred was not an emotion she had ever felt before. It was alien to her, and she bit at the inside of her cheek as she tried to swallow the bitterness of it.

Just a few minutes of rest was all she needed...

Blizzard's sudden barking jolted her. The fog of sleep burned away with the sudden hit of adrenaline as she realized it was light outside.

How the hell did that happen?

She glanced at her watch. It was early morning, but still later than she expected. Blizzard was staring at the door, his tail down, the hair on his back standing at attention as he growled and barked his warning.

Jessie was on her feet immediately, head cocked to one side as she listened to the world around her. Gentle morning breeze playing against the side of the house, birds chirping, loons calling softly from the lake...everything seemed as it should.

But she trusted Blizzard. Had someone ventured onto the porch while she slept? Maybe tried the door latch? She moved swiftly to the kitchen and retrieved a butcher knife from one of the drawers and then crossed over to peek through the closed blinds.

No one was there, and she couldn't see any signs of a disturbance on the porch. "Heel." She waited until Blizzard had moved to take his place at her side, then she reached for the front door, unlocking the bolt and the handle. She gripped the knife in a way that would allow her to jab quick and low if needed. Briefly, she considered going for the small gun Alex had gifted her, but immediately decided against it.

If someone was out there, she didn't want to kill them. Dead men can't speak, and she would need whoever it was alive in order to answer her questions.

Taking a breath, she steadied herself and cleared her mind. The door opened with the slightest of tugs. She eased out, hugging the door frame, her back to the side of the house, knife in front of her at the ready.

With her free hand, she flicked two fingers at Blizzard and the big shepherd made his way onto the porch, sniffing at the floor and then the steps. He looked from her to the sandy area around the dock where the lake lapped slowly at the tall reeds.

"Track."

The white shepherd headed for the dock, sniffing intently as he went. Whoever it was, must have been scared off by Blizzard's barking. She placed the knife inside the door on the tiny entry table and then followed the dog.

He had stopped on the dock and was circling back and forth, giving out a tiny whine as he licked at Jessie's hand. He had lost the scent.

She rubbed his head. "It's okay, boy. Good job. Maybe it was just a kid being a kid and you scared them off."

It wasn't a kid, and she knew it.

No sign of crushed reeds, footprints in the soft, wet sand, and the water didn't look recently disturbed. "Or maybe it was a deer. Or a squirrel." Blizzard's head whipped around looking at her at the mention of the animals and his tail wagged uncontrollably as he scanned for either of his two nemeses that she never let him chase.

She sighed. "Alright. go do your business and let's bet back inside."

He ran from the dock to a stand of saplings near the water to relieve himself. Then, instead of returning, he stood perfectly still, nose to the ground. Jessie could hear him huffing in air as she approached.

"Blizzard, track."

This time, he took off through the tree line that sprang up near the inlet of the lake. Jessie followed as quickly as possible to keep up with the dog. He wound around a couple of times, almost losing the scent of whatever he followed, but inevitably picked it back up and kept going.

They were traveling parallel to the lake, heading into the more scenic areas with large docks and elaborate boathouses. Spacious seasonal homes dotted the lake as they headed into the more populated regions.

Blizzard stopped, the hair on his back standing up, a low rumble of a growl building in his chest. He stared straight ahead, and Jessie followed his eyes.

He was locked onto a house. A beautiful, large house of modern design that commanded a breathtaking view of the lake from atop a perfectly manicured lawn.

32

Inside the Big House

Making her way to the early morning shadows of the large tree grove that bordered the lawn, Jessie crouched, not moving, for thirty minutes watching the house. Her knees screamed at her, and her thighs burned. She ignored the pain, keeping her eyes locked on the large home.

So far, she had only seen a woman and a girl, walking around the spacious kitchen and the large, well-appointed deck. She watched the child laughing and playing with the woman, who occasionally picked her up and spun her around, both laughing hard at something that passed between the two of them.

She didn't see anyone else enter or leave the house. If the woman was married, there was no evidence of a man in view. It didn't make sense that the two of them could have wandered onto Jessie's property, and Blizzard had caught their scent. The distance between the houses was too great for that.

But there was something about the situation that didn't sit quite right with Jessie. Part of it was the dense foliage that ran along one side of the lawn. They were Green Giant Thuja's and could easily reach a height of thirty feet. Planted close together, they formed a living wall that would be all but impossible to walk through.

The other side of the lawn, the side Jessie had approached the house from, seemed to be under heavy construction, with a couple of large, Bobcat excavators sitting quietly. If they were planting more of the giant Thujas, the entire property would be cut off from view, unless you passed by on the lake.

Unlike many of the other grand homes along the lake, this one seemed a bit out of place as well. It was a bit too modern. It didn't fit in with the other grand traditional and Victorian houses the lake community was known for.

This was a new build. The existing home had been torn down to make way for it. She searched the backside for signs of security cameras, but saw none, which also stood out as odd to her.

Finally, convinced the woman and child were alone in the house, she made a move. She made her way up the hillside to the main road that curved along the lake and walked to the entrance of the massive house. She motioned to Blizzard, and the dog disappeared into the foliage down the side of the home.

The front door to the house was just as massive and imposing as everything else about the home. It was comprised of a single ten-foot slab of Brazilian hardwood with a massive black handle. There were no visible locks to be seen, only a digital screen set in the siding next to the door.

The screen brightened at her approach and a woman's voice spoke through invisible speakers. "May I help you?"

She sounded cheery enough, and Jessie tried to mimic her tone as she answered. "Uh, hello. I'm sorry to bother you, but I was walking my dog and he got free of his leash when he saw a squirrel. He ran into your property...I think he's in the backyard, and I didn't want to just walk back there unannounced."

There was a moment of silence followed by a soft whirring sound as locks built into the doorframe retracted. The large door cantilevered open as one unit revealing a smiling woman in her early thirties on the other side.

She extended her hand to Jessie. "Hello there. I'm Ellie, and this little shy one" —she stepped aside to reveal a little girl clinging to the back of her stylish sundress— "is Sarah."

Jessie smiled broadly at them. "Jessie. And I hate to bother you so early in the morning."

Ellie shook her head and stepped aside. "Don't think anything about it. This one gets up with the chickens. Which means I do as well." She playfully ruffled her daughter's hair.

"Mom, no!" the girl replied, attempting to smooth her dark strands back into place.

Jessie forced a laugh. "Like I said, my dog ran into your yard, so I just need to grab him."

Ellie nodded, looking down at Jessie's hands. "You don't keep him on a leash?"

Jessie took a deep breath, her mind racing. "Normally I do. But we are at the end of his training, and I'm supposed to work on making him heel with just my voice. I got distracted and didn't see the squirrel in time to stop him from taking off. I really am so sorry to be bothering you." She pointed with her thumb over her shoulder. "I don't mind going around the outside to get him—"

"Absolutely not," Ellie said cutting her off. "That way is too steep. You'll fall and break your neck." She ushered Jessie into the house. "My husband is having another retaining wall built to level it out a bit, but it won't be finished for another few weeks. It's much easier to access the back from the deck."

"Oh, thank you so much," Jessie said, taking in the high ceiling of the entryway. "You have a beautiful home. And I hope I'm not disturbing your husband in any way."

Ellie laughed as she led them through the entry and into the great room with its wall of glass overlooking the lake. "No, not at all. He leaves very early for the office. He works with a team of consultants in London...or something like that. So, his workday actually starts around four in the morning."

Jessie took the house in. The decor was immaculate, with expensive, oversized furniture in neutral tones, and pine hardwood floors that gleamed in the sunlight. They walked into the chef's kitchen, and Jessie marveled at appliances she had never seen before. "I can't get over how beautiful your home is. It must take an army to keep it this clean."

Ellie sighed as she made her way towards the custom doors leading outside. "Oh no. It's just me. I am lucky enough that I don't have to work, so the least I can do is keep the house tidy."

"Mommy, I'm starving," said the little girl, pointing to one of two large center islands cast from white marble.

"Oh, Sarah...give Mommy a minute." She turned to Jessie with an apologetic look. "I'm so sorry. Let me just get her set up with some pancakes and I'll help you look for your dog."

Jessie held up a hand. "Oh, not at all. I'll go out and get him and we can probably make our way back up to the road through the woods off to the side of your house. I don't want to burden you anymore than I already have."

Ellie lifted Sarah into one of the highchairs and began filling a plate with a couple of pancakes from the built-in griddle. "Oh, nonsense. Get your dog and bring him back through the house. I haven't mopped for the day, so it won't be a big deal."

"Are you...sure?"

She waved her off. "Absolutely. By the time you get back I'll have some coffee for you. It's awfully chilly out there and you look like you just ran out of your house without realizing that."

Jessie tried to hide her blush and nodded. "Thank you, very much."

She walked out onto the deck and made her way to

the wide set of stairs that led down to the steep yard. She made a play of calling out and clapping her hands together as she took in the landscape. Ellie was right. The pitch of the land was severe. Beautifully manicured, but not particularly useable. She looked for a basement or any type of entrance from the outside but found nothing.

Finally, she placed her hands on her hips and let out a deep sigh. Maybe there really was nothing here. "Blizzard, heel."

The dog materialized out of the undergrowth to her left and plodded across the grass to her side. Together, they made their way up to the deck and the glass doors. Jessie stuck her head inside. "Are you sure you don't mind him coming in?"

Ellie was at the stove and walked over, motioning for her to step through. Her eyes widened at the sight of the large shepherd. "Oh my, that is one big dog." Her brow furrowed as she glanced from Blizzard to her daughter sitting at the island.

"Oh, he's okay. He's big but would never hurt a fly," Jessie said, nodding to Blizzard.

The dog trotted over to Ellie, sniffing her leg, tail wagging.

Jessie smiled. "See, he likes you already."

Ellie nervously held out a hand and let him get her scent. Then she reached forward, rubbing his head and then down his back. Blizzard stretched forward, gleefully meeting her hand. "He's so soft...and warm. What a beautiful dog." She pointed to a cup sitting on the end of the island. "I poured you some coffee, and before you thank me just know I'm not the best at making it. It's the one thing my husband says I need to improve."

Jessie frowned but didn't respond as she took up the cup and sipped at it. She did her best to maintain a neutral face as she forced it down. "It's good. And I can't say anything. My only experience with coffee comes from a bakery."

"Well, thank you for saying that."

"I get mine at Angela's in town. Have you been there?"

Ellie hesitated before turning back to the stove. "No. We, um, don't really venture into town. Everything we need is right here."

"Yes. I can see that." Jessie glanced down at Blizzard. Something had caught his attention, and he was staring off through the living room, his nostrils quivering. "Um, look, thank you for your hospitality. Can I bother you for one last favor? Is there a powder room close by? Then I promise we will be on our way."

Ellie wiped her hands on a towel and nodded through the great room. "On the left, just outside the living room is one you can use."

"Thank you so much. I'll make sure Blizzard stays by my side."

She headed out of the kitchen, and when Ellie turned her back, she whispered to the shepherd. "Track."

Following him down the hall, she passed a narrow console table pressed against one wall. On it was an array of small, framed photographs. Jessie recognized Ellie and Sarah in many of them. There were also a few with a man standing next to Ellie, his arm around her. He was shorter and seemed to be squinting in most of the photos. Jessie looked around, and then grabbed one of them and shoved it into the waistband of her pants.

Blizzard was at one of the closed doors off to the left, his nose to the floor as he huffed in the air coming from the tiny crack under the door. Jessie put her ear to the door but couldn't hear anything.

"The bathroom is on the other side." It was Ellie. She had appeared at the end of the hall. "The door that isn't locked."

Jessie gave her a nervous laugh. "Sorry. Got turned around." She motioned for Blizzard to follow her into the powder room and shut the door. She stood for a moment, then ran some water in the sink before making her way out and back to the kitchen. "Thank you, Ellie. So much for this. I'm sorry for intruding."

"Oh, not at all. It was kind of nice having another adult to talk to. No matter how brief."

Jessie sensed a sadness to her tone that she briefly considered exploring further. But she had already over-stayed her welcome and didn't want to raise the woman's suspicions. "Well, again, you have a lovely home. And if you ever need to talk...or anything, I'm the last house at the inlet of the lake. The...tiny one."

Ellie smiled. "Thank you. Who knows. Maybe I'll get that cup of coffee with you in town someday."

"I'd like that." Jessie smiled, waved, and turned to hike back up the drive, Blizzard in tow, as the massive door whooshed shut behind her.

Once on the road, she took out the picture she had stolen from the house and studied it once again, before continuing home.

She was unaware of the sophisticated grid of surveillance cameras that had followed her every move inside the house and sent recordings to a cell phone belonging to a very dangerous man who had a habit of squinting instead of smiling.

33

A Shocking Revelation

The tires on Jessie's Jeep screeched to a stop outside the Gray Eagle. She jumped out and rushed to the front door. It was locked, and she was both annoyed and grateful that John was keeping his word to make sure Kevin was safe and secure. Her hand slapped loudly against the solid wood. For a moment, she worried that no one was inside. Would John have taken Kevin back to his cabin, even after she told him to stay put?

She was about to call out John's name, when the door was unlocked. Josie pushed the door outward for her to enter. Stepping past the large man, she looked up at him and shook her head. "Do you ever go home?"

He only grunted, rolled his eyes and stomped back towards the bar.

Jessie strolled past him and walked straight into John's private office behind the bar. He was sitting at his desk and looked up at her with a frown as she looked around the room. "Where's Kevin?"

"He's upstairs, sleeping in the loft. He was down here originally, but I had work to do, and that kid asks too many questions."

Jessie was about to argue the point but decided against it. "Thank you, John. For keeping him safe."

The bar owner looked surprised for a moment, but then nodded, glancing behind her. "So, where's your shadow?"

"Oh, I left him with Eric and Mark at the bed and breakfast. There's something I need to do and didn't want to risk bringing him along."

John raised a single eyebrow at her. "I meant Alex."

"Oh." Crimson crept up her neck. "Of course you did. I called him. He should be here any minute now."

As if on cue, Alex walked into the office, acknowledging both Jessie and John with a nod. Once again, he was not in uniform and wore a denim jacket over a form-fitting green tee shirt tucked into a pair of jeans. Years of training to spot such things, told Jessie he was carrying a gun, though she couldn't see the outline of it on his hip.

"Everything okay?" he asked, turning to face Jessie. "I got your text to meet. Sounded urgent."

"It could be," she said. She pulled the picture she had taken from its frame out of her pocket and placed it on John's desk. "Do either of you know him?" She pointed to the man in question in the photo.

Alex stared at him before shaking his head. "Never seen him before."

"That's Phillip Winters," John said after glancing

briefly at the picture. He reached out and pointed to the woman. "That's his wife Ellie." He paused scratching his chin. "I guess that would be the daughter. Didn't know they had a kid, though."

Jessie looked at him in shock. "You know this man?"

"Well, I don't know him personally, but I know of him."

Alex held up a hand. "Wait. Jessie, maybe tell us why you have a picture of this man and what he has to do with things."

Jessie took her time and relayed everything that had transpired since waking. She told them every detail she could remember about the house and her conversation with Ellie. "I can't say for certain, but it just felt like she was reaching out...but without actually reaching out. Maybe she was just lonely, but it felt like something more."

Alex folded his arms. "Why did you go back to your house? I thought you were staying at the bed and breakfast."

She knew Alex well enough not to play games with him. There was too much respect for that. "I went to the bed and breakfast because I needed to leave something there for later." She looked Alex in the eye, holding contact. "But it was personal. It had nothing to do with this investigation. And once I was there, I knew I had to go home. I don't know, I just thought maybe I'd see or find something there that might spark an idea for next steps. I needed to be in my own space to free my head. And I wasn't about to call you because you needed to get some rest as well. We all did."

He didn't say anything but held her gaze. "You shouldn't have been alone."

"I wasn't. If someone was on my porch, I'm pretty sure the reason they didn't try coming in was because of Blizzard."

John gave a low whistle. "I know I wouldn't risk anything with that dog around. I'm betting she was just as safe as if one of us had been there."

Alex narrowed his eyes at the man. Jessie saw the vein on the side of his head start to throb and stepped in before he could reply. "The bottom line is, I'm fine and we might have a break in this case. Because the last time I checked, we've only got hours left before whoever has Cora does something unthinkable." Both men gave her a look that said they were onboard and agreed with what she was saying. "Now, John, tell us about this guy."

John looked at the photo again before speaking. "The only reason I know him is because he hired a couple of my guys to help with the build out at that monstrous house of his. He pays everything in cash, and he is incredibly protective of his wife."

"What do you mean by that?" Jessie asked.

"Well, he went off on one of my guys; accused him of eyeballing his wife. The one rule he apparently had was no one was to look at his wife. Apparently, he lost his mind whenever he caught someone ogling her." He hesitated, trying to frame his words the right way. "The way he doted on her, and how he was so protective...I just don't see how you'd pick up on any weird vibes from her. She's with a guy who only wants to keep her safe and protected."

Jessie arched her eyebrows as she stared at him. "Well, you've never been a woman in a relationship before. This explains a lot of what I was sensing from her."

Alex nodded in agreement. "I agree that maybe what you were picking up on was some kind of domestic situation. But that doesn't mean this guy is involved in Cora's kidnapping."

Jessie exhaled sharply. "You're right. But why would Blizzard have led me to that house?"

"You said that the husband wasn't there; that he works early with overseas clients," John said. "How could he do that and have been stalking around your place as well?"

Jessie shook her head in exasperation. "I don't know. I only have his wife's assurance that he's at work. Maybe she doesn't know what he really does. In my experience, men like that aren't always truthful with their spouses about what they're up to. And maybe it wasn't him. Maybe it was someone else that was in the house. Blizzard hit on someone's scent from there. And he picked it up inside the house as well. But that's a lot of maybes." She wrinkled her brow.

"What is it?" Alex asked.

"The look on her face when she saw me at the door in the hallway. For a moment, she looked so afraid that I was going to open that door. But also, she looked protective... if that makes any sense."

"Maybe it was her husband's office. Or the basement," offered Alex.

Jessie shook her head. "I checked for that when I was

in the backyard. They were excavating to level out the space a little, but there wasn't a basement."

"Well, sure there is. Sort of," said John, looking up from the picture to the two of them. Their wide-eyed stare urged him on. "At least there was with the original house that was on that property."

"I thought this one looked a little out of place, even if it were remodeled," Jessie said.

"The house wasn't just remodeled," John clarified, his voice becoming reflective. "They completely tore it down to the ground. Originally, it was a grand Victorian, a real piece of history. Belonged to the O'Connell family—you know, the old Pine Haven lineage. Their house was almost as magnificent as the one that's now the bed and breakfast. I remember Angela and Ariel, the O'Connell twins. They were in my high school class. Those two were notorious for throwing some wild parties when their folks were out of town."

He paused; his eyes clouded over with memories. "But it was what was under the house that was really something. Beneath that elegant Victorian were all these dark, sprawling spaces. No natural light ever touched those rooms; they were like forgotten caverns. But they were vast, winding through the whole space. The twins turned that eerie, windowless room into the heart of their ragers." He chuckled at something his mind replayed. "Good thing those walls couldn't talk."

Jessie and Alex exchanged looks. "Another underground railway. Just like the bed and breakfast."

"Sure sounds like it," Alex responded.

John stared at both. "What are you talking about?"

Jessie quickly described what they had found at the bed and breakfast.

John looked at her solemnly. "Wow. Well, I'm pretty sure there were no chains, cages or anything like that under the O'Connell house."

"And what about a tunnel leading in?" asked Jessie. "Anything like that?"

John thought for a moment then shook his head. "If there was, I never heard about it."

Alex thought for a moment. "It could be hidden. The way it was at Mark and Eric's. The family could have never known it was there."

Jessie tapped her lips with her forefinger. "And the entrance or exit could be somewhere along the lakefront as well. If it's like the one leading into the bed and breakfast, it could be hidden in the banks close by."

"I have access to a small boat that we can take out and see what's out there," Alex said. "That is, if you think this is something to pursue."

Jessie thought for a moment. There was nothing tangible that connected this house to Cora's kidnapping, but her gut told her there was something there. Cora was running out of time. Who knew how long it might take to find the entrance that led to the space beneath the house? If there even was an entrance.

Alex's phone buzzed, interrupting her thought process. He looked at the screen and frowned. "Looks like one of the CSI officers specializes in forensic accounting and was able to trace the payments coming into our mystery doctor's account. It's from an offshore land and leasing company called Trident, Incorporated. No luck on finding out who owns the company, though. We would probably need a court order for that. But...he was able to trace another set of payments to a second account and, unlike our doctor, that account isn't shielded by dark web apps." Alex looked up, smiling. "That account is an online banking one registered to an Anthony J. Miraldi. I guess that's a start."

John's body stiffened and he stared at the two of them, eyes wide, mouth open.

"What is it, John?" Jessie asked. "Do you know this person?"

His hand shook as he raised it over his mouth before letting it fall to his side. "Anthony *Joseph* Miraldi. That's Josie's full name."

Jessie felt a bolt of adrenaline shoot through her as she raced from the office, followed by Alex and John. The bar was empty; the big bartender was nowhere to be seen.

"Kevin," she breathed, before heading up the stairs to the loft. She felt the room sway as she tried to steady her breathing. Just like the bar area, it was empty as well. The blanket that had been on the couch was strewn across the floor and there was an overturned bottle of water on the coffee table. Alex rushed into the room. "He's gone."

34

A Tongue Lashing

"She was in my house! How the hell did that happen?"

Josie gritted his teeth, trying to relax his grip on the phone. "I swear I have no idea. Maybe she was, I don't know, canvasing the area or something."

There was a pause on the other end of the line, and Josie was sure his partner was massaging his eyes as if he had a headache coming on. It was something the man often did when they were together. "Josie, she was snooping. I have her on camera...and she took a picture from my hall stand. A picture of me and my family! Now why would she randomly do that?" Another pause. "Is there something you need to tell me?"

"No, honestly, I mean...okay, maybe I went to her house. But I swear she didn't see me. Her friend just made me so mad...I just wanted to..."

The voice on the other end of the line was like ice. "You wanted to what?"

Josie heaved a breath. "I was just going to sneak into her place, grab something that belonged to her, to show it to her uppity friend. Let her know if she didn't shut her mouth and keep it shut, I'd hurt Jessie. She wasn't supposed to be there! I heard her tell the cop she was staying at the bed and breakfast, so I didn't think there would be any harm in it."

The man on the other end ground his teeth, trying to control his anger. "Did she see you?"

"No. Not at all. As soon as I heard that dog of hers bark, I got out of there."

More silence on the other end followed by a deep exhalation. "And when you left her house, where did you go?"

Now it was Josie who seemed to lose his voice. "I... went back to the cells. But only long enough to give the girls water and their morning feeding. Then I went straight to the bar, I swear. I just did what you always said to do. Keep them girls watered and fed. That's what I did."

"Where is she now?" the man asked.

"She's back in John's office with that deputy she works with."

"Can you hear what they're saying?"

Josie bit at his lower lip. "No. But I saw Jessie showing them the picture she must have taken from your house."

"Christ. Where is the boy?"

"He's up in the loft," Josie replied.

"Can you get to him without them seeing you?" the man said.

"I think so, yes."

"Okay, while they're meeting, get him and bring him to the cells. Throw him in with the girls until we figure out what to do with him. Be sure they don't follow you."

Josie hesitated. "But that will mean blowing my cover with John..."

The man snapped. "Maybe you should have thought about that before playing creeper! Just, get the boy, we'll figure out the rest later." He let his words sink in, before adding. "And Josie, if they see you, shoot the boy, and try to take one of them out. Aim for Jessie first. She's the most dangerous. Got it?"

Josie swallowed hard, nodding. "Got it." He hung up the phone, checked that the pistol was secure in the waistband of his jeans, and then peeked into the office. They were still holding court, John speaking animatedly about something. He took a deep breath and headed for the stairs where the boy was sitting on the couch, thumbing through his phone.

"Hey, Josie," Kevin said, looking up briefly.

Josie walked over to him and whipped the blanket off that was draped around the boy's shoulders. It struck the bottle of water on the coffee table, knocking it over. Kevin jumped, eyes wide, his voice catching in his throat.

"Get up," Josie said, his voice like gravel. He lifted his leg, placing his boot on the coffee table. Kevin began to tremble when he saw the six-inch fixed blade that Josie pulled out. "And if you make a sound, I'll gut you like a fish."

Kevin raised his hands, his eyes locked on the tip of the steel aimed at his midsection. Josie flicked the knife at the entrance to the loft space.

"Here's what's going to happen," he growled. "We are going down the steps and straight out the door. Stay to the right of the bar and out of sight. I'll be right beside you and if you do anything to attract attention, or so much as make a peep, I'll slice your stomach open. No paramedics would get here in time to save you and you'll die in agonizing pain. Do you understand?"

Kevin's eyes had teared up and all he could do was nod his head emphatically. His body shook as he headed for the stairs, nearly tripping over his feet in his haste to make his way down. Josie followed close behind, his own heart trip hammered as they walked through the bar and out into the nearly empty parking lot.

"This way," Josie said. They walked around the building to the side where his pickup truck sat. The door creaked as he opened it, and he stepped aside for Kevin to climb in. He calmly made his way to the driver's side and climbed behind the wheel. Slipping the knife back into the holster inside his boot, he climbed into the seat and fired up the engine. He gave Kevin a hard look as he pulled away. "Just so you know I have a gun on me as well. Try anything and I'll shoot you between the eyes."

Josie smiled as the boy swallowed hard, and tears flooded his face. He gave a long look into the rearview mirror as they exited the parking lot of the Gray Eagle. No one was following, and he relaxed his grip on the steering wheel as he headed down the road.

THE SMALLER MAN hung up the phone, his eyes narrowing to a squint as he then dialed another number. The phone rang once and was answered. The man spoke swiftly, relaying the conversation that had just taken place with his business partner. The silence that followed caused a line of cold sweat to break out along his spine.

"I am very disappointed in this development."

The sweat along his spine spread and he reflexively mopped at the wetness along his brow with his sleeve.

"Is this location viable in your opinion?"

The man considered the question carefully before answering. "It would mean a complete revamp of the space. There are a lot of obstacles that would need to be... removed. Todd might have been an ass, but without him at the police department, we don't have the eyes and ears we need to ensure everything could be handled properly. Alex is going to be a problem moving forward." He hesitated before speaking again, choosing his words carefully. "And the woman has proven to be a considerable thorn. I know you said she is not to be taken out of play, but..."

"That was before. Unfortunately, she has become too much of a liability. Pine Haven is too important to our future growth to allow her to continue unchecked. She needs to be removed from the playing field."

The man's eye twitched at the words. Jessie Night was proving to be more formidable than he thought. But she had invaded his personal space; jeopardized his family. "I would be more than happy to personally see to that. And when I do, maybe we can talk about a...bump in my compensation." He held his breath waiting for a response.

"If you can clean up this mess, and take Jessie Night off the board, then maybe we can discuss moving you into the role her brother once occupied."

The man smiled, calculating what he could do with such an increase.

"But there is one other thing. Josie has now become a liability."

He swallowed. He knew this was coming but had hoped his offer to clean up the situation might change their minds.

"Is there a problem?"

He closed his eyes. "No. No problem at all. I'll take care of it."

"Also, we have decided there needs to be a purge of any of the women that do not have current buyers. We will rebuild our merchandise once things have calmed down."

"Understood." He hung up the phone, reviewing his orders.

It was a shame, having to dispose of such hard-earned merchandise before they could be sold off. But in truth, he was less upset over that than he was at having to get rid of his partner. Josie had his moments, but he had been a friend and someone whom the man could count on for over a decade.

Maybe he'd throw his friend one last bone. Josie hated the woman called Cora. He'd give her over to Josie to do with as he pleased as a parting gift. The man smiled, pleased with himself and his generosity.

35

A Framed Revelation

"Pine Haven police!" Alex wasted no time waiting for an answer as he slammed his foot into the door's lock. It gave way in a splinter of wood, slamming open. He stepped into the tiny house; gun drawn. "If there's anyone here, show yourself now!"

When there was no answer, Jessie brushed past him, looking around the two-bedroom shotgun-style house that belonged to Josie Miraldi. John followed them in and went from the front of the house to the back, sweeping aside a couple of doors as he went, in less than a minute. He returned to where Jessie and Alex stood at the front of the house. "He's not here."

Jessie placed her hands on her hips, pacing a couple of steps back and forth. "Where else would he have taken him? Think, John."

The bar owner frowned. "I don't know. I mean, I've

known Josie for five years. He's been reliable and trustworthy. I'm as shocked as you by this."

Jessie turned to Alex. "We need to go back to the Winters' house. It doesn't make sense that Josie would bring Kevin here. He's working with whoever orchestrated this whole thing. Has to be." She turned to John. "You know I'm right. He isn't a leader, is he?"

John exhaled sharply and shook his head. "No. He doesn't think for himself. If he's involved in this, he's following orders."

"But we can't go into someone's house because you had a hunch the wife was uncomfortable about something," Alex said to Jessie before walking around the small room and into a tiny eat-in kitchen. There wasn't much to see there, and he slammed his fist down in exasperation on the wobbly table. "There has to be something here to give us an idea of where he took Kevin." He took a breath and turned to Jessie. "I'm making a call. I know we weren't supposed to involve the department, but I'm putting out a BOLO for Josie's truck." He took out his cell and swiped at the face of it.

For once Jessie didn't argue. She looked at her watch. The time frame the kidnappers had originally given her to hand over Kevin was less than an hour away. Assuming Josie was working with them and was on his way to hand Kevin over, then they would need as many eyes looking for them as possible.

"We saw how much money was in his account," said Alex, after his quick communication with the department. "He has to be spending it on something." He turned to John. "Does he have another house or cabin or anything else where he may have taken the boy?" The timbre of his voice was rising, and he wasn't bothering to hide his frustration. John moved into the kitchen with him, scratching his head. Jessie could hear their discussion as to where the barkeep might be but tuned them out.

Her mind was racing. There had to be something she had missed. Something that might clue her in as to where Josie was. He wasn't a big talker, so it wasn't like he could have accidentally said anything that would give him away.

Correction.

He wasn't a big talker to her. She had assumed that he just didn't like her; but now she knew it went much deeper than that. He didn't speak around her because he was afraid she might pick up on something that would give him away. She thought back to every brief encounter they had ever had. There had to be something there. Something that would—

Her mind froze in place as her eyes focused on something above the fireplace mantle. She moved closer and her breath caught in her throat. "Hey guys. Shut up for a minute and come over here." She was pointing to a framed picture displayed on the mantle.

"What is it?" asked Alex. He glanced at the photo of a group of five men dressed in waders standing in front of a stream. One man stood in the center, nearly a foot taller than everyone else. He held up a fishing line, a large trout dangling from his meaty fist. "Is that Josie?"

Jessie nodded. "Yeah, but look at the smaller man standing to his right." She dug into her pocket and took out the picture she had taken from the Winters' house. Her hand trembled as she held it up next to the framed photo.

Alex gasped. "That's the same guy. Phillip Winters. They know each other."

Jessie grabbed the picture off the mantle and turned to face the officer. "Does this give you probable cause to enter the house?"

"It sure does," he said, as the three of them hurried for the door.

Jessie let out a long breath as they climbed into Alex's cruiser. It was a forty-minute drive back to the lake from where they were. She glanced at her watch. Cora would be out of time before they could reach her.

36

Never Question the Boss

Kevin was nearly hyperventilating by the time Josie dragged him down a set of stairs and through a heavy steel door into the chilly, concrete holding room. He gasped as he was led past a large, free-standing cell that held a half-dozen women huddled together in the center of the cage. None of them looked his way as the big man all but dragged him past.

Josie pushed him down next to another woman who crouched, chained to a wall. His knees hit the concrete and he cried out in pain, instinctively cowering next to the woman.

Josie pointed at him. "Don't move from this spot. You can't open the door to get out anyway, and all you'll do is make your death painful and slow." He stared at Cora, and blew her an invisible kiss, his lips peeling back in an evil grin. He stepped away, disappearing around the corner. There was the sound of another door opening and closing, and then silence.

Kevin drew his legs up beneath him, sobbing as he leaned against the wall.

"Hey," Cora said softly. Her voice was harsh, her throat dry and her chapped lips burned as she forced them to form words. "Are you hurt?"

Kevin shook his head but was still unable to look at her. He drew his knees to his chest and hugged them tight, rocking back and forth.

"Hey, do you know where we are? Did you see a way out?"

He didn't answer, only continued to rock himself. Cora could tell from his body language that he was most likely close to going into shock. If that happened, she might lose her only chance at finding out what he may or may not know. Information that might help her escape.

Her throat felt like someone had burned it from the inside as she tried again to get his attention. "Hey, can you tell me your name? I'm Cora. What's your name?"

For the first time he stopped rocking and slowly looked up at her with red, watery eyes. "Cora? You're Cora?"

She looked at him. "Yes. Do I know you?"

His eyes were frantic suddenly as he released his knees and grabbed at her bound arms. "You're Jessie's friend."

Now it was Cora's turn to be shocked. She nodded her head vigorously. "Yes. I am. How do you know that? Is she here with you?" She knew that couldn't be possible, but her mind was reaching for anything to make sense of what was happening.

The boy started to cry at that moment. Not his previous tears that were born from fear, but something else. "My name is Kevin. And...and it's my fault you're here."

"ARE you sure that's what they want?" Josie asked.

Phillip shrugged. "We don't question or argue with the boss."

They stood in the small study Phillip had built. A space where they could openly discuss their business affairs and keep an eye on the women they were auctioning off.

"It just seems like a waste is all," Josie added. He looked down at the array of monitors on Phillip's desk. They were all focused on a different room in his house. He felt weird watching his friend's wife fold laundry while his daughter played with an expensive doll house in her room. He averted his eyes and cleared his throat. "Hey, I'm really sorry I messed things up. I had no idea she could follow me back to your place like that."

Phillip looked at his friend. He knew Josie was genuinely sorry for what he had done. He also knew that if Josie were allowed to live, he would never make that same mistake again. "I know you didn't, buddy. You did nothing wrong. But the fact remains that we need to purge our data." He leveled a hard look at Josie. "All of it. You can start with Jessie's friend if you want."

The big man's eyes lit up, reflecting his penchant for cruelness. "She has a mouth on her, that one. And the boy?"

"Did you get his phone?"

Josie reached into his pocket and took out Kevin's cell and handed it over to Phillip.

"Good. He needs to be eliminated as well. But not before he tells us who potentially has seen or has copies of the footage. Did you get the actual drone controller that houses it?"

Josie suddenly looked confused. "He didn't have anything like that with him. At least, I don't think he did."

It was a struggle, but Phillip hid the annoyance he felt. They had the boy and that was the biggest thing. He watched Josie drag him in and knew the kid would fold immediately under the slightest hint of duress.

"Phillip, do we have to move?" Josie was looking down at his shoes. "Because I kind of like it here. It's quiet."

Phillip liked it in Pine haven as well. Ellie and Sarah seemed settled. It was finally beginning to feel like they were a family. "No. We won't have to move. We just need to clean everything up, then lay low for a while. We'll get a new shipment to tag and hold once the boss says it's safe to resume operations."

Josie's confusion deepened. "How will we tag new ones? I heard that cop talking to John. Sounds like Jessie really messed up the doc. Who's going to do what he did for us?"

Phillip sighed. "They'll send us a new doc when the time comes. Everyone is replaceable, Josie."

"Yeah. I guess you're right. So, what do you want me to do first?"

Phillip swallowed hard and smiled at his friend. "Jessie will be on her way here. We need to be ready for that."

The big man seemed startled. "What? How do you know?"

"Because she's very good at what she does." Honestly, he hoped she would show up. It would make killing her that much easier if she came to him. "Do me a favor. Go get Ellie and my daughter and escort them to the panic room. Tell Ellie they are to stay in there until I personally come for them. Got it?" He waited for Josie to nod. "And don't scare them. Tell them it's one of our drills, nothing more."

When Josie turned to leave, Phillip turned to the laptop that sat in front of the row of monitors. He triggered a complicated series of programs that were meant to digitally shred everything on the hard drive, as well as install a layer of impenetrable decryption on top of that. When he was finished, he would drill a hole through it as well. The computer was air-gapped and had never been connected to the internet. Still, he knew better than to leave anything that could potentially be traced back to his employers.

Ten minutes later, he left his small office, secured the door, and headed back to his house.

～

CORA STARED DEFIANTLY as each of her captors walked past her at different times. Kevin buried his face, turning away from them. To Cora, it looked as if the young man had regressed to a child's game of peek-a-boo.

If I can't see you, you can't see me.

She hissed at him. "Kevin. Look at me. Something is happening. The big guy is always cruel to me and those women. He walked by us without even glancing my way. And his friend is just as bad. Whatever they are up to is not going to be good for us. Do you hear me?"

The young man groaned. "Leave me alone...please. I told you what happened...what I did. I told you why you're here. All I can do is say I'm sorry."

Cora sneered at him. If she could have gotten one hand free, she would have slapped him. "Well sorry is not enough. There is more that you can do. You're the only one of us not locked in a cage or chained to a damn wall. Get up off your ass and see if there is a way out of here."

He raised his head, eyes filled with disbelief. "Are you crazy? Josie told me to stay put or he'd kill me slowly."

Josie.

So that was his name. Cora glared at Kevin. "He's going to kill you anyway. But not until they have tortured you to get whatever it is they want out of you. Does anyone else other than you have this footage you told me about?"

He nodded quickly. "Jessie has a copy of it as well."

Cora rolled her eyes. She knew he wouldn't last long when they started applying pressure. Cora clenched her jaw. No way was she going to sit by and watch this kid roll over on one of her closest friends. "Listen to me. I need you to focus and find some balls. Help us!"

Kevin stared at her, his lip quivering. Finally, he took a deep breath and stood up. "What do you want me to do?"

"How did you get in here? What kind of structure is this?" Cora asked.

"We're under a house. A big one on the lake. I used to clean the pool for a nice lady a couple houses down, but I've never been to this one before."

"Okay, that's excellent. How far is this house from the lake? How close is the nearest house?" Cora asked.

Kevin thought for a second. "From what I remember we are about a hundred feet from the lake and the nearest house is maybe twice that."

Cora's mind raced. "Is there a dock or does the back lead directly to the lake?"

He frowned. "No, I don't think there is a dock now that you mention it. Maybe that's why there were always those large digging machines back there."

Cora's breath caught in her throat. "Does it slope into a landing for boats, or is it too bushy with overhanging vegetation for a boat to pull right up to the property?"

"Nah, a boat couldn't pull up. Tree roots and all kinds of bushes at the water's edge."

"Okay, that's good to know. I think we are in an old underground railroad system that they have taken over. If that's the case, there is probably a way out; a tunnel leading to the outside. It might be boarded over, but there should be a way out. It would be on a wall closest to the water. If we can find that, we might have a way out." She rolled her tongue, working her mouth until she spit out the nail she had been hiding in her cheeks. "Take this and see if you can pick the lock on these manacles. I was close...but couldn't get the right positioning to do it."

Kevin took the nail from her and bent over the lock around her wrists. "You're in luck. This is just a basic pin lock, and my dad taught me how to pick these when I was a kid." He turned the manacles a bit to get a closer look before carefully inserting the small nail. "It might take a second to rake the pins. It's harder with just one tool to pick, but these aren't very complicated..."

Cora looked around anxiously. While she didn't want to get caught, she also knew there was nothing they could do to them at this point that they weren't planning to do already.

Kevin murmured something to himself that she couldn't understand. Before she could ask him what he was saying, she heard a distinctive click as the manacles relaxed around her wrists.

"Did it," Kevin said, his voice tinged with equal parts surprise and excitement. "Never thought I'd be grateful for having a career criminal for a dad."

Cora pulled free of the restraints and rubbed at her aching, raw, wrists. "I don't know the man, but I'm thankful for him as well. Come on."

She stood, trying to ignore the searing pain in her knees and back. She felt crippled from the position she had been locked in. But she was also grateful for the pain.

It meant she was still alive.

"Time to find a way out of here." She looked over at the women in the cage. "For all of us."

37

Divided Can We Conquer?

"You can't be serious," Alex said. "Your plan is to just walk in the front door?"

"For once, I have to agree with him," John added. "It's suicide."

The three of them were standing at the lake's edge, three houses down from the large, modern home Phillip Winters had built.

"It gives the two of you time to find an entrance into the underground beneath the house. If this is like the bed and breakfast, there should be one that opens along the water somewhere close to the house. That has to be where Cora is being held. If I can talk to Phillip's wife, find out what is going on, maybe even speak with the man himself...it gives you two a chance to save Cora," Jessie said.

John was scratching his cheek. "There are a lot of things that need to go right for that to happen, you know.

And don't take this the wrong way, but a lot of this hinges on Cora still being alive. For all we know, she and Kevin could have already been killed and these guys have pulled up stakes and ghosted the whole operation."

Jessie's eyes darted to the man as she fought to control her temper. "She's alive. I refuse to even consider that she isn't. And I was inside that house. It didn't feel like something transient. There was a permanence to the life being created there. Whoever this guy is, he isn't leaving." She cast her glance down the lake towards the house. "My brother made it sound like there was a major operation being set up in Pine Haven. This is definitely a part of it. I've seen this kind of behavior before. People like this don't just up and leave once they've established a foothold. They burn everything around them until the environment conforms to their needs. That's what this man is doing."

"Then all the more reason for us to go in with you," said Alex, raising his arms. He let them drop to his sides loudly for emphasis. "You can't just play fast and loose with your life like this."

She was shaking her head. "It's a very calculated gamble. I've known men like this. He's narcissistic and overconfident, and believes himself to be superior to all others; especially women. His wealth and perceived social standing make him think he's above the law. His overconfidence will lead him to think that a woman, especially one who has no backup, poses no real threat to him. I'll use that to my advantage."

"Jessie, your reputation is all over town," John said. "People know you can hold your own and that you are not to be fucked with. My bet is he's waiting on you alright. With a shotgun."

She squared her shoulders and stared him down. "Someone like this is usually a sociopath. His willingness to kidnap, kill and traffic women indicates a lack of empathy and reinforces his tendencies. You're right...he wants me dead. But someone like this will want to do it up close and personal. He's going to want to watch the light fade from my eyes. He won't use a gun." The two men glanced nervously at one another. "Look, the longer we sit here arguing, the greater the chance that Cora or Kevin is going to die."

"You're right," said Alex. "But what if there is no entrance along the lake?"

She was already putting her hair up in a knot on her head. "Then you come back and bust down the door. Whatever it takes to get inside that house."

The men nodded and turned to head for the lake. Alex spun to face Jessie one last time. "Don't die."

She didn't say anything, but gave him an ironclad nod, before heading up the embankment towards the road. She forced herself not to look back as she heard Alex and John wade into the water and begin their trek through the overgrowth, searching for an entrance to a labyrinth of horrors.

Jessie made her way along the road to the large house, down the long driveway, and up to the imposing front door. The digital screen appeared before she could knock.

"I'm sorry, but I don't believe we have any more business to complete," came a cold voice.

Jessie frowned. She wasn't in the mood to play games. But if that was what this asshole wanted to do, then so be it. She dug her cell phone out of her pocket, called up the video footage from Kevin's drone, and held it up to the screen as it played.

Almost immediately, there was a click and a series of electronic whirring as the door locks retreated. Jessie reached out a tentative hand and gave the door a push. It opened with a whoosh, inviting her in. She stood there, her heart pounding away as she peered at the opening, her ears straining to pick up anything that could represent danger.

John's words echoed in her mind. What if Phillip Winters was standing just inside the door...or behind it... with a shotgun. If that was the case, at least she wouldn't feel anything.

She took a deep breath and forced the thought from her mind as she stepped into the house.

KEVIN WAS bent over at the door on the cage that held the trafficked women, working at the lock.

"Anything?" asked Cora.

He dropped his hands in exasperation. "This is most definitely not a basic pin lock. It's electronic and keyed to biometrics. I told you I couldn't open it."

Cora was at the wall where one of the office doors was located. She was feeling along the base and sides as she called back over her shoulder. "Well, keep at it. There has to be a way to override the lock. Didn't your dad teach you how to do that?"

Kevin sighed. "The only way to do that is to cut the power to it...and what are you doing?"

"I believe this structure we're held in is part of an old underground railroad system. Some were used to house runaway slaves. If it's like the one I saw earlier, there should be an exit that leads out of here that they may not know about. The problem is, they've put up so many walls and dividers they might have unknowingly covered it up." She crossed the space to the opposite corner of the room. "The floor is damper here...and I swear I can feel a draft in this corner..."

Before she could explore further, metal grinding against metal echoed slightly through the space.

"He's coming back!" one of the women spoke from inside the cage.

Kevin froze, his eyes wide with terror. Cora sprinted for the wall where she had been chained, motioning for Kevin to join her. She quickly resumed her place crouching along the wall and draped the manacles over her wrist as best she could. Kevin crouched next to her, just as the door into the chamber squeaked open.

The women once again shrank to the center of the cell, huddled with their backs to the bars.

Josie swept into the room, his footsteps heavier than usual, his face dour with dark intent. He passed the cage, giving the women a passing glance as he made his way to Cora and Kevin.

He stood over them, placed his hands on his hips, and let out a heavy sigh. He zeroed in on Cora. "Well, looks like you and I have come to the end of the road, little lady." He turned his attention to Kevin. "I need you to watch me kill her. Because after I do, we are going to talk about where any and all traces of that drone footage might be. And you're going to answer...unless you want to go through what she's about to."

Cora sneered at the man. "You know, it's not lost on me that you've got a woman of color chained to a wall in a space once used as a refuge for runaway slaves. You're putting out a lot of really bad karma, and that bitch is going to come for you like a freight train."

His lip drew up, a nasty glint coming into his eyes. "You know, you aren't the first person to tell me that. Yet, I'm still standing. Now, let's get this over with."

He reached forward and pulled her to her feet.

38

Like Your Life Depends on It

The inside of the house was eerily quiet compared to what Jessie had experienced earlier. There were no inviting smells coming from the kitchen, no child's laughter; nothing to signify there was life of any kind in the home.

She entered the large, light-filled great room, to see Phillip Winters sitting in one of the leather chairs he had pulled into the center of the room. He stared hard at Jessie as she walked in, his eyes narrow and dark.

"So, you're the one who's been such a pain in my side, huh?" His tone was measured and casual. "You just don't stop."

Jessie willed herself to remain calm. "Strange way of putting it, considering you pulled me into this by kidnapping my friend and demanding I do your dirty deed for you."

He motioned towards the couch with his chin. "Have a seat."

Jessie took a glance around the room. "I'll stand."

Phillip moved his hand, and she caught a glimpse of the pistol he was holding. She clenched her jaw. Had she read him wrong? Maybe he was just going to shoot her and be done with it.

He must have read her mind. "Why did you walk in here? I have cameras in and around my house and I didn't see your friends with you. What's to stop me from just shooting you right here and now?"

"If you were going to do that you would have already. My guess is you want to know what I've done with that drone footage."

The corners of his mouth turned down and he gave her a half nod. "I have the boy. Something tells me he'll be more forthcoming about it than you would, so I really don't need you. Or your friend."

"That's true," Jessie said. "Except, I sent the footage to a cloud server that I have to log into every hour on the hour; otherwise, it will automatically be emailed to the FBI. So, you can kill me, but then you're going to be running for the rest of your life." She looked around the house. "And something tells me you don't want to do that." She gave him a smile. "Where are your wife and daughter?"

He snorted at her. "That's not your concern. They're safe...which is more than I can say for you."

Jessie's mind was racing. "It's not too late for that deal we had."

He pursed his lips. "You're law enforcement. What makes you think I believe anything you're saying?"

"Because I only want my friend back. Hand her over and we can still do business."

"You know, they were right about you. You're not like your brother at all. Unlike him, you don't get down in the mud. I can see that now. I also think you're bluffing about the footage."

She raised her chin, refusing to break eye contact. "Try me. And you didn't know my brother at all."

He scoffed at her. "Sure I did. Brody was one mean bastard." Jessie flinched hearing her brother's name come out of his mouth. "He used to tell us what your father put the two of you through...what he tried to turn you into. Shame that it succeeded with your brother and not you. You would have definitely been the better choice. You did my employers a favor, putting down that rabid dog." He laughed unpleasantly. "Certainly did me one...it got me a promotion."

Jessie felt red-hot anger well within her, threatening to cloud her vision. She strummed with her right hand, her fingers playing in rhythm against her leg."

He stood slowly from the chair. "See, there's one thing about me that you don't know."

Something about the look in his eyes, the tone in his voice gave Jessie pause. "And what is that?"

"The people I work for know about the footage and about you. They've already commenced damage control. I have been granted immunity from doing whatever they need done. And right now, they need you taken out of the picture." He smiled and raised the gun. "So goodbye, Jessie Night."

JOSIE PULLED Cora to her feet. "You know, it's almost a shame I have to waste you. It would have been fun finding just the right type of buyer for you who would put you in your place on a daily basis." He leaned close to her face. "I even had your own marker made for you. The doc was going to install it tomorrow actually."

Cora's lip quivered in fresh anger. "I don't know what you're talking about, and I don't care. If you're going to kill me, get it over with. I'll die happy knowing that Jessie is going to find you, and what she's going to do to you."

He laughed hard, spittle striking her face as he looked upward. "She's up there right now, you know. She's probably already dead. I offered to do it for him, but this was one Phillip wanted to handle personally."

Cora laughed, shaking her head slowly as she mumbled, her voice too low to be understood.

Josie frowned. "What's that?" Then his black-hearted smile returned. "Are you begging for your life? It's not going to change things, but I do like it when you women beg. So go ahead. Let me hear it." He turned his head to the side and leaned in close to Cora's lips.

It was an opportunity that she intended to make the most of. She quickly maneuvered the nail in her cheek until the point protruded from between her lips, her teeth holding the head as solidly as possible. Then, she swiftly drew her face back from his ear and rammed it forward, driving the nail deep into Josie's ear.

The big man howled in pain, rearing back as he grabbed at the side of his face. He let go of Cora and she took her hands out of the manacles and pulled the chain as far out of the wall as possible before swinging the end up to catch Josie in the face. His nose split and she heard him choke on blood.

She fell back against the wall, the effort nearly exhausting her in her weakened state. Josie opened red-rimmed eyes, his mouth opened wide as he pulled his hand away from his ear and saw the amount of blood covering it. His nose didn't seem to bother him, but the pain in his ear caused him to stagger backwards a couple of steps as he once again protectively cupped it.

"Bitch!" he roared. His face pinched together in an ugly rictus as he made a fist and lurched forward.

Cora flattened herself against the wall as much as possible, turning her face away from Josie just in time to see a blur of motion. Kevin unfurled from his crouch and charged at the larger man. He led with his shoulder, a terrified scream escaping his lips as he dove into their attacker's midsection.

Josie let out a surprised whoop as he was driven backwards by Kevin's feeble attack. Reaching down, he wrapped his arms around the smaller man and with a twist of his torso sent him sprawling across the floor. He stomped over to the young man and delivered a kick to his midsection, sending him even farther across the floor.

Josie moved to stand over him, his bloody hand trembled as he reached for Kevin. Before he could grasp him,

Cora leaped on his back, one hand clawing around for his face. She managed to hook one finger in his mouth and pull his head around towards her before he was able to shoot an elbow into her stomach, stunning her. Reaching over his shoulder, he grabbed her by the hair, bent forward, and threw her to the ground.

The impact stunned her, but instinctively she rolled onto her stomach, grabbed his leg and pulled herself to him. With all the strength she could muster, she bit into his leg. Again, he yelled out and kicked forward trying to dislodge her.

By then, Kevin was on his feet and was grabbing at the man from behind, trying to drag him away from Cora. Josie gave her one last kick that made her release him as he turned to Kevin. A strong punch to the younger man's stomach caused him to double over. Josie reached for his head at the same time Cora made her way to her knees behind him.

She swung her arm upward as fast and hard as she could, catching him in the groin from behind. Josie lurched forward and Cora struck again, this time grabbing onto his testicles and pulling back as hard as she could. Josie screeched in real pain this time, his eyes wide in horror as he reached between his legs to try and dislodge her hand.

Kevin straightened, standing on wobbly legs, his breath coming in gulps. With a shout, he launched into the big man again, driving him backwards away from Cora. They both stopped when Josie slammed into the bars of the cage. Kevin tried to hit the man, but he was so winded and weak that it was little more than a slap at Josie's face.

Josie placed a large, meaty hand on Kevin's face and shoved him backwards to the ground. He spit at the young man, and reached down, drawing his knife from his boot as he growled. "I was supposed to wait with you, but fuck it." He moved to take a step towards Kevin, knife raised, only to find himself stuck in place.

One of the women in the cell had reached through the bars and grabbed his belt. He felt other hands grabbing at him as well, latching onto his shirt, sleeves, trousers...and they pulled him backwards, pinning him against the bars.

Cora struggled to her feet and ran at the man with a scream. She gouged her nails into his eyes, trying to dig them into his skull with all her strength. The big man screamed and threw himself forward with enough force to pull free of the women who held him. He slashed the knife in a horizontal arc. Cora was able to get her arm up to shield her face just in time as the blade cut across the flesh of her forearm. She screamed, grabbing at the wound and skittered backwards.

Josie held one hand across his bleeding face, his eyes swollen nearly shut. He roared curses in Cora's direction as he sliced the knife back and forth in front of him, slowly advancing on her position.

He stopped, frozen in his tracks by the loud click of a gun's hammer being cocked, and the feel of a large muzzle pressed against the side of his head.

"Take one more step and I will blow your face off,"

Alex said. His voice was calm and measured and left no doubt that he would follow through on his threat.

Cora looked up to see him standing beside Josie, his hand steady as it held the heavy gun. She tried to make her way to her feet but found her legs wouldn't support her weight as she sank back to the floor.

A man she didn't know, wearing a leather vest that looked like the one Josie wore, crouched next to her, placing a comforting arm around her shoulders. Kevin made his way to them and dropped down next to her, leaning his head against John's arm.

"The...the women," Cora managed, pointing to the cage. "Please...get them out of there." Her voice was little more than a whisper.

Alex grabbed Josie by the collar and yanked. "Drop the knife." He waited until it clattered to the floor. "What's the lock code? Tell me or I swear I will handcuff you and let Cora finish what she started."

Finally, Josie recited four numbers to him, and together, they made their way to the locked cell door. Alex punched the code and the door locks popped and he was able to swing it open.

"It's okay," he said softly to the terrified women. "You're safe now."

Slowly, one by one, they made their way out and into the open.

"Thank you," Cora breathed. "Thank you." She turned, looking around. "Where...where is she? Where is Jessie?"

39
———

Last Person Standing

Jessie controlled the fear that threatened to seize her as Phillip raised his gun in her direction. While she had extensive training in dealing with assailants and guns, none of the techniques for evasion or concealment and cover applied in a situation like this. Phillip was too close for her to use her training. All she could hope was that he wasn't trained to use the firearm against someone with her skill set. She wasn't as young and nimble as she once was, but perhaps a quick drop and roll towards him might throw his aim off long enough for her to get close enough to disarm him.

She focused on his trigger finger, preparing to launch herself as she saw his hand tense to squeeze the trigger.

Movement from behind the man grabbed both of their attention. Phillip half turned his head and saw his wife approaching.

"Phillip? What's going on?" she asked.

"What are you doing here?" he demanded. "We are in the midst of a drill. I need you to go back—"

She stared over his shoulder at Jessie. "Jessie? What are you doing here?"

Jessie's breath caught in her throat at the sight of the woman. "Ellie, get out of here!" She looked around wildly, thankful there was no sign of Sarah.

Phillip wheeled on her. "You shut your mouth. Don't you speak to my wife."

For the first time, Jessie noticed a tremor in the man's voice. One that was matched by a slight shaking of his gun hand.

Jessie understood immediately what was going on. He didn't want to do it in front of his wife.

"What's the matter, Phillip? Don't want your wife to know what you've been up to lately?" Jessie said coldly.

Ellie looked confused. "Phil...what is she talking about?"

He turned his face halfway toward his wife but didn't take his eyes—or his gun—off Jessie. "Ellie, get back to the room with Sarah. I'll tell you when it's safe for you to come out."

Jessie raised her hands slowly as she took a tiny step to her left.

"Don't move!" Phillip said, stabbing the barrel of the gun in her direction.

Ellie gasped, throwing a hand over her mouth.

"Is this a surprise to you, Ellie?" Jessie said. "A side of your husband you've never seen before?" She studied the look on the woman's face. "Or is it? Let me guess, maybe he hasn't pulled a gun on you, but I'm betting there have been signs of aggression or subtle hints at a need to control and dominate you. Maybe with a possible threat of violence if you get out of line?"

Phillip's lip began to quiver. "You shut your mouth. I'd never hurt her, and she knows it."

Jessie stared at Ellie, the look in the woman's eyes was one Jessie had seen too often in her past. "So you say, but does she know that? Ellie, this is who your husband is. He's a violent man, with a deep-seated hatred of women." She took a deep breath. She's gone this far, might as well cross the goal line. She turned her attention to Phillip. "Does she know what's in the basement?" Phillip's face twitched, and she could feel the hatred radiating from him.

Ellie's eyes grew wide. "Phillip? What is she talking about?"

A shadow passed across her features. It was brief, barely noticeable. But Jessie saw it and pounced. "You know, don't you? You know that your husband has been kidnapping women and doing God knows what with them. Hell, for all I know you're an accomplice."

Ellie was shaking her head furiously. "No. No, it's not like that. You don't understand...I have a daughter now...I can't..."

"Can't what?" Jessie said. "Go to jail? Because I can assure you that you can and will. And you'll never see Sarah again...neither of you will."

"No. That's not true..." Ellie argued, desperation creeping into her voice.

"Of course it is," Jessie added. "Your husband is a violent man who probably enjoys doing terrible things to women. And if you think your daughter is safe around him, she isn't. At some point, he will turn his anger on her."

That was the final bait and Phillip took a big bite. He spun towards Jessie, mouth hanging open, but the gun wavered as his hand dropped just a bit, away from Jessie. In a flash, she moved to the side table she had been inching towards and grabbed one of the decorative, crystal rocks on display. She heaved it at his head while throwing herself sideways. The rock missed, striking him in the shoulder rather than the face, but it gave her time to get her bearings.

The crack of the gun was deafening, and she had no idea how close he came to hitting her as she rolled to one side. She was up and on her feet, charging at him as he tried to level the gun at her once again. She reached his side, swiping the gun away as she pivoted to place her back against his torso.

She dropped her elbow into a cluster of nerves along Phillip's forearm, causing him to drop the gun. Once it clattered to the floor, she spun her body to face Phillip. Clasping his shirt, she pulled him forward while simultaneously driving her knee into his side. There was a satisfying crunch as she cracked a couple of ribs. He grunted heavily in response and stretched a hand out to slap it across Jessie's face in an attempt to push her off him.

She struggled, realizing she couldn't match him strength for strength. Her mind flashed back to what her father had taught her. Men, even the small ones, were incredibly strong when compared to most women. Especially when they were enraged. But the thing that gave them their strength was also one of their biggest weaknesses.

Their balls.

She ducked under his arm, made a fist, and struck him between the legs with an uppercut. He groaned and doubled over, his grip on her loosening. As he fell forward, she met his face with her knee, breaking his nose. She expected that to take the fight out of him, but all it seemed to do was anger the man further.

With a shout, he lurched forward, grabbing her in a bear hug. His head shot forward, his forehead slamming into Jessie's. She saw stars and staggered backward from his grasp. His right arm shot out in a haymaker that connected with the side of her head. She rolled with the punch, escaping the worst of the blow, but was still disoriented by the glancing shot. He drew back to throw another shot at her face, and this time Jessie raised her own arm, sweeping the blow aside. She followed through, letting the momentum spin her until her arm was facing the ground. Then, with as much strength as she could muster, she pulled her elbow back and up, catching Phillip under his broken nose.

The blow threw him back as Jessie planted her left leg and raised her right. Pivoting her hips for power, she lashed out with a roundhouse kick, the top of her boot catching the man in his temple.

He went down in a heap, crumpling like a rag doll.

Jessie stood and looked at him. There was no sign of movement, other than the slight rise and fall of his chest. She looked up at Ellie who had stood there during their fight with one hand covering her mouth.

"Is he…" Ellie whispered.

"No," Jessie replied, though she wasn't as certain as she tried to project. She walked carefully over the man and bent down next to him.

"I'm so sorry," Ellie whispered, her voice trembling. "He said he wouldn't do it again."

Jessie looked up at the woman. "What do you mean?"

It was all the distraction that was required. Phillip rolled over; he swung the crystal rock Jessie had thrown at him. Years of training kicked in and she avoided the brunt of the blow, but still, the glancing strike made her see stars. Before she could recover, Phillip was on her, straddling her abdomen and pinning her to the ground.

Fingers wrapped around her throat and he began to squeeze the life out of her body. "I told you not to speak to her!"

Jessie gasped, trying unsuccessfully to draw in breath. She struggled, realizing the man had leverage and strength on her as he pinned her arms against her body with his knees. Her head swam from the blow she had just taken, and she couldn't focus her thoughts enough to devise a countermove from her position. Her knees…if she could just twist her knees enough to throw him off balance until she could free one arm, then maybe…

The boom from the gun rattled her molars as she felt Phillip stiffen, before slowly relaxing his grip on her neck and falling forward across her body. She took a deep breath, flooding her oxygen-starved lungs, before summoning the strength to roll the man off her. Breathing hard, she sat up to see Ellie still pointing the pistol Phillip had fired at her.

"Ellie, it's okay," Jessie said, keeping her voice calm and reassuring. She held up one hand slowly. "Just put the gun down."

The woman's arms shook as she stared at the body of her husband. Blood seeped from the wound in his back, spreading in a dark circle on his shirt.

Jessie slowly got to her feet and moved to the woman's side, gently placing her hands on Ellie's arms and taking the gun from her grasp. The woman's breath came in shallow gasps as Jessie wrapped an arm around her shoulders. "Ellie, I need you to take some deep breaths for me. Can you do that?"

The woman tried to nod her head, but then burst into tears, her body folding itself in against Jessie. Footsteps echoed through the house and Jessie looked up to see Alex rushing through the house from the front. He had his gun drawn, his eyes immediately going to Phillip's body. Jessie shook her head as he approached them and continued to console a sobbing Ellie.

The woman lifted her face from Jessie's chest and took one last look over at her husband's body, and then at Alex, and finally back to Jessie. "I...I don't know why I did that. He was hurting you, and he promised...he promised he would never do that again. I just...I had forgotten..."

She held out her arm and pushed her sleeve up. There, on the inside of her upper arm, Jessie could make out the sliver of metallic balls and dashes embedded just below her flesh.

It was too much, and Jessie felt her own tears flood her face as she held onto the woman and rocked her back and forth. Movement caught her attention, and she looked up through watery eyes to see Cora standing before her.

She locked eyes with her battered and bruised friend, and suddenly, even though they were surrounded by darkness, everything seemed alright in the world. Cora made her way to her friend, wrapped her arms around the two women, and cried with them.

40

Not So Hard to Adjust

Despite the commotion and noise around her, Jessie refused to take her attention off Cora. They both sat on the bumper of an ambulance as paramedics examined them. Due to the sheer number of women needing potential medical attention, Alex had put out a call to the neighboring county for assistance as well. Surprisingly, other than being slightly dehydrated, the women all appeared in fairly good health.

At least physically.

"These poor women," Cora said, speaking around an ice pack one of the paramedics had given her for her swollen lip. "Most don't even speak English. And they are all going to be dealing with post-traumatic stress for years to come."

Jessie held one of the ice packs to the cut on the side of her head. She reached out and squeezed her friend's hand. "I'm just glad you're not one of them. When I think

about what you went through...all just to get to me—"
She couldn't finish the sentence.

Cora lowered the ice pack, much to the annoyance of
the paramedic trying to listen to her lungs. "No. Don't you
blame yourself for the actions of evil men. If you weren't
the person you are, I might be in a cage somewhere or in
a grave. I will be forever grateful to you, Jessie Night. You
gave me my life back." She winced as she reapplied the
cold pack. "But don't take it the wrong way when I say I
will not be visiting you and these mountains again."

Alex walked over to the two women, notepad in hand.

"Anything?" asked Jessie.

"The couple of women who speak English all have
the same story. They worked as prostitutes in different
cities, were lured into a van or a hotel room with the
promise of quick cash for...work...and were then
drugged. Next thing they knew, they were in a truck,
blindfolded, and traveled for what felt like a couple days.
Then, the doors opened, they were drugged again, and
woke up in the cell in Phillip's basement, with that
metallic strip implanted in their arms. They were
photographed from different angles, height and weight
recorded, and then left in the cage. They said every now
and then a new woman would show up and one or two
would be removed. They didn't know what happened to
the ones who disappeared or where they went."

Cora shook her head. "We know what happened. We
just don't know where they went or who their buyers
were." Her gaze grew distant and sad. "I saw it happen.
One of the girls, with dark hair and eyes, was led away to
a buyer. The way she looked at me...I'll never forget the

look in her eyes. Like she had just given up. Also, I'm pretty sure some of the girls were sold and resold. At least I'm pretty sure that was what happened from some of the conversations I overheard." She looked at Alex. "There has to be a way to track these women down?"

Jessie and Alex exchanged glances.

"To do that, we need to start identifying them," Jessie said. "And thanks to Ellie, that just got a lot easier."

"How so?" Cora asked.

"Those implants," Jessie said. "They are an identification system used by the traffickers to keep track of where a woman came from, her age and ethnicity, and how many times she has been sold. The dots and dashes making up the implant are a code. Once it's broken, it should tell us a lot more about these missing women."

"We have a log with multiple entries that we are hoping can be broken," Alex added. "It was found in the possession of a murder victim that Jessie helped us solve. Now, I think we have a reason behind why she was killed. These traffickers would undoubtedly do anything to keep that list from getting out."

Cora's head hung heavy as she looked up at him. "And that's what they had planned for me? They were never going to trade me for Kevin, were they?"

Jessie looked her friend in the eye. "I'm pretty sure that was the plan all along."

Cora smiled at her. "But you never gave up. Thank you."

Jessie tried to hide her blush. "Well, losing my therapist would be bad enough...but one of my closest friends? No way."

"So, what's going to happen to Ellie?" Cora asked.

"She's as much a victim here as everyone else," Jessie said. "Apparently, she's been with Phillip for years. He received her as one of his first shipments in this business and decided he wanted to keep her. It's disgusting. My guess is, she'll be questioned and then she and Sarah will be ready to start their life over."

"Maybe," said Alex, furrowing his brow. "She just confessed that Sarah isn't her child. She said Phillip showed up with her a year ago and said she was the newest addition to their family. We are waiting for social work to show up so they can dig into that a little deeper."

Jessie could only stare at him, her mouth agape. "Christ. That poor child..."

Alex nodded. "From what Josie has confessed, he and Phillip were just middlemen. They received these women and held them here, arranging for the buyers and facilitating the deal. They used that doctor set up at the farm as a cleaner and also to take care of branding the women with those implants. But Josie's knowledge doesn't go any further than that. He never had contact with the person or persons they worked for. That was all handled by Phillip."

"And the doctor?" Cora asked.

"Most likely a freelancer. Hired to do one thing and nothing else." He sighed, looking at the swarm of activity going on in and around the large house. "We've had to turn this one over to the feds. These victims are all from different states, and who knows how far the corruption goes with this. Plus, they have access to databases and services that we don't. They are confident they can break the code on that ledger. Their Human Trafficking Task Force already has some promising leads."

Just then a woman dressed in an expensive-looking pantsuit walked up. She placed a hand on Jessie's shoulder. "Looks like we have you to thank for shutting down another horrific operation trying to take a foothold in our beautiful town."

Jessie looked away. "Thank you, Mayor, but it was a team effort. I couldn't have done it without Alex and... others." Her eyes drifted down the hall to where John stood, hands in his pockets as he watched more officers and federal agents come out of the house carrying boxes of materials and loading them into black sedans.

"Well, we will be holding a celebration to thank each and every person that helped in breaking this terrible, terrible human trafficking ring." She wheeled to face the ever-present Will Mason, his camera flashing to capture the mayor's radiant smile. "Come, Will. We need pictures of me inside this house of horrors. Maybe even down in that shelter place the kidnappers created."

"No." It was Cora who spoke up. "That is not a shelter they built. It wasn't a basement. It was part of an existing underground railroad system for runaway slaves that those men corrupted and defiled. If you're going to report on this, you call it like it is." Her eyes locked with those of the mayor and her tone left no room for discussion.

The mayor broke her stare and looked nervously at Will. "Very well. Will, why don't you run the final edition of your coverage on this by" —she frowned for a moment — "Jessie's friend. she seems to be an authority on this matter, and I am granting her final editorial say on whatever you print about it." She turned on her heels and headed down the driveway back toward the house.

"Wow," said Alex. "I've never seen that side of the mayor before. I'm going back down there. Chief Trent is in there and way over his head. I'll check back in with you later."

"Alex...one thing," said Cora before the officer could get too far. "How did you get into that underground space where we were held? I couldn't find the exit from the inside."

Alex gave her a tight smile. "We have to thank John for that. We couldn't find an entrance to the underground from the banks on the lake. But then John noticed the weird way the landscaping was built up on the left side of the house. They had created a second entrance to the old underground railroad to the side of the house, connecting it to one of the catacombs off to one side. Once inside, they built a false wall, with a couple of cots and bunkbeds installed. God knows what they planned to do with those. But there was a door leading from those spaces into the room where you and the other women were being held. Luckily, we were able to get through it just in time."

Cora let out a low whistle. "I'll say you were just in time."

Alex gave her a nod and headed back down the drive.

"I'm sorry you missed your conference," Jessie said. It seemed like a small thing, but the words were filled with emotion that she hoped her friend would understand.

"Not a problem. I wasn't really that interested in it to begin with. I just used it as an excuse to come see you."

Jessie leaned over, resting her head on Cora's shoulder. Every part of her body ached and there probably wasn't enough aspirin in all of Pine Haven to take it away. Still, despite the bloodshed and violence, she felt strangely at peace.

"It's just too bad you don't have any clue as to who is ultimately behind this. Those women were brought here and placed for sale by someone. Josie certainly didn't have the brains for this, and Phillip was obviously just following orders. Who set all this up? It just feels like there's another piece to the puzzle out there somewhere."

And just like that, Jessie felt her calm crack ever so slightly.

JESSIE LOOKED out over the lake, watching the autumn-hued light and shadows at play. She sat on the front porch, one foot lazily pushing herself back and forth on a white rocker. She glanced over at Blizzard and smiled at the big dog as he lay on his back, legs spread akimbo as he basked in the rays of the setting sun.

She looked from the shepherd to the thumb drive that rested in her hand. At some point, she was going to have to open it and see what her brother's final words to her were.

But that could wait just a bit longer. She was tired. Emotionally and physically. Deep down in her bones, tired.

And she knew she would need strength to look at whatever was held on the drive. So, it could wait. Right now, all she wanted was to enjoy the quiet and the view, relaxing with her dog.

A soft buzz disrupted the solitude, and she looked down at the phone resting beside her. She saw the name displayed across the screen and picked it up. "Hello?"

"Hi. I was just checking in to see if you were doing okay," John said.

She breathed easily, settling back into the rocker. "I'm okay. Aside from the bruised ribs and slight concussion. Getting old sucks; I don't heal the way I used to."

He chuckled into the phone. "Well, I hate to tell you, it's all downhill from here."

There was a moment of silence that Jessie finally broke. "How's Kevin settling in?"

John's voice lifted. "He's doing great. I was surprised at how well he's adjusting to life in college."

"You know, that was extremely generous of you. Paying for a full ride like that. I can only imagine how shocked he must have been."

In her mind's eye she could see John shrugging. "It's two years of art school. It's not that big a deal. Besides, he's a good kid. All he wanted was to get himself out of the dead end that is the Narrows. He made some bad decisions, but that shouldn't be held against him or used to keep him from making a better future for himself."

"We still talking about Kevin?" There was no answer; and she hadn't expected one. "It was a good thing you did, John. Thank you."

He cleared his throat. "Well, I wasn't the only one. You could have had him up on charges for what he tried to do."

She sighed. "Yeah, there was no way I would have let that happen. Neither would Alex." She could only imagine the conversation he must have had with Chief Walker after all was said and done. She didn't want to think about what that favor might have cost Alex. Thinking about favors brought back an unwelcome memory she had been pushing to the back of her mind. "Have you heard anything from Terry Blackburn?"

A sound of disgust in the form of a snort came from the man. "I heard that the land next to his daddy's farm has been purchased. Basically, for a song, he just had to pay off the back taxes and it was pretty much his. I really wish you hadn't made that deal with him. Lord knows what he'll ask for."

"So, whatever he is up to I just helped him expand his territory. At least everything in that maintenance building has been confiscated." There wasn't much to be said. She couldn't turn back time and undo the deal she made. All she could do was deal with the fallout when it came. She didn't mean to continue that line of the conversation but found herself speaking up. "He knew my brother. They worked together. That means he probably knows more about what's going on around here than he let on."

John waited for a beat to be certain she was finished talking. "Yes. And whatever he's up to now is no doubt an extension of their work together."

She sighed. "Well. I have a feeling it will all come to light at some point. I just have to be ready when it does."

"And something tells me you will be. Well, I just

wanted to check and see if you needed anything. I'll let you go. But if you need something, just yell," John said.

"I will do that. Good night. Oh, and John? Thank you. For everything."

She hung up and turned to look at Blizzard. Her conversation had roused him, and he sat up, tail wagging, eyes focused on her.

"You know what, boy? Let's go for a walk. I think we could both use a good leg stretching before turning in for the night."

She reached inside the door and grabbed his leash. She looked down at her hand and the metal drive, turning it over a couple of times. She would get around to it. But whatever secrets it may or may not hold weren't something that needed to be delved into tonight. She placed it in a basket on the entryway table next to her car keys, before turning and leading Blizzard off towards the lake.

Tomorrow would come soon enough, and that would be when she would deal with missives from her dead brother. Until then, Pine Haven Lake, and all its splendor, was calling to her.

41

Messy Business

The unassuming brick traditional house on the banks of the Potomac River, sat back from the road, hidden from cars and neighbors by a white privacy fence, and a gated entry. Inside, a large fireplace roared, fending off the chill that crept in through single-pane windows that should have been replaced years ago.

At the table, a woman who told everyone her name was Hillary Jamestown, sat at the kitchen island, pen in hand as it hovered over a crossword puzzle. The smell of a pot roast in the slow cooker wafted throughout the house and made her stomach growl from time to time. She should have gone with the oven method; the roast would have been done and ready to eat in a couple of hours. But she had given in to nostalgia when she woke up and decided to go the crock pot route instead.

She had one word left on the puzzle and wagged her

pen furiously between two fingers as she studied the words around the open boxes. A small burner flip phone that rested on the tiled granite next to her buzzed. She lifted it to her ear without taking her eyes off the puzzle.

"Yes?"

"Will there be blowback that could reach us?"

She sighed. "No. As ever, we are fully shielded."

"We have clients who are very unhappy about the missed deliveries they were promised."

"I have spoken with those clients and assured them they have been moved to the top of the list and will get their pick of deliveries from a different hub, once it is up and running. I have also given them a considerable credit to use for...accessories, once they settle on a new product. All is well in that department."

"And the loose ends?"

"There are no loose ends. The doctor is being paid in full for services rendered as we speak, so nothing to worry about there. There was nothing that could be retrieved from the laptop that was found at the scene. The big bartender's contract is being paid in full as well."

"Excellent. And what about our lost merchandise?"

"Unfortunately, that we will have to take a write down on. It is not covered by insurance, so that is a loss we will have to accept. But luckily, it is easily replaceable."

"What is our time frame for replacement?"

Hillary shifted in her seat. "Negligible. We already have new routes being opened and product is starting to flow."

"A shame we had to leave such a scenic operation. The clients rather enjoyed the place."

Hillary didn't respond. She had a feeling where this conversation was going and didn't want to indulge it.

"You know, there is still the matter of the woman. Do you think she will let the matter drop?"

Hillary hesitated but kept her voice calm and detached. "If we cease operations in that town, I don't see why not."

More silence from the other end. "Our partners don't see it that way. We knew bringing her brother into the operation was a risk. But it was a risk that his skill set mitigated. However, we both know that *she* is a different breed."

"And as you may recall, I was the lone voice of dissent when it came to utilizing her brother in that manner. The man was a sleeping tiger whose tail should have never been pulled."

The reply was a bit snappier than Hillary would have liked. "Nevertheless, we did what was in the best interest of the business. Now, we have to do what is in our best interest again. When her father was alive, she was untouchable. But with him no longer being in the picture..."

Hillary took a breath to steady herself. "I'll oversee it myself this time. Winter's coming, and that means there are always opportunities for...accidents."

"Indeed."

There was a click, and the line went dead. Hillary let out a breath and returned her attention to the puzzle. She filled in the final word, a feeling of satisfaction rushing over her with its completion. Standing up, she stretched her arms over her head, enjoying the feeling of her old bones cracking. She had so been looking forward to spending the winter in Florida for once.

The thought of being in those mountains when the snow came did little to make her feel better about what she had to do. Still, it was necessary. Maybe she'd make it quick and still get down to Florida for a bit.

Yes. That's what she would do. She made her way to her bedroom and found her business planner. She sat down on the bed as she opened it and flipped ahead a couple of months. There was a lot to do between now and when she needed to make her way to North Carolina.

She sighed heavily. Killing family was such messy business.

***

Book Three is coming very soon and is now available for pre-order!

Veil Of Night: Jessie Night thriller Book 3

ALSO, if you'd like to stay up to date on all new releases, including the third book in this exciting new series, join the author's mailing list, at:

sendfox.com/emberscottauthor

ABOUT THE AUTHOR

Ember Scott is an author of thrillers and mysteries living in the great state of North Carolina. He is a lover of dogs, mountains, lakes...and some people.

He loves to create tale about very bad people that do very bad things and ultimately get their comeuppance.

If you like fast paced thrillers that are built around unforgettable characters, then this is the author for you.

He can be reached at:

emberscottauthor@gmail.com